Summer Has Ended

Ray Wright

This book is a work of non-commercial use and distribution of literature.
Typical of a literary contribution.

Summer Has Ended, by Ray Wright. ISBN 9781638680277

Published 2015 by Virtualbookworm.com Publishing Inc., P.O. Box 9949,
College Station, TX 77842, US. ©2015, Ray Wright. All rights reserved.
No part of this publication may be reproduced, stored in a retrieval system,
or transmitted in any form or by any means, electronic, mechanical, recording
or otherwise, without the prior written permission of Ray Wright.

"Summer Has Ended," by Ray Wright. ISBN 978-1-63868-027-7.

Published 2021 by Virtualbookworm.com Publishing Inc., P.O. Box 9949, College Station, TX 77842, US.

1

IT WAS LATE IN THE AFTERNOON when Jeremy noticed the two men. They were standing outside a car, just across the fence and at the end of the two rows he and his father were working. They seemed to be waiting. Lem Stroop, Jeremy's father, gave no indication he had seen the men. "They's two fellers down there at th' fence, Paw," Jeremy said.

"Yep," said Lem, stopping and straightening his back and squinting in the direction Jeremy indicated.

Jeremy was glad to see the two men. He had no idea who they were or what they wanted, but he knew that his father would stop and talk to them at least for a while, and that would provide some respite from work. He wished there was shade. As Jeremy and his father drew nearer the two men, Jeremy realized that he knew one of them; it was Jacob Mutchell, the man who had earlier gone turkey hunting with Jeremy and his dad. Now Mutchell was waiting at the end of the row.

Jeremy did not recognize the other man, but he could tell he was no farmer. He wore a white shirt and a wide floral tie; his hands and face were pale in the sun. The hat he wore was not the typical straw hat of the farmers that Jeremy knew. It was made of white straw with a wide black band around it. A small feather was stuck in the hat band. The shoes he wore were not brogans; they were wing-tipped, shined leather shoes, although they were already beginning to accumulate a fine pall of dust.

"Howdy, Lem," Mutchell said, nodding and smiling under the straw hat pulled down over his forehead. He wore overalls and a blue denim shirt. The underarms of Mutchell's shirt were white with salt leached from his perspiration. Jeremy remembered that he smelled like pigs.

"Jacob," was the reply.

"How's th' crop a-comin', Lem?"

"Fair tuh middlin'."

"Why, it looks like a fine crop tuh me."

Lem did not reply. He pulled at a strip of bark on the cedar post that he leaned against.

"My crop ain't no good." Mutchell shook his head. "Seems like it never got started. Yuh know how some crops is." Still no reply. "Course I guess I did git started a little late this year. They uz just so much tuh do, what with mother a-bein' sick an' all. An' uv course I got them hawgs tuh take care uv, an' they do take up a lot uv time." He paused again and began to roll a cigarette. "But actually I didn' come out here tuh talk crops with yuh." Mutchell's face broke into a smile, revealing gapped, yellow teeth. "Mine wouldn' never compare tuh yores nohow." He turned to the man with him. "Lem's th' best farmer in these parts."

"Good fer him," said the stranger, quick to engage himself in the conversation. He had removed his hat, and his face was dotted with perspiration. "Praise th' Lord."

Mutchell returned his attention to Lem. "Lem, you remember last Sattidy when I tole yuh about our meetin' at th' church?"

Lem nodded.

"Yeah. Well, I seen yuh ain't made it tuh none uv th' services yet, Lem, an' we been a-havin' some powerful testifyin', an' Brother Flancher here—" Mutchell paused and made a sweeping gesture toward the visitor, "—he has been doin' some great preachin'. Full gospel preachin'." Mutchell beamed. "Lem, this here is Brother Cleo Flancher. Brother Flancher, this here is Lem. Lem Stroop."

"Howdy," said Lem noncommittally.

"Glad tuh meetcha, Sir," said Flancher, reaching enthusiastically across the fence for Lem's hand. "Shore am. An' who is this?" he asked, directing his attention to Jeremy.

Jeremy was surprised. Grownups seldom acknowledged his presence at all. He looked down at the ground and pushed his hair back from his eyes.

Mutchell spoke. "This here is yer boy, ain't it, Lem? What's 'is name?"

"Jeremy."

"Howdy, Son." Flancher smiled broadly. He extended his hand.

"Hi," said Jeremy. He took Flancher's hand and was surprised at how large and soft it was.

"'Bout tuh git this fiel' done, Lem?" Mutchell asked.

"I'm behin'," replied Lem. He looked about.

"Well, you've got some mighty fine help here, it looks like," said Flancher, still smiling, looking directly at Jeremy. He pulled a large white handkerchief from a back pocket and wiped his face.

"He works when he has to."

"All boys is like that. I bet this is a fine boy," said Flancher, still smiling approvingly at Jeremy.

There was a long silence. Mutchell and Flancher looked at each other. Lem studied the ground.

"Well, Lem," said Mutchell finally. "We don't wanta interfere with yer work none, but we did wanta come out an' remin' yuh 'bout th' revival. Yuh'll hear some mighty fine preachin'. I'll guarantee yuh that." He looked at Flancher as if for confirmation.

Lem did not reply.

Flancher spoke, "Be glad tuh see yuh, Sir. Like fer yuh tuh bring yer boy along too—an' all th' rest uv yer fam'ly. The Lord is a-savin' souls, an' th' people in th' little church here in Dorman, well, lemme tell yuh, th' people in th' church er true people uv God. Real Christians. Amen!"

"Amen!" chimed Mutchell. "Praise th' Lord!

Lem still said nothing.

"Th' Lord's a-comin'. Bless his holy name. *Bible* tells us so."

Flancher concentrated on Lem. "You go tuh church with Brother Mutchell?"

"Mr. Flancher," Lem said slowly and deliberately, "I work hard, real hard ever' day. Ever' day 'cept Sunday, that is. I don't work none then, er not much, but I work hard ever' other day, an' Sunday is my only day tuh git any rest a-tall. I ain't got no time fer church."

"Ah, Brother, don't yuh believe th' Bible?" Flancher took a small, well-worn Bible from his pocket and held it in the palm of his large, outstretched hand. Jeremy's interest increased.

Flancher slapped the book for emphasis. "Brother, beware! Avoid th' flamin' pit uv hell, th' lake that burns with everlastin' fire. Hallelujah!" Jeremy remembered the lake of fire he had read about in the family Bible. He was greatly interested in what Flancher was saying.

"Brother Flancher," Mutchell broke in. "Perhaps we best come back another time tuh visit Lem." He put his hand on Flancher's arm to lead him away.

Flancher turned. "You come too, Jeremy," he said. Jeremy did not know what to say. He pushed back his hair and said nothing. Then Flancher said to Lem, "Nice tuh meetcha, Mr. Stroop."

"Yeah," Lem replied.

3

After the two men left, Jeremy and his father returned to work. As far as Jeremy could tell, his father quickly forgot about the visit. But Jeremy dwelled on it. The preacher had attracted him. He had noticed Jeremy, and few adults did that. He had not asked Jeremy how old he was or what grade he was in, as most adults did, and he had invited him to church. He was a preacher, and Jeremy had never met one before. He had been impressed. Jeremy's mind wandered back to the comment Flancher had made about the flaming pit. He remembered that he had read somewhere in the Bible about a flaming lake into which sinners were thrown, and he had tried to visualize such a lake in his mind. He pictured men and women tumbling down from the sky into leaping flames and bobbing about on the flaming crest of the lake. He tried to imagine it. Did people swim around in the fire? How could they do that? Maybe they just stood around on the bank.

Lem shattered Jeremy's reverie. "Mind yore bizness, Boy, and come on. Yer fallin' behin'."

Jeremy sped up, but he couldn't dismiss the thoughts of the lake of fire. He was careful not to fall behind again, but he was still engrossed in the visit of the two men. Mutchell, he knew. He remembered how Mutchell had shown up early one morning to invite Lem to join him in a turkey hunt. Lem had shown only mild interest, telling Mutchell that there had not been any wild turkeys in the country for several years, but Mutchell had insisted that he'd found a bunch of the birds and even knew where they roosted at night. "It's that big ole pecan tree down on th' river, there on ole Sam Watson's place," Mutchell had insisted. "I uz by there th' other night a-huntin' coons, and I walked right up under 'em, Lem, afore I even seen 'em. They exploded outta that tree right over my head. Scared th' hell outta me. They musta been a hunnerd uv 'em, Lem. Big turkeys."

"How many?"

"A hunnerd an' two." Mutchell smiled at his own joke.

"Hell, Mutchell. They ain't been a hunnerd turkeys uv any kind in this part uv th' worl' fer years."

"Well, they uz a bunch."

Lem had said that he was not interested, but Mutchell had insisted. "Come on, Lem. Them turkeys is sittin' ducks. We kin slip in there tuhnight an git 'em afore they know what hit 'em."

"Hell, Mutchell. Huntin' at night is illegal. You know that."

"Aw, that don't matter none. Ever'body knows they ain't no game warden since Mack Schuler left."

"We didn' have much uv a warden when he uz here," observed Lem.

4

"Maybe so. But I ain't afraid uv Schuler. I come tuh git you tuh go with me tuh git them turkeys. I'm a-tellin' yuh, they're right there on Watson's place."

"What about Watson? He ain't gonna take too kindly tuh anybody a-comin' on his place, 'specially at night."

"Hell, that ole man'll be in bed by sundown," snorted Mutchell. "He'll never know we uz there. Besides, he's half deaf, an' I don't think he even stays on his place much anymore, since his wife died las' year."

"Mebbe so." Lem paused. Then he said, "Do yuh think yuh could fin' that tree ag'in?"

Mutchell was encouraged by this turn in the conversation. "Oh, shore. It's about a mile below th' bridge, there at th' bend in th' river whur th' water is shaller. An' now's th' time tuh go, Lem, while all th' leaves is offa them trees. It'll be easy tuh see th' birds. An' I know th' water's shaller. I waded it th' other night."

Lem nodded. He knew the place. "Yeah, but Sam's house is purty close tuh th' river as I remember it, an' he shore as hell don't like no trespassin'."

"He ain't gonna do nothin', Lem. I tole yuh. Ole Watson spends most uv his time in town these days with 'is daughter. We kin go in there tuhnight, git us a few uv them turkeys, an' git out without anybody ever knowin'. Whatta yuh say?"

"Well, it's all right with me, I reckin. What Watson don't know won't hurt 'im, an' they ain't none uv his birds. What time yuh thinkin' uv goin'?"

Mutchell was pleased. "I'll be by tuhnight 'bout dark. They'll be a moon tuhnight, but it won't come up till purty late. We'll hafta sort uv feel our way. Cain't take no flashlights er nothin'. But th' land is purty level there at th' river, an' they ain't many bushes in that pasture. We can park our car there on th' road an' cut across th' fiel' tuh that tree. We won't have no trouble. Might want tuh take our shoes off once we come tuh th' river."

Lem snuffed out his cigarette. "Okay. Count me in."

Once Mutchell had left, Jeremy began to beg to go on the hunt. "Please, Paw. I won't be no trouble. I just got my new shotgun, an' I wanta try 'er out."

"Likely you'd just blow yer fool head off. Er some other fool's head."

"Aw, Paw, I'll be keerful. Yuh know I will, an' I can he'p you an' Mr. Mutchell carry th' turkeys yuh shoot."

"They ain't likely tuh be many turkeys tuh carry, an' you ain't likely tuh be much help," muttered Lem.

"Aw, Paw. Please. I done all my chores, an' . . . ."

"Oh, hell. All right. But you do as I say."

"Oh, I will, Paw. Thankee, Paw. I cain't wait tuh try out my new gun."

"Now, just a damn minute. I never said nuthin' about you a-takin' no gun."

"But, Paw. I gotta take my gun. Please. Please."

"No. Ain't nothin' more dangerous than a damn excited kid with a gun."

"Oh, please, Paw. I'll do just what yuh say. I won't make no noise, an' I'll behave. You'll see."

"Oh, shut up. Ain't never satisfied. But all right. All right. But you be keerful with that gun. You keep it on safety, an' don't shoot unless I say yuh can. I ain't a-gonna have you a-shootin' nobody down there in th' dark, 'specially me."

"I'll be keerful, Paw. I won't take my gun offa safety till you tell me I can."

It had seemed to Jeremy that the day would never pass, but at last Mutchell had come, and the two men and the boy had loaded their gear into Mutchell's car for the trip to the turkey roost. Immediately as Jeremy had entered the car, he had become aware of the unpleasant odor of pigs—an odor he experienced every time he passed Mutchell's pig farm.

On the way to the river, Mutchell had explained, "We'll park about a quarter-mile from that tree whur them birds are. If th' moon is good, we'll be able tuh see Watson's house from there. Th' turkey roost will be right between us an' his house. We'll cut across th' fiel' till we come tuh th' river, an' then when we cross it, we oughtta be right at that tree. We cain't miss it."

"Whur we'll be is right at Watson's house," groused Lem.

"Naw. That won't be no problem. Hell, Lem. Stop worryin'. Ole Watson may not even be home tuhnight."

The three had sat in the car, waiting for the moon to rise. Jeremy had rolled down his window and listened to the night sounds. He could hear the faint gurgle of the river. Somewhere a bullfrog boomed his song, and in the distance, a fox barked. He began to doze, but at last Mutchell had leaned over the front seat and said to him, "Roll yer winder up, Boy. It's time tuh go."

Jeremy opened his door to get out, and the dome light came on. "Hey, hey, close th' door," cautioned Mutchell. "When you open that door, th' dome light comes on. Yuh gotta open an' close th' door real quick, so nobody'll see th' light."

Jeremy closed the door quickly, and finally the three stood on the road. Lem had supervised Jeremy's loading of his shotgun and had checked the safety. "Now you keep that damn safety on," he warned. "You take it off before I tell you that you can, an' I'll take off a bunch uv yer hide."

"Shore, Paw. I promise."

They made their way across the field, always bearing toward Watson's house, dimly visible in the moonlight. A light gleamed in one of the windows of the house.

"I don't like th' looks uv that damn light in Watson's house," said Lem.

"Lem, will you stop complainin'? I said it ud be okay, an' it will. I don't know whether er not ole Watson is home. They's always a light on in th' house. He leaves it on alla th' time."

Lem was still concerned. "How much farther is it to th' river?"

"Not much."

"You shore you can fin' that roost?"

"Shore. I know right whur it is. You see that tallest tree?" asked Mutchell, indicating the dim silhouette of a tree in the moonlight. "It's a pecan tree, right there below Watson's house. I think you an' me gathered pecans there one time."

"I seen lotsa trees on his place."

"Shore. But this tree is that really big un down below Watson's house on th' river. Right there whur we picked them pecans."

"Yeah," said Lem. "I remember we wuzn't supposed tuh be on 'is place that time, either."

Mutchell did not reply, and the three had walked on in silence. The air was damp and cool. Jeremy could smell the river before he saw it.

Soon, they reached the river and stood on its bank, its waters gurgling past their feet.

"This damn river looks purty wide to me," observed Lem.

"Well, I don't know," replied Mutchell. "Maybe it's on a rise. I don't remember it a-bein' this wide th' other night."

"Mutchell, it ain't rained aroun' here fer two months. Whatta yuh mean, rise?"

"Hell, I donno. Maybe it rained up in th' nex' county."

"Whur's th' roost?"

"I thought it uz about right here," Mutchell replied, "but I don't see it just yet. I guess my bearin's that night wuzn't perfect."

"Prob'ly drunk," snorted Lem.

Mutchell laughed good-naturedly. "Well, I mightta had a drop too much."

"You better not uv brought us out here on no damn wild goose chase."

"Take it easy, man." Mutchell was exasperated. "Hell, it uz dark. Gimme some time, an' I'll fin' th' damn tree. Right here is whur th' river starts a-gittin' shaller, an' that tree should be just on th' other side. See, there's ole Watson's house right up there on th' hill."

"Yeah, with 'is light just a-glowin'."

Lem was mumbling something under his breath. Then, all at once, Mutchell seized Lem's arm. "Look! Look!" he whispered. "Right there. There they are."

"Whur? Whur?"

"There. Just across th' river in th' top uv that tree. See 'em?" Mutchell shifted about excitedly.

Jeremy could see the birds himself. There were several large, dark shapes sitting high in the tree.

"Shhhh," whispered Lem, taking charge now that the birds had been found. "Don't make a sound. Man, them is big turkeys."

"Now, lissen," continued Lem. "We'll hafta wade over tuh th' other side tuh git a good shot. Let's move down th' river a piece so's we've got some trees between us an' them birds. We'll cross th' river then, an' we can slip right up under 'em. How far down th' river can we go before it starts a-gittin' deep ag'in?"

"Oh, it's shaller fer a hunnerd yards."

"I hope you know what yer a-talkin' about. I don't cater tuh steppin' off in some deep water."

"Trust me. It's okay."

Lem and Mutchell had sat down and took off their shoes in preparation for wading the river. Both of the men stuffed their socks into their shoes, and then tied the shoe strings together and slung the shoes around their necks. Jeremy was not wearing shoes. Then the three had begun to wade the river. Jeremy quickly found himself in water up to his knees. The cold water tugged at his legs, and at first the water made his feet ache, but in the excitement of the hunt he overlooked the cold. Once on the other side, the three hunters had inched forward, keeping low to the ground. Neither Lem nor Mutchell put his shoes back on. Jeremy started to ask his father if he could take his gun off safety but thought it might upset him if he did, so he took it off safety without saying anything.

At last, Mutchell and Lem had stopped under a tree. "There they are," Mutchell whispered triumphantly. "But I cain't tell th' toms from th' hens," he complained.

"Don't matter," Lem replied.

"Hens ain't legal," muttered Mutchell.

"At night like this, ain't none uv these damn birds legal."

The two men stood surveying the birds. Then Lem said, "We cain't git no closer. We'll hafta shoot frum here. Now, Mutchell, you take th' top bird on th' right. You see 'im? Right there on that highest branch on th' right. I'll take th' top one on th' left. You hear me? You got it?"

"Yeah. Shore. Hell, I can see."

"Be shore yuh do. Ain't no use uv us a-shootin' th' same bird. Remember. You shoot th' one on th' top right. Now, take aim, an' let me know when yer ready. Then, I'll count tuh three, an' we'll blast 'em together."

"Paw," Jeremy tried to attract his father's attention.

"Shut up, Boy," Lem ordered.

Jeremy started to say something else, but his father had begun to count.

"One. Two. Three."

There was a tremendous roar. Even expecting the shots, Jeremy jumped. Wings thrashed as the tree exploded into activity. At the same time, heavy bodies plummeted through the limbs of the tree.

"Git 'em quick!" Mutchell leaped forward even as the birds thumped to the ground.

Confusion reigned. A dog began barking somewhere nearby, and Jeremy thought he heard a door slam.

"Hurry an' fin' them damn birds," Lem urged. "I think we got a couple uv 'em." Both he and Mutchell were down on their knees in the leaves, feeling around in the dark, searching, trying to find the birds that had fallen. Quickly, each grabbed a bird from the ground.

"Ain't they another?" asked Mutchell frantically.

Now two dogs were barking.

"Fergit it, an' head fer th' car!"

"Who's down there?" a voice yelled. The dogs seemed closer.

"What th' hell's a-goin' on down there?" The voice was more distinct.

"Oh, God, they's a flashlight a-shinin'. It's Watson. He'll see us shore. Run! He might shoot!"

Jeremy followed the two men, who seemed to have forgotten him. In his fright he forgot the safety on his gun, and as he ran, he stumbled over a tree root and fell to the ground. His gun discharged with a deafening roar, kicking up a shower of dust and leaves.

"Oh, God!" screamed Mutchell. "He's got us! He's got us shore as hell."

"Dammit! Wha'd I tell you, Boy?" growled Lem. "Put that damn gun on safety, an' leave it on, an' come on." Lem stopped for a moment, and Jeremy was afraid of what he might do, but Lem continued on his way. "Come on, Boy. I'll take care uv you when we git home."

"Gawdamighty! He's got us!" Mutchell gasped, trying desperately to run with his gun in one hand and a heavy bird in the other. In the pale moonlight, Jeremy could see Mutchell's shoes flopping around his neck.

Mutchell plunged recklessly into the stream bed, where he slipped and fell noisily into the creek. He came up, cursing, flailing and stumbling, still holding to his gun and to the bird. Then he stopped in mid-stream. "My shoes. My shoes. I lost my damn shoes," he panted. "I got tuh go back."

"Leave them damn shoes," snapped Lem. "You don't git outta here, yuh'll lose more than yer shoes."

Somewhere, from the direction of the house, a shotgun boomed—and Mutchell, forgetting his shoes, began running awkwardly across the stream.

Jeremy followed the two men as they ran across the pasture, retracing their steps to the car. Now the two men ran slowly, especially Mutchell, who was breathing heavily. Jeremy easily kept up with them. The voice from the house on the other side of the stream did not call again, and the dogs' barking seemed further away. "Oh God, my feet hurt," complained Mutchell, but he continued to run heavily, still holding to his gun and his bird.

All three of the hunters had arrived at the car at the same time, and Lem hastily opened the car door and threw his bird into the back seat. The dome light light came on, revealing the ugly, naked head of a buzzard. Lem sagged against the car, gasping for air, staring at the bird. "I'll be damned," he sighed.

Lem looked at Jeremy. He said, " Come on, Boy. Yer gittin' behin'."

It was a quiet field during the afternoon.

2

AT LAST THE WORKDAY ENDED, and Jeremy and his father turned from the field toward home. On the way, Jeremy decided to ask Lem about Flancher's visit. "Paw, did you like th' preacher?"

"Not pertickerly."

"What did yuh think about what he said about th' Lord a-comin'?"

"Not much."

"Paw, do you know when the Lord's a-comin'?"

"No, an' neither does nobody else," snapped Lem, and Jeremy was surprised and disappointed.

"Yuh think maybe that preacher we met tuhday knows?"

"Hell, I know he don't know, an' neither does any other fly-by-night, two-bit preacher know. Don't you git caught up in that preacher. He's just like alla th' rest. He's a slick-talkin', fancy dresser a-goin' aroun' th' country preachin' tuh people an' a-gittin' 'em all riled up. Oughtta be run outta th' county. All these preachers want is money, money, money."

"But, Paw, he never ast us fer no money."

"Time wuzn't right, Boy. Just give 'im time, an' he'll pick yuh clean. They're all alike. You just watch. He'll hang aroun' here till he gits most uv th' folks' money, an' then one mornin' we'll all hear that he just lit out fer parts unknown. Preachers er all the same." Lem nodded affirmatively.

Lem and Jeremy continued their walk toward home. Their path from the field led them down the slope of a dry wash, across broad, flat sheets of shale.

Jeremy was never comfortable among these rocks. For one thing, during the summer months they became scorching hot in the afternoon, burning his bare feet. This time of day the rocks would be so hot that he would have to pick his way carefully in order to find patches of cooler dirt where he could step. Usually the patches of dirt would have prickly pear growing on them, a fact that complicated Jeremy's walk among the rocks. Jeremy also knew that the rocks served as hiding places for all manner of lizards. Small lizards with horizontal yellow and green stripes and long tails would appear out of the cracks in the rocks, and then dart back under cover, but they were no threat to Jeremy. He enjoyed chasing them and throwing rocks at them. He had heard that if someone cut off the tail of one of these lizards it would grow again, and this theory interested him. Working in the fields with his hoe, he had had several opportunities to cut off the tails of such lizards, and he always wondered whether or not the tails grew back. The problem had been that Jeremy had never seen any of these lizards again to check out the theory. He had tried to keep a couple of them in a box, but they had died.

There were also horned toads in the rocks, but they did not concern Jeremy either. He knew that they moved about slowly, and he had never heard of anybody being bitten by one. On the other hand, he had been told that if someone picked up a horned toad, it would squirt blood from its eyeballs. He had picked up any number of them and had held them patiently, waiting for them to squirt blood from their eyeballs, but it had never happened. He had even squeezed a couple of them as hard as he could with both hands, pressing his thumbs into their stomachs, but he had never seen any blood. He had asked his father about it once, and Lem had only replied that he had heard the story was true. Jeremy had tried everything. He had held horned toads upside down as he squeezed their stomachs or he had squeezed their heads, but to no avail. The horned toads had not squirted blood.

But there were other lizards among the sheets of shale, the mountain boomers. They appeared here frequently, especially in the heat of the day—large grey lizards that would stand in the glare of the sun, doing push-ups with their front legs while they held their heads high, expanding and contracting the pink sacs under their mouths. Jeremy knew that these lizards were lightning-fast, and he had heard that they chased people and could inflict severe bites. He had asked his father once why they were called mountain boomers, and Lem had said that it was because they sometimes made a booming sound. But he didn't elaborate.

Jeremy's greatest fear among the rocks, though, was rattlesnakes. He knew that they were common on the farm, especially during the summer months. He and Lem had killed any number of them, some in these very rocks. Lem never seemed so afraid of snakes as Jeremy. He laughingly told of a time when he had accidentally walked up on a rattlesnake, and in his words, "I just sort uv slipped up behin' 'im, an' I picked 'im up by th' tail an' swung 'im aroun' a coupla times and popped 'is head off."

"Paw, sometime can we find a rattlesnake, an' you pop off its head?"

"Now, Boy, I don't want you a-thinkin' thataway. You leave them rattlesnakes alone."

"But I'd just like tuh see you pop a snake's head off."

That night at supper, Jeremy still remembered the visit in the field, and he wanted to talk about it. "Maw," he said, "Mr. Mutchell brought th' preacher tuh see Paw tuhday." He looked at Lem for some indication that he might join in the discussion, but Lem was bent over his plate, eating. "And me," he added.

No one responded.

"And he invited us all tuh come tuh church tuhnight." He looked from his father to his mother.

"It's too late tuhnight," said Lem, wiping his mouth with the back of his hand. "An' you still got chores tuh do."

Lem now addressed Jeremy's mother. "Olga, I swear this is th' day-dreaminest boy I ever seen. After that preacher left tuhday, I had to yell at 'im twice tuh keep up with 'is work." Lem broke a large slice of yellow cornbread from the pone and began crumbling it into his plate. "I think I've even heard 'im a-talkin' tuh hisse'f a couple uv times lately." Lem shook his head in disbelief. "An' I know he reads a lot. An' frankly, I think alla them things is just foolishness." Lem picked up the pot of beans and began to pour potlicker from it over the pile of bread crumbs on his plate. "Hand me some uv them onions, Maw."

"Well," began the mother. "I don't know 'bout his talkin' tuh hisse'f, but I don't see nothin' wrong with 'im a-readin.' I've noticed 'im a-readin' frum th' Bible lately, an' I think that's a good idee. When I uz home, my paw always taught us tuh read th' Bible."

Lem looked up. His hand, lifting a spoon piled high with moist bread crumbs, stopped in mid-air. "Th' Bible! Th' hell you say. Now, I never knowed he uz a-readin' th' Bible. Damn! Daydreamin' an' a-talkin' tuh yerse'f and now a-gittin' religion, an' who knows what else." Staring at Jeremy, he punctuated his remarks with a huge bite of food. Jeremy squirmed on his chair.

Lem pointed his fork at Jeremy. "Now you lissen tuh me. Ain't no sense in a-readin' that Bible. It just makes people crazy. My paw never wasted no time a-readin', much less th' Bible. Hell. He uz too busy a-workin', trin' tuh make a livin' fer us ten kids. An' I never done no readin' neither. I worked at home, an' I've worked hard ever since I left. I ain't done no kind uv readin', especially that Bible, which I think is a complete waste uv time. All them damn religious people think uv is a-goin' tuh church an' a-tryin' tuh git pore people tuh give their money tuh some church er other, an a-tellin' ever'body how tuh take care uv their bizness. Had an aunt once. She uz married tuh one uv these Bible-quotin' preachers. Both uv 'em claimed they had been saved an' had th' Holy Ghost. Got tuh whur ever' time they come tuh see us, all she did wuz try tuh convert my paw. Always a-jawin' at 'im, a-quotin' scripture."

Lem leaned back in his chair and began rolling a cigarette. He continued his story. "One day at dinner, she uz a-standin' behin' my paw at th' table. He uz just a-sittin' there, mindin' 'is own bizness. Well, she just kept a-quotin' scripture at 'im an' a-tellin' 'im how he ought tuh believe in Jesus an' be saved, an' that if he didn' accept Jesus he uz a-goin' straight tuh hell, an' all that kinda trash."

"Paw tole 'er tuh shut up, but she just kep' on. 'Yer a-goin' tuh hell! Yer a-goin' tuh hell!' she ud say. Fin'ly Paw, he put down 'is knife an' fork, an' stood up, turned aroun' an' said, 'You just shut up, er I'll knock th' livin' hell outta yuh.'"

"Well, she looked at 'im fer a minute. Then she started in ag'in. But she never finished her first sentence. My paw just coldcocked 'er, backhanded 'er clear across th' damn room. Knocked 'er plumb silly. She hit that wall an' just sort uv slid down it till she wuz a-sittin' on th' floor, her eyes all rolled back in 'er head, an' 'er laigs all stuck out in front uv 'er." Lem became reflective for a minute. "Plumb indecent th' way her dress wuz all bunched up around 'er butt. Hell, I wuzn't shore she uz ever gonna git up. Might not have, if that shiftless husband uv hers hadn' hepped 'er up. He wuz a-holdin' 'er up against th' wall th' best he could, but she uz a-saggin' purty bad. He kep' a-pattin' 'er an' a-sayin' 'If someone strikes you on one cheek, then turn th' other. Can yuh hear me? Can yuh hear me?' Well, she never give 'im no satisfaction a-tall fer th' longest. Fin'ly she sort uv come aroun', an' then this preacher husband uv hers started in on Paw, sayin', 'Vengeance is mine,' says th' Lord,' but he didn' git very close tuh Paw while he uz a-preachin'. But I'm a-tellin' yuh, that aunt uv mine never tried tuh convert my paw ag'in. No, sir." Lem laughed mirthlessly.

"That's awful," whispered the mother.

Lem looked at her quizzically. "Well, you better just be glad that my paw put down that knife afore he hit 'er."

There was silence. Then Jeremy, feeling a need to defend himself, said, "I just been a-readin' th' Bible."

"You just been a-readin' when you coulda done somethin' useful."
Lem spewed crumbs of food from his mouth as he spoke. "You keep a-
readin' that Bible, an' then yuh'll git religion, an' then yuh'll want tuh
go tuh church ever' Sunday, which is just another damn waste uv time.
Maybe yuh'll want tuh become one uv them Holy Rollers. That what
you've got in mind?"

"I just been a-readin'."

There was a long silence, broken only by the tinkle of forks and
spoons against dishes. The conversation was over. Lem's cigarette
burned unnoticed on the table's edge.

Jeremy excused himself and walked outside. The conversation
with his father had been unsettling. He had heard before of his
grandfather's violence, and he had come to realize that his father had
inherited a similar nature.

He knew that his father was capable of violent, uncontrolled anger,
and that he was susceptible to sweeping mood changes. He could go
from calm to violent rage. Jeremy could remember one time when his
father had been repairing a piece of harness. The leather was tough, and
Lem had trouble punching the awl through the material. Lem continued
to work with the leather, humming a song that Jeremy had heard his
mother sing, something about amazing grace. Suddenly, Lem had
missed the awl and had smashed his thumb with the hammer. "Oh,
God! Oh, da-a-a-amn, damn!" he gasped. "Oh, damn it tuh hell! Damn
sorry good-fer-nothin' hammer." He threw down the hammer. He rose
to his feet and stomped the hammer. He stalked around, going through
a litany of curses and then going through that litany again. "Oh, my
God A'mighty! Sorry son uv a—" Then he stopped and stuck his
thumb into his mouth. He continued stomping about. He took his
thumb from his mouth and alternately cursed the hammer, the awl, and
the leather. Then to make sure he had not left anything out, he cursed
them all again. He picked up the hammer and threw it across the yard.
"Oh, Gawd. Oh, Gawd. Oh, that hurts!" He squeezed his thumb in
dismay.

But at last, Lem had quieted. He walked back and forth, holding
his injured thumb. He stuck it back into his mouth. He took it out and
looked carefully at it. Finally, he walked over and picked up the
hammer where he had thrown it, returned to his seat, and resumed his
work, picking up his song about amazing grace where he had left off.

But another incident of Lem's anger had made a more lasting
impression upon Jeremy. Lem had just come in from riding the horse
and was heading for the barn when a scrap of newspaper had blown
under the horse's feet. Seeing the paper, the animal had shied

violently—and Lem, not expecting the move, had been pitched to the ground. He had rolled about clumsily, trying to get up and catch the reins of the horse at the same time. At first the horse had tried to elude him, but the paper having blown away, the horse quieted, and Lem calmly and quietly walked up to him and caught the reins. Jeremy had watched him, wondering what he would do. He had expected an outburst from his father, but none was forthcoming.

Lem moved slowly and deliberately as he led the horse over to a post and tied the reins securely around it. He pulled the knot tight. Still not a word. The horse lowered its head, attempting to graze but the reins were too short. Lem walked away, flexing his hands, watching the ground in front of him until he found what he was looking for. Jeremy's heartbeat quickened when he saw the four-foot length of two-by-four that Lem picked up from the ground. Hefting the club, Lem walked toward the unsuspecting horse.

The horse did not look up until Lem swung the first blow, striking the horse squarely between the ears. Suddenly, Lem began to scream curses, striking the horse repeatedly about the head and neck. He gripped the two-by-four as one might grasp a baseball bat, and he swung with all his might.

"Damn you!" He screamed. "Think you can throw me. I'll beat th' livin' hell out uv you, you bastard." Bits of flesh and blood spattered from the force of the blows as the horse reared and tried to escape the man and his fury, but the reins held, and the blows continued.

"Hold still, you bastard! I ain't through with you yet," Lem raged, his face flushed with anger and his breath coming in gasps. He moved about to get a better angle to deliver his blows, then planted his feet squarely and swung viciously into the horse's head.

At first Lem had swung wildly, and sometimes the two-by-four struck its legs. If the horse was down on all four feet, then the blow struck its head. But now Lem slowed the beating and became more deliberate. Now he waited until the horse was standing on all four feet, then he would swing overhead and bring down the club squarely on the horse's head. The sound of the blows sickened Jeremy. The animal's head and neck were covered with blood. Its right ear was almost severed. The horse whinnied and jerked its head to no avail, and, at last, it slumped to its knees on the ground, its head held at a crazy angle by the reins tied around the post. Blood trickled from the animal's nose. Lem, perspiring heavily, stopped in exhaustion. He stood, leaning on the club, his free hand held against his chest, breathing in heavy gasps, surveying the horse; then he threw down the blood-stained club and turned and walked away, leaving the animal tied to the post.

Jeremy approached the agitated horse, which struggled to its feet and strained against its reins, trying to escape. Once again it reared and weakly lashed out with its hooves.

"Be still, horse. I ain't a-gonna hurt yuh," Jeremy whispered. He gingerly touched the horse's bloody shoulder.

At last he succeeded in releasing the horse. He stared at the animal's left eye, dangling upon its cheek.

3

SUNDAY CAME, AND JEREMY KEPT THINKING about church. He got up too late to go to church in the morning, but after lunch he began to think about trying to go that night. He assumed that neither his father nor his mother would go with him—they had never gone to church, as far as Jeremy knew, but he hoped to be allowed to go by himself. The more he thought about it, the more he wanted to go. He had never been to church, and he wondered what church was like. He tried to imagine a church service. In books he had seen well-dressed men, women, and children, all in their Sunday best, solemnly filing into a high-ceilinged building. He had seen pictures of churches with brightly painted windows, and he assumed that all churches had such windows, although as he thought about it, he did not remember having seen any church with such windows in his community. He had decided that perhaps the windows of the churches that he knew were only painted on the inside. He kept wondering what it would be like to hear Flancher preach.

He whiled away the morning and the early afternoon. At last he made up his mind, and he began to prepare for his visit. His father had gone into town to see about buying a cow, and Jeremy knew he would not be back until late. With his father gone, he was sure he could talk his mother into letting him go to church.

He even did his chores early in case his mother raised the necessity of doing them as an objection. He dressed in secret, because he wanted to be fully dressed before he confronted his mother. Seeing him already dressed for church might sway her in his favor. He put on his good shirt, the only shirt that he had that was not too little for him. His parents had not yet bought his clothes for the coming school year. He did not change his trousers, nor did he put on shoes, although he had a respectable pair under the bed, a pair of "school shoes" left over from the past school year. He splashed water on his hair and combed it until it stuck to his head, and then he went to look for his mother. She was just coming in from sweeping the yard.

"My, ain't you all duded up? Whur do yuh think yer a-goin'?"

"Maw," Jeremy blurted out. "Do yuh min' if I go tuh church tuhnight?"

"Tuh church?" His mother was surprised.

"Yeah. Remember I tole yuh about Mr. Mutchell an' Brother Flancher a-comin' out tuh invite me an' Paw tuh church."

"My, I don't know, Jeremy. I hadn' thought about it. What church does Mr. Mutchell go to?"

"It's the church over on the Dorman road. Remember? We pass it ever' time we go tuh town."

"Oh, yeah. That one. Well, I just don't know, Jeremy."

"I'd like tuh go, Maw. An' Mr. Mutchell an' th' preacher invited me tuh come."

"I know, Jeremy, but like I said, I just hadn' thought about it. You ain't never ast about church before."

"I know. But this is special. It's a meetin'. An' some uv my friends will be there." Jeremy added the last comment for emphasis. He had no idea who might be there.

"Oh. Who?"

"Leland," Jeremy said quickly.

"I didn' know th' MacMillans went tuh that church."

"So, can I go?"

"Now, Jeremy. I just don't know about that church."

"Why?"

"Well, Jeremy. There's churches, an' there's churches. An' that tabernacle is a Holy Roller church. I just ain't too sure about yuh a-goin' there."

"What's a Holy Roller church?" Jeremy had never heard of such a term.

"It's just differ'nt. I don't know if yer paw would approve uv you a-goin' tuh that church er not."

"Aw, Maw. It's just church. It won't hurt nothin'. I just wanta see what it's like. Brother Flancher invited me, an' Paw won't keer."

His mother was not convinced. "Well, Jeremy, yer paw an' me, we never had nothin' tuh do with them Holy Rollers."

"Aw, please, Maw. Just this one time. I already done my chores."

"Well, I guess it'll be all right this once. I don't guess yer paw will need you fer anythin' else th' rest uv th' day. But you be keerful, an' you come straight home right after church."

"Thankee, Maw. I will."

His mother continued to justify her decision. "I think young people oughtta go tuh church."

"Thankee, Maw." Jeremy sprinted for the door. His mother followed him, reaching the door just in time to catch it as it was closing behind Jeremy. "Now mind you, you go straight tuh church. An' don't you be cuttin' up an' actin' like no fool. You lissen tuh th' preacher, Jeremy. An' Jeremy! Jeremy Stroop! You git back here an' put on yer shoes."

4

WITH HIS DOG, PATCHES, TROTTING BESIDE HIM, Jeremy had walked only a short distance when he stopped. "I betcha I shoulda brought my Bible," he said out loud. He stood still a moment. He looked at Patches, a long-haired white dog with patches of black scattered over its body. Impressed by the dark patches, Jeremy had named the dog within minutes of the time his father had presented it to him as a gift.

Now Jeremy watched the dog for a moment; then he started to turn back home. Maybe I better go back, he thought. Then he remembered his mother. "She might not let me out ag'in," he said to himself, "an' shore as shootin' she'll make me put on shoes." So he decided not to return for the book. "I prob'ly won't need it nohow," he reasoned aloud, and he continued on his way, but he wished he had brought his Bible.

Patches started following him once again, but Jeremy scolded the dog and ordered him not to follow him. "Go home, dawg. You cain't follow me ever'whur." Patches stopped and watched Jeremy for a while, and then turned toward home.

The church building to which Jeremy was going was about a mile away on the Dorman road. If one went around the county road, it was further, but Jeremy knew the countryside well, and he did not need to follow the road. He cut directly across the field to the north of his house, knowing that soon his route would intersect the Dorman road heading east. Once he intersected the road, he would turn to his right for about a quarter of a mile, and he would be at the church.

In the oppressive heat of the August afternoon, the mile seemed a long way. Man, I wish I had a bicycle, he thought, but I just wish and wish and nothin' ever happens. He remembered he had talked to his mother several times about his desire for a bicycle, and each time she had told him that he just needed to wish harder. She had said, "If yuh wish hard enuff, yuh'll git yer wish."

"Really?"

"Why shore."

"But I do wish hard, an' nothin' ever happens. An' I wish fer lots uv things. I started wishin' las' week that I could fin' my book about dawgs, an' I ain't found it yet."

"Just keep wishin', Son. Yer wishes will all come true if yuh just keep on a-wishin'."

Now as Jeremy walked along in the summer heat, he was not sure that his mother was right.

The sun was still up, but it was low in the western sky as Jeremy made his way across the field. Large bunches of Johnson grass grew along the edges of the field, and occasionally small patches of sunflowers. Once across the field, he entered a pasture filled with mesquite trees, algerita bushes, and catclaw. Earlier in the year the algerita bushes had produced small, tart berries. Jeremy liked the taste of the berries, but he seldom picked any of them because the leaves on the bushes were so sticky. Lem had observed that "th' damn berries er so small a guy could starve tuh death eatin' 'em."

He passed two stock tanks on his left. The smaller one, the first one he came to, was his swimming hole now that he had graduated from the creek. He was afraid to swim in the second because it was much larger and deeper. On the other hand, the smaller one where he swam had cottonmouth water moccasins in it. At least Jeremy was convinced that it did. He had seen snakes sunning themselves on the bank of the tank, one particularly large black one, and while he had never seen one in the water, he was always a little apprehensive, afraid one might slip up on him and bite him while he was swimming. He had told his father about seeing the large snake there on the bank, and after he had described it, Lem had said, "Yep, that's prob'ly a cottonmouth."

"Why do they call 'em cottonmouths?"

"'Cause uv their mouths. If yuh ever see one up close, an' he opens 'is mouth, yuh'll see that th' inside uv 'is mouth is white as cotton. That's why folks call 'em cottonmouths. I'll tell yuh somethin', though. One uv 'em that gits close enough yuh can see 'is mouth, that snake is way too close. You watch out fer 'em. They can kill yuh."

"Do they chase yuh, Paw?"

"Oh, I don't think so. They wuz a nigger worked here a while back, an' he claimed that a big un chased him."

"You think a snake really chased 'im, Paw?"

"I got my misdoubts. It may have been a hoop snake. That same nigger claimed that a rabbit run up tuh 'im an' bit 'im, an' I ain't never heard uv no rabbit a-doin' that."

"Boy, I don't want no cottonmouth tuh chase me."

"Water moccasins ain't gonna chase yuh. Yuh just hafta watch out fer 'em."

Next, on his left, he passed a fenced enclosure which Lem used to pen the sheep anytime he needed to work them: to shear them, to brand them, to dock their tails, to "cut" the young bucks, or to treat any injuries. He knew that his friend Leland's house would be next on his left about halfway to the Dorman road. Then he would pass the house where a black family, the Roosevelts, lived. Now on his right, there was nothing but mesquite trees and open pasture, the ground heavily infested with prickly pear.

At last Jeremy was abreast of the Roosevelt house. He had gotten to know the Roosevelts only slightly. There was a young girl named Phrony, about the same age as Jeremy, and they become casual friends picking cotton in the previous year during cotton picking time.

The Roosevelt family was a large clan, and other than Phrony, Jeremy did not know any of the others, though he had seen some of them. Mr. Soules, who lived in Milburn, owned the farm, but he turned all the operations of the farm over to Lem. One of Lem's duties was to hire extra help during harvest or cotton-picking time, and he always hired the Roosevelts. But the Roosevelts, especially the two sullen young sons, George Washington Roosevelt and Reuben Roosevelt, never had anything to do with Jeremy except to tell him to get out of their way.

But cotton picking time was about the only time Jeremy ever saw Phrony or her two brothers. He had asked his father once why he never saw them at school, and Lem had explained that they attended the "colored" school.

Jeremy did not know much about the "colored" school, but he had heard that it had a good football team. Its star player was Puddin' Jones.

Jeremy had heard his father brag about what a good runner Puddin' was. The boys at Jeremy's school had also heard of the "colored" school and Puddin' Jones, but they were not impressed with Puddin'.

"Hell," said H.C. "He ain't nothin' special. Just kick 'im in th' shins."

"Kick 'im in th' shins. Whatta yuh mean?" one of the other boys had asked.

"Don't you know nothin'?" H.C. was indignant. "Yuh always kick a nigger in th' shins. Paw says that's th' onliest way yuh can hurt one. Ain't no use uv a-hittin' 'em in th' head. Cain't hurt 'em there. They all got heads like rocks."

"Mebbe so, but I heard Puddin' can run like hell."

"Yeah, he made five touchdowns in one game once last year."

H.C. was not much impressed. "I'm tellin' yuh, just kick 'em in th' shins."

As Jeremy walked past the Roosevelt house, he pictured Phrony, a skinny girl with large round eyes. Jeremy had never seen her wear shoes, and her dress was always simple and straight, hanging loosely around her neck, drooping off one shoulder. She was constantly pulling the yoke of her dress up around her neck. Jeremy remembered that she always seemed to have a runny nose.

He walked past the house now. Unpainted, it sat up on concrete blocks in a grassless yard. A bent stovepipe sticking through the roof emitted a thin wisp of white smoke. Two trees grew in the yard, and almost every branch of each tree had a brightly colored bottle hanging on the end of it.

He remembered a time earlier when he had passed the house. It had been late morning, and Phrony had been outside, sitting on the edge of the porch by herself, kicking up small clouds of dust with her bare feet. She had greeted him shyly, swaying gently from side to side: "Hi, Jermy." She pronounced his name as if it had two syllables.

"Hi," he replied without looking directly at her. He was always self-conscious around any girl, and especially Phrony, since his mother had told him that all blacks were under a curse. He had wanted to ask Phrony about the curse but had never found the right time.

"We gots a new calf." Phrony motioned toward a small barn behind the Roosevelt house.

Jeremy did not reply.

"You wanta see it?"

Jeremy shrugged his shoulders. "Okay, I guess."

"It was just born yestiddy." Phrony was up off the porch and moving toward the barn. "I got tuh be at th' barn when it uz born."

Jeremy was not sure he wanted to go to the barn. "Maybe some other time."

Phrony stopped. "You don't wanta see th' calf?" She seemed perplexed.

"Aw, I got other things I need tuh do."

"It's a purty little calf. Daddy's gonna let me name it."

Just then, an old black woman, small, stoop-shouldered, and wizened, appeared on the porch. Her grey hair hung in strings about her head. She leaned heavily on a cane. "Phrony, git yorese'f up tuh this house an' eat yore lunch 'fore I throw it out tuh th' hawgs." She turned aside to spit.

Phrony had immediately begun moving toward the house. "I gots tuh eat," she said, adjusting the collar of her dress around her shoulders and already running toward the house.

Now, for the first time, the old woman seemed to become aware of Jeremy. "Tell yore fren' he kin eat, too. Ain't you got no manners?" She turned aside and spat a dark liquid onto the ground.

Phrony had stopped and turned. "You wanta eat, Jermy?"

"Naw, naw, thanks, I ate a big breakfast." He was not sure that he wanted to go into Phrony's house. Blacks were strange to him, and he was afraid of them, especially now that he knew they were cursed people.

He wished he knew more about the curse. He wondered if the bottles hanging on the branches of the trees had anything to do with it.

"Well, you wait fer me. I won't take long," said Phrony. She started into the house.

Reuben walked out onto the porch. Jeremy had seen him before in the cotton patch. Now he was naked to the waist, his muscles rippling under his dark skin. He stood on the porch and emptied a pan of water into the yard. "Who that?" he asked Phrony, indicating Jeremy.

"It's Jermy," said Phrony. "He's my fren', Reuben. I ast him tuh eat with us, but he cain't."

"Ain't that he cain't. He won't," snarled Reuben, staring at Jeremy. "Likely he thinks he's too good tuh eat with us coloreds." He scowled at Jeremy. "What's yore name, Boy?"

"Jeremy. Jeremy Stroop."

"Whatcha doin' here?"

"Nothin'. I uz just a-walkin' by, an' Phrony ast me if I wanted tuh see th' new calf."

"You messin' with my sister, white boy?" Reuben moved a step closer to the edge of the porch.

Jeremy watched Reuben warily. "Naw, I ain't doin' nothin'."

Reuben stared at Jeremy. "You ain't got no damn bizness here, Boy."

"Now, Reuben," warned the old woman, turning aside to spit again.

The Roosevelts disappeared into the house, and Jeremy walked over toward the porch, planning to sit on it while he waited for Phrony.

A single rocking chair sat on the porch. At one end of the porch lay a small stack of firewood, and beside the wood was a washtub turned upside down. A cat lying on the porch raised its head and surveyed Jeremy briefly. Then, stretching itself luxuriously, it extended its four paws and withdrew them under its body, curling up on the floor as if it were already in a deep sleep.

He did not see the dog until he was almost to the porch.

The dog emerged from under the porch, its head lowered, a deep growl in its throat. It was a large dog; most of its hair was missing along its shoulders and flanks. Where there was no hair, the dog's skin was crusty and inflamed. Jeremy stopped in his tracks. He was not sure what to do. He stood very still, his heart pounding. The dog lifted its massive head as if to investigate Jeremy's scent. It stared at Jeremy through rheumy eyes.

What to do? Jeremy thought about trying to speak to the animal but decided against it. The dog and boy stood facing each other, neither moving, except for the dog's lifting its head and snuffling loudly. After what seemed like an eternity to Jeremy, the dog turned and went back under the porch, where it turned around once or twice and then slumped heavily to the ground. Jeremy slowly walked to the other end of the porch and quietly sat down.

He was uneasy about the dog that he couldn't see from his position on the porch, and Reuben had made him nervous. He didn't want to stay, yet he knew that Phrony thought he was going to. So he did.

He had been sitting there for only a few minutes, however, when suddenly two blacks smashed through the screen door of the house and out onto the porch. They were struggling furiously with each other. "You black bastard. I'll teach you to steal my stuff." Jeremy recognized the speaker as Reuben. Kicking, swinging their fists wildly, and cursing at the tops of their lungs, the two boys stumbled down off the porch and out into the yard, where they continued their fight. Jeremy watched in amazement. Reuben's nose was bleeding profusely. Jeremy heard him say that he was going to get his knife and kill the other boy.

Then, suddenly, the old black woman who had summoned Phrony to lunch burst out the door and down off the porch. She no longer used a cane. She moved swiftly and with agility. She carried a broomstick in her hands, and she plunged between the two combatants. Jeremy could hear the sharp whacks as she struck now one and then the other. "Stop it! Stop it, you damn kids. Stop it this instant. I'll beat th' livin' hell outta both uv yuh, right here on this yard if'n you don't stop it right now. You know I will. I ain't a-gonna put up with none uv this nonsense frum none uv you kids." She continued to rain blows on the two boys, and at last they parted sullenly.

"Now, George Washin'ton," the old woman said, "you just go in that house, an' don't you come out till I tell you that you can. You hear me, Boy? You damn well better." She raised her broomstick in a threatening gesture. "Go on before I break this damn broom handle over yer head." Jeremy remembered how H. C. had said that you could not hurt a nigger by hitting him on the head. The old woman apparently had not heard that. She turned to Reuben. "And you, Reuben, you go over there an' sit on that porch, an' you stay there. You hear me? Both uv you. Now git. Go on. Git!" She swung her broom handle in the general direction of the two boys, both of whom drew back from her.

George Washington walked back into the house, viciously slamming what remained of the door. His antagonist walked over and took a seat on the porch. Jeremy was glad to see that he sat on the far end of the porch, away from him. The old woman spat, and then hobbled awkwardly up onto the porch. She had lost some of her agility. On the porch she stopped.

From inside, George Washington called out, "Lemme come out. I'll whip that nigger's black ass."

Reuben, sitting on the porch, had produced a knife and was sharpening it. "Let 'im out," he said, studying the knife in his hands. "Let 'im out. I'll damn shore cut 'im ever'whur but th' soles uv his damn black feet. I'll carve my 'nitials on his black ass."

The old woman had sat down on the porch. "Washin'ton, you ain't comin out. Just fergit it," she yelled.

George Washington called out again. "I want out. I wanta kill that nigger."

Reuben continued to sharpen his knife. "Let 'im out. Let 'im out. I'll cut that black bastard so many ways he won't know whur tuh bleed tuh death first."

"Hush up, both uv you," said the old woman. Then she looked at Jeremy. "Son, you best go on home now. Phrony ain't likely tuh come out no more tuhday."

Jeremy had needed no further encouragement. He rose from the porch, and watching carefully for the dog, ran out across the yard and into the pasture. He never knew how the altercation was resolved, and he never found out why the bottles were on the tree branches.

Jeremy continued on his way to church. He loved this time of day, when the heat finally broke and all the world seemed subdued. Rabbits appeared at this time—tall, rangy jackrabbits which sprang away in long, loping strides, and cottontails, which would start up suddenly, sometimes right under his feet. Patches would chase either kind, but he never got close to any of them, especially jackrabbits.

Jeremy encouraged Patches in his chases. "Go git 'em, Patches. Catch that rabbit." He always hoped that Patches would be successful. In his mind's eye he could see Patches racing up beside a jackrabbit and throwing it down on the ground. "Go git 'im. Git that rabbit, Patches!"

In the distance he heard sheep bleating, but he tried to shut this sound out. He hated sheep. His father had told him that sheep were the dumbest creatures in the world, and Jeremy believed him. He hated the dust they raised as he and his father tried to drive them from one place to another. It always made him sneeze. Even now as he thought of the sheep, he imagined them with their straggly wool encrusted with filth and full of cockleburs and grass burs.

Also, at this time of day, gray doves would begin their evening flight to the stock tanks in search of water. Jeremy enjoyed watching their graceful, swift flight and hearing the whir of their wings as they passed overhead.

5

THE COMMUNITY IN WHICH JEREMY LIVED was sparsely settled; there was only one house on the Dorman road between Jeremy and the church now, and Jeremy knew the house well. It was the home of David White, the richest and most popular boy in the ninth grade. Jeremy always knew when he was nearing David's house. For one thing, unlike all the other farms in the area, the White farm had no mesquite trees. Mr. White had hired a man who owned a Caterpillar tractor to come in and push all the mesquites into great piles and burn them. The only trees to be seen in the White pasture were oaks, and Mr. White mowed a large area of the grass around his house regularly so that it was always neatly trimmed. He had also constructed a board fence and painted it white. The fence ran the full length of the front of the place, and Mr. White saw to it that it was always freshly painted.

The Whites' house was a large two-story affair with multiple gables. It sat well back from the road at the end of a curving, graveled drive that was lined with oak trees. Between the house and the Dorman road was a large pond lined on one side with great boulders and on the other by an earthen dam. A huge sign featuring a picture of sleek, grazing cattle had been erected on top of the dam. Jeremy knew what it said: *White's Hereford Ranch. Cattle for sale. Theodore White, Stock Breeder, Owner and Manager.*

As Jeremy walked by now, several Hereford cows wandered about the pond. Surrounded by a well-kept yard in which several trees and bushes grew, the house was white with green trim. The front porch was supported by two stout columns. He had never been in the house, but he had been told that the Whites had water piped into their house and that it was even wired for electricity. He had heard that the Whites simply turned on a faucet for water, or flicked a switch and lights would come

29

on, but Jeremy found that hard to believe. Jeremy's house had neither running water nor electricity.

As he walked by the house now he could see a large, shiny car sitting in the driveway, and he knew that Mr. White had a new pickup too. Jeremy also knew that the oldest White boy, Larry, who had just graduated from high school, had his own car.

For Jeremy, another indication of the Whites' wealth was the fact that their youngest son, David, wore different clothes to school every day of the week. Jeremy was not clothes-conscious, but he could not help noticing how often David changed his clothes. Jeremy would wear the same shirt to school on Monday, Tuesday, and Wednesday, and then wear another shirt on Thursday and Friday. The following Monday he would wear the same shirt, washed and ironed by his mother, that he had worn the previous Monday. He wore the same trousers—khakis— every day for a week. One of the Stroop rituals was to go to Ayers Store in late August, just before school started for the fall, to buy Jeremy's school clothes. The purchases were always the same: two pairs of trousers and two shirts. Mrs. Stroop made the selections. Jeremy would not see the clothes until she brought them home.

Jeremy did not really care what kind of clothes she bought for him. Sometimes the purchase of shoes was necessary, and about every other year Jeremy would need a new coat. Mrs. Stroop explained that it was important to get a coat that was too big for him, because he was growing so fast, and he outgrew his clothes quickly. Jeremy did resent, however, his mother's insistence on buying him a set of long johns each fall season.

David White always wore shoes. He wore them on the first day of school in September and, what was more amazing to Jeremy, he would wear them up to the last day of school in May. And what Jeremy noticed even more was the fact that David sometimes wore cowboy boots to school. Jeremy had never owned a pair of cowboy boots, and he never wore shoes the first weeks of school. He began to wear them only after the mornings became frosty, and in the spring, as soon as the weather began to warm, he stopped wearing them.

But the one single feature of David's clothing that most impressed Jeremy was his underwear. David always wore white tee shirts and white boxer shorts. Jeremy knew about David's underclothes because he and David were in the same gym class at school, and the boys were required to "suit out" for activities. Each day, David would strip to a gleaming white tee shirt and white boxer shorts.

One of Jeremy's most mortifying concerns was his mother's insistence that he wear long johns during the winter months.

"Aw, Maw," he would plead over and over again. "None uv th' kids at school wears th' things."

"Now, Jeremy," his mother would reply, "I bet lotsa boys in yore room wear 'em, an' besides I don't want yuh a-catchin' no cold. These long johns will keep yuh warm, an' yuh know how yuh hate tuh wear a coat."

"No! Please, Maw. Please! None uv th' kids wear 'em."

"Oh, I bet they do."

"No, Maw, they don't. An' I don't like them ole things. They itch me, an' they git hot, an' I don't wanta wear 'em no more."

"Jeremy, yer paw wears 'em, an' I reckin if they're good enuff fer him, they're good enuff fer you. Now you hush, and put on yer clothes."

"Dang it, Maw! Please. Th' kids'll laugh at me."

All of Jeremy's pleading with his mother had accomplished only one adjustment: his mother had at last consented to let him cut off the sleeves and leggings of the long johns so that they would not stick out from beneath his trouser legs and shirt sleeves.

At first the cutoff long johns had seemed like a workable solution to Jeremy, and the first morning he had worn them to school, he had felt confident. On the bus that morning he had wanted to tell everyone that he no longer wore long johns, but no appropriate time presented itself. Instead, he carelessly rolled up his shirt sleeves so that everyone could see that he did not have long johns on. He even nonchalantly pulled up his trouser leg and scratched an imaginary itch to show anyone who was watching that he did not have on any long johns at all, neither tops nor bottoms.

His confidence had only lasted until gym class. When Jeremy stripped to his cutoff long johns in the locker room, he heard peals of laughter from the other boys as they pointed out to each other the skinny boy in his cutoff underwear.

"Oh, dear me," Ernie had roared. "Wontcha just look at that?"

"Ha, ha, ha," laughed Ben, leaning against a locker door and slapping it with his hand. "Look at 'is laigs a-stickin' out uv his shoes."

Ernie continued to laugh. "Jeremy, you look like a kildee, yer so skinny."

"No, no," chimed in Ben. "He looks like a crane a-standin' in a pair uv watermelon rinds." He could hardly finish, he was laughing so hard. The entire class enjoyed this last comparison immensely. Even the gym instructor had smiled.

"Whur'd yuh git 'em, Stroop?" asked Ernie, but Jeremy was too near tears to answer. And all this time David White had stood there secure in his gleaming white tee shirt and boxer shorts, enjoying the whole scene.

"Why dontcha git some real men's underwear?" he had asked.

Jeremy had hurriedly put on his gym suit. He had joined the other boys on the gym floor, and in the process of the activities, the boys seemed to forget Jeremy and his underwear. Throughout the class period, however, Jeremy had felt no relief. He had dreaded to see the class end, for he knew he would have to undress before the boys and stand before them in his hated cutoff long johns. When the bell rang, signaling the end of the period, he had hung back as much as he dared, offering to help the teacher put away equipment, rearrange chairs, anything to avoid a repetition of his shame at the beginning of class. By the time he had come to the locker room, he was the only boy in the room except for little Johnny Rodriguez. Johnny had a twisted leg, and he always required extra time to go from class to class. He never teased anyone.

As a consequence of his loitering, Jeremy was late to his next class, but he preferred a reprimand from Mrs. Russell to the teasing about his underwear. At least in the classroom, he thought, no one can see my underwear.

The students had only been seated for a short while when David White raised his hand and asked permission to sharpen his pencil. David had then risen from his seat and walked to the pencil sharpener mounted on the wall directly behind Jeremy. Jeremy had paid no attention to David; in fact, he was hardly aware of him at all until David thrust his hand under Jeremy's shirt and pulled up the collar of his long johns for everyone to see. "Lookee! Lookee!" he had shouted, holding firmly to the collar of the underwear as Jeremy tried to wrench free. "Jeremy is still a-wearin' long johns!"

His announcement had brought down the house. Jeremy had twisted violently, trying to escape David's grasp, even swinging at him. "Git yore hands offa me," he screamed. Everyone in the classroom laughed, and some of the students stood up so they could see better. Even Mrs. Russell had to turn her head aside to keep from laughing outright. It had taken a moment for her to compose herself and to tell David to take his seat.

6

AND SO JEREMY HATED DAVID WHITE. He hated David's assurance. David always knew the right thing to say, the right thing to do. He had a muscular build, and he always had a girlfriend. Indeed, it seemed to Jeremy that most of the girls in the school wanted to be David's girlfriend. Jeremy had heard them talk about David in the halls, and he had seen how they flirted with him in class.

David had already begun dating, and he loved to talk about his dates in class or out. Jeremy could remember a time only a few months before during math class, when David had raised his hand to ask Mrs. Russell a question. Jeremy had been thinking it was time for him to raise his hand to ask to be excused to go to the privy, as he did every math class, but Mrs. Russell had recognized David first.

"What is it?" the teacher had asked.

"Well, I wuz a-wonderin', what if I go tuh pick up a girl on a date, see, an' I go in my car, an' when I git there, see, I go up to th' door tuh git 'er, an' I walk 'er out tuh th' car an' open th' door fer 'er, but, see, she slides over under th' wheel an' wants tuh drive. What should I do?" Jeremy had thought the question was ridiculous, and he had laughed. Mrs. Russell, however, had silenced him with a stare.

"Why, David," she had replied, "I think that is a very good question, don't you, class?" The students had nodded in agreement, partly because David had asked the question, and partly because they welcomed the diversion from math. "Now, who can help us?" continued Mrs. Russell. "What should David do?"

A long discussion had followed, mostly among the boys who, attempting to appear gallant in front of the girls in the class, had generally agreed that the girl should be permitted to do whatever she pleased. David had sat back, smugly enjoying the discussion he had provoked and the admiring glances of the girls in the room who hoped that he would come to their door, whether or not they got to drive his car. Jeremy had not entered into the discussion. He had not had anything to say. He had never asked a girl for a date.

But Jeremy's problems with David White went beyond his underwear, and there was one event that burned fresher than any other in his mind as he walked past the Whites' house and thought of his experiences with David. On the last day of school the past term, there had been the usual confusion. The students had been excited and restless in anticipation that school would soon be out, and the teachers had been less strict. The students had just come into the classroom from their lunch break and were milling around in the room. No one wanted to sit down. Mrs. Russell had not yet returned to the room.

Jeremy had been one of the few students who was seated. Across the room, David White and several other boys had leaned on the sills of the open windows; David had a knife that he was showing the boys. As he had watched the boys, Jeremy saw David motion toward him, and then call the boys together for a whispered conversation. As the boys talked, one and then another would look in Jeremy's direction, and then they would all laugh. At last, with a vigorous nodding of heads, the group had broken up and had headed toward Jeremy's desk.

"Why, hello, Stroop," said H.C., the biggest and burliest of the boys.

"Hi," said Jeremy. He had tried to say it carelessly, but he suspected that the boys were up to something, and he was nervous. He looked from one to another of them as they surrounded him. He wiped the palms of his hands on his trousers.

"Whatcha doin' this summer?" Lupe had asked in a friendly tone.

"I gotta work," Jeremy had replied, feeling that the conversation was pointless and yet afraid not to continue it lest he offend the boys, and thus encourage them in whatever they planned.

Lupe had stood on his right and H.C. had stood on his left. Each had casually put his hands on Jeremy's arms, but Jeremy sensed the extra pressure. He realized that the boys planned to pin his arms. At first he thought of trying to break away, but then he decided not to struggle. Perhaps if he did not struggle, they would let him alone.

"Whur yuh workin'?" asked David.

Jeremy had not known whether to answer or not, but he saw that some of the students were watching, and he had decided to put up a front.

"Fer my dad," he said.

"Wha-wha-whatcha gonna do, do, Stroop?" Fred always stuttered in tense situations.

"Why, his Dad is a-gonna use him tuh punch holes in th' ground, he's so skinny," H.C. had laughed. "He'll just walk down one uv th' rows, an' poke his laigs in th' ground tuh make holes, so his paw can plant." All the boys enjoyed the joke. Two girls who had been watching looked at each other and giggled.

Suddenly David had reached for Jeremy's collar, and Lupe and H.C. had tightened their grip on his arms. "Got yer longies on today, Stroop?" David asked, and the boys had laughed again.

"No!" replied Jeremy hotly. He began to struggle in helpless rage.

"Why, I thought yuh'd wear 'em th' year 'round, them bein' so cool cut off th' way yuh wear 'em," David had continued, still holding Jeremy's collar. "But I see yuh don't have 'em on tuhday."

H.C. and Lupe tightened their grip. Jeremy struggled in vain. David leaned near him. "Listen, yuh little bastard. You ain't no part uv a man. Yer just a jerk-off kid, an' we plan tuh teach yuh a lesson yuh won't never fergit. How about that?" He shook Jeremy by the shoulder. When Jeremy did not reply, he shook him again, and then slapped him, not hard. "I ast you a question, stoopid. Answer me."

Then David had released Jeremy's collar and seized his head. "Yuh like things cut off, do yuh, dumb ass?"

Jeremy did not reply.

"Less cut off 'is hair," Lupe had suggested.

"Naw, I got a better idee," David had replied. "Let's cut off 'is ear."

"Hey, that's a great idee." Lenny spoke up for the first time.

David had turned to Lenny and said, "Lenny, you watch th' door an' sing out if ole lady Russell comes."

"Yeah, let's do it." Lupe had been enthusiastic.

Jeremy had squirmed, but there was nothing he could do. Sitting in his desk with his arms pinned, he was helpless.

"Yuh want us tuh cut off yer ear, Stroop?" David had asked.

In fear and desperation, Jeremy had cast about for something to say. All he could think of was a comment he had read in a novel. The hero, when threatened, had said: "Do what you think you can do." The instant Jeremy had said this, he realized it was exactly the wrong thing to say. He wished he had not said it. In the novel it had sounded heroic; now it sounded stupid.

"Do what I think I can do, huh?" David had been pleased with Jeremy's response. "Hear that, boys? Stroop thinks he's tough. Don't think that we'll cut off 'is ear. Let's show th' little bastard."

Jeremy tried to break free. Then he stopped. It was hopeless. He looked up to see the two girls who had been watching earlier still looking at him. He hated them for watching him in his helplessness. And now he had become aware that the eyes of every student in the class were fixed on him.

"Aw, that's enuff. Let 'im go," said H.C., suddenly releasing his grip and turning toward his seat. "Miz Russell will be comin' in here any minute."

H.C.'s withdrawal seemed to break the spell. All the other boys now moved away, watching the door as they moved toward their seats. All the other boys except David. In a quick move, he seized the top of Jeremy's ear, pulled it down, and drew his knife across it where it joined Jeremy's head. Then wiping his knife and putting it into his pocket, he rushed to his seat, chuckling to himself. Jeremy felt a burning sensation in his ear, and when he put his hand to his ear he felt a warm stickiness. Relief and fury swept over him, but at that instant Mrs. Russell came into the room.

Jeremy had waited until she was seated at her desk. Then carefully shielding his ear with his hand so Mrs. Russell would not see the blood, he had approached her and asked to be excused.

"But you just came in from lunch," she said. David laughed.

Jeremy struggled to control himself. He was furious; he felt humiliated. He took a deep breath before he said, "Yes ma'am, but I need tuh go."

"I think you're just taking advantage of its being the last day of school, Jeremy."

"No," Jeremy was losing his patience. He could feel the stickiness spreading over his ear and his hand. "No. I got tuh go now."

"What's wrong with your ear?" Mrs. Russell asked. "Why are you holding your hand over your ear?" She looked around to see who was laughing.

"Nothin'. Nothin'. But I got tuh go!"

"Oh, all right. Go ahead," she had said in exasperation.

As Jeremy had turned to leave the room, someone in the back of the room called out, "Hey, Stroop. Don't wetcha pants!" The roar of laughter had drowned out Mrs. Russell's demand to know who had made that remark.

7

JEREMY LOOKED UP TO SEE THAT HE WAS DRAWING near the church building, and he dismissed thoughts of David White and school from his mind and fastened his attention on the adventure before him. He had passed the church building many times, for it was on the main road from his house to Dorman. The school bus passed it twice a day; the Stroop family passed it twice each Saturday as they went into town to buy groceries and back, but he had never been in it. Now as he approached it in the fading light, he was apprehensive. He even began to have second thoughts about entering. He hated crowds, and he was not comfortable in new experiences. He stopped in the road and turned about, pondering, *Should I go in?* At last, he decided he would.

The building sat on a piece of land higher than the road. A gravelled, deeply-rutted driveway led into the parking lot, which was covered with freshly mowed dry grass. Two large oak trees grew on the lot behind the church, but there were no trees or shrubs on the front lawn. The building was a weathered, square, frame structure in need of paint. It had no steeple, no cross, nor any other external decoration except for a small sign made of warped boards and faded paint that was nailed just over the front door. Jeremy had read it before, and he knew that it said Tabernacle of the Holy Spirit. Behind the building on either side sat two smaller buildings, the outhouses.

There were no windows in the front of the church. The only opening was a single screen door. On either side was a row of windows, some of them missing panes of glass. None of them was stained glass. The church sat up on blocks, and underneath it Jeremy could see several dogs which had retired there to avoid the afternoon sun. Although the sun had set by now, the dogs still had not stirred; they lay panting, watching the people arrive at the building.

A few vehicles were already parked when Jeremy arrived. There were more pickups than cars. Scattered among the vehicles, small groups of people stood, laughing and talking. "H'lo, Jeremy," sang out a small boy as he came tearing past, pursued by two girls. Jeremy recognized the boy, but in these unfamiliar surroundings he did not reply.

All of the people were dressed simply, and Jeremy was a little surprised. He had expected them to be dressed more formally, the way he had imagined them. Most of the men had on khakis or Levis and boots. They wore short-sleeved shirts or had rolled their sleeves above their elbows, and almost every one of them had a straw hat on his head or in his hand. Many of them were smoking. He decided not to linger outside, but to go directly into the building to find a seat.

The building seemed bigger on the inside than it had on the outside. There was no foyer; Jeremy stepped through the screen door at the front of the building and was immediately in the meeting room. Two rows of worn wooden benches sat on the unvarnished floor. The benches faced the speaker's platform and pulpit, and a single aisle extended between them all the way from the entry to a small, elevated platform, covered with a carpet.

The pulpit stood in the center of the platform. It was not high on the wall as Jeremy had expected. Draped over it was a yellowed, flimsy white cloth. Directly behind the pulpit was a single door, which Jeremy surmised led out into the backyard. Beside the door, on either side, sat a small wooden stand with a vase of artificial flowers on it. The windows, on both sides of the building, were all opened in an attempt to catch whatever breeze might be blowing on this sultry August night. There were no screens on the windows. In the ceiling, two large fans turned slowly, clanking ominously with each turn and succeeding at best in stirring up the warm air in the building.

Jeremy stood and surveyed his new surroundings. There were many seats available. He had not known when church would begin, and he had arrived early. He selected a vacant bench and slid its length to the end nearest the wall. He sat down and waited for the services to begin. He had no idea what to expect. As far as he could see, there was no robed choir. Maybe the choir will come later, he thought to himself.

As Jeremy continued to look around, he saw that several people were already seated, and he noticed that some people were on the floor, kneeling before their benches, their arms resting on the seats and their heads on their arms. The kneeling people were motionless; he hoped that he would not be asked to assume the same position. The ladies who had already seated themselves in the building fanned themselves with whatever was convenient: purses, songbooks, and one lady was using a handkerchief. The men for the most part sat in preoccupied patience. One man, gazing into space, turned an unlighted cigar in his hand.

8

AROUND HIM THE BENCHES WERE BEGINNING TO FILL. The kneeling people still had not changed their positions. Occasionally, Jeremy could hear them mumble something. He decided he would ask his mother about the kneelers when he got home. Meanwhile the dull buzz of conversation had increased to a substantial noise, punctuated by the dull grind of the two large ceiling fans and by loud laughter.

"Why, hello there, Tom," someone behind Jeremy said. "Glad yuh could come tuh services tuhnight."

"Wouldna missed it after that sermont this mornin'."

"Wasn't that a good un? Boy, people don't know what they're a-missin' by not comin' out tuh this meetin'. Lemme tell yuh. This Brother Flancher is some kind uv preacher. Best I ever heard. I never heard him before. Had you?"

"Naw, I hadn', but he is good, an' it's a shame that more don't come tuh hear 'im. People don't come like they useta. They just ain't inter'sted in religion no more."

"I know. I think it's mostly young people. They don't come 'less their parents make 'em. They'd rather go tuh some movie er somethin'. My brother's got two kids, both uv 'em boys 'bout growed up now. I tole 'im about this meetin', an' I tole 'im he should oughtta bring them boys to these services, but he don't keer. An' his boys don't keer. Don't none uv 'em keer. Them boys uv his is growed up now, an' all they wanta do is go over tuh Peach Springs ever' Saturday night an' dance. I come by his house this mornin' an' ast 'im tuh come tuh church an' bring 'is boys, but he tole me them boys had been tuh Peach Springs las' night, an' they uz still in bed. I tole th' missus that I bet they uz a-sleepin' off a big drunk."

"More likely they had been tuh Mexico tuh that 'Boys Town' down there."

"Well, now, they mighta been. I have heard 'em speak uv it."

"Ain't nothin' but a cesspool uv sin down there."

"I know. I know. But yuh cain't tell youngsters nothin' these days."

"Well, th' time's a-comin'."

"I know. It's shorely a shame. I just don't know what th' worl's a-comin' to."

"Well, it's th' devil's work fer shore. He's a-conquerin' th' whole worl', an' only th' righteous remnant shall stand. Bible says that."

"Amen, Brother. Amen. Yer dead right. Only th' righteous. Yes, Sir."

Jeremy turned his head to see the two speakers solemnly nod their heads to confirm their concern.

A lady sitting behind the two men leaned forward and said, "Well, I can tell yuh what th' worl's a-comin' to. It's a-comin' to an end."

"That's right, Sister," replied one of the men. Jeremy could not tell which. "Th' Lord's a-comin'."

"Oh, shore. I expect 'im tuh come any day now. All th' signs point tuh it. Why, las' week they uz this big earthquake somewhur over in China er somewhur, an' you know th' Bible says that sich signs shall appear just before th' Lord comes."

"Amen. Yer dead right, Sister."

"Yeah, an' there's been this turrible drought here in our own county."

"Yep. All signs a-pointin' tuh th' end."

"They shore are, an' then there's alla th' false prophets now."

"Yep. A person cain't be too keerful these days. I've 'bout quit listenin' tuh preachers on th' radio 'cept the good uns. Anymore I just read my Bible. At least yuh can trust it."

The lady nodded solemnly and leaned back against her bench, secured in her faith by the acceptance of her companions.

Jeremy looked around. People still filed into the building. A family of two adults and five children arrived. They stopped beside the bench where Jeremy was sitting, and after a brief discussion, to Jeremy's consternation, the mother indicated that they were all to sit on his bench. A boy larger than Jeremy slid down the bench until he was beside him. As the other family members joined the boy on the bench, he moved closer and closer to Jeremy to make room for them. Jeremy slid down to make room for the family, and soon he found himself crowded against the wall of the building. He decided that he had made a poor choice of benches, for the bench in front of him and the one behind him was in front of a window, but his bench butted against the wall between the two windows. He thought about getting up and moving, but he did not want to attract attention to himself—and besides, as nearly as he could tell, all the benches were filled except for one or two right in front of the podium. Jeremy thought about moving up to them, but then he realized that these two benches were occupied by the kneelers, who still had not changed their positions.

All over the building people were fanning themselves with whatever they could find. Jeremy's hair had become damp, and he felt a drop of perspiration slide down his spine. The boy next to Jeremy began to unbutton his shirt and to blow on his chest and stomach. His mother, a short, dumpy lady with sparse, black, stringy hair—it occurred to Jeremy that her face looked like a potato—leaned across the child between her and the boy and tried to slap him, saying, "Button yer shirt. Yer in church!" She blinked furiously.

The boy dodged her hand, and she missed him, hitting instead the back of the bench. She put the two fingers of the injured hand into her mouth and sucked them vigorously, then shook her hand in pain. She swung at the boy again, but this time he used a book as a shield.

"You button yer shirt," she hissed, "er I'll turn you over tuh yer paw when you git home." Her eyes snapped.

But then, her attack on the boy over, she resumed her position on the bench and began to fan herself. She put her fingers back into her mouth, and then as an afterthought she gave the boy a dirty look. He looked at Jeremy and winked, but he buttoned his shirt except for the two top buttons. His sister, sitting between the boy and his mother, looked at him and said, "You better button yer shirt, er I'll tell."

"Go tuh hell," whispered the boy, but he watched his mother.

"Mama," the girl said, tugging on her mother's arm. "Nolan told me tuh go tuh hell."

His mother looked at him, shook her head, and scowled fiercely. "You jest wait," she rasped. "Yer paw will beat yer butt raw once we git home."

The girl looked at her brother. "You ain't suppose tuh tell me tuh go tuh hell."

The boy, facing the podium, reached out and pinched the girl on her leg where the mother could not see what he did. Not looking at the girl, he said, "Go tuh hell."

"Ow!" shouted the girl. "Mama! He pinched me."

The woman turned in exasperation. "Lordy, what's a body tuh do. You two kids'll be th' death uv me, and then I guess yuh'll be sorry enuff." She faced the podium and resumed fanning herself. The little girl gave Nolan a dirty look, and then snuggled close to her mother.

It was very hot. All over the building there was the swish of improvised fans. Children moved about restlessly, irritated in the heat. The parents scolded in frustration, trying to make the children behave. Somewhere a baby began to cry. Jeremy wished the services would begin.

Suddenly, someone said "Shhhhh!" and then the same sound was repeated all over the building, and the crowd quieted. Every eye turned toward the podium and watched as two men walked into the building through the door at the back of the room. Jeremy recognized both of them: Jacob Mutchell and the preacher, Flancher.

Everyone strained to see; even the children stopped their activities and craned their necks to watch the new arrivals. Some of them stood up in their seats to see better. The kneelers, as if in response to some unspoken cue, shifted back from their benches, rose, and turned to sit on the seats. "It's th' preacher," someone whispered.

"Hush now. Here's Brother Flancher," said another.

Jacob Mutchell wore khaki trousers and a khaki shirt opened at the collar. He rubbed a hand over his scrubby beard. Over his khaki shirt he wore a dingy black coat frosted with lint. He had carefully combed the long hairs on the left side of his head over the crown of his bald pate. He moved with authority as he walked in, not looking to the right or to the left, not looking at anyone in the audience, heading directly toward a front bench, one of the few where there was room for him to sit. As he sat down, he picked up a songbook and began to leaf through it, oblivious to his surroundings.

Flancher, however, stopped at the podium and stood, hands on hips, surveying the crowd before him. He was larger than Jeremy remembered; Jeremy thought he must weigh three hundred pounds. He had a florid complexion, thick lips, and bushy eyebrows that gave the impression that he was always looking through them. His nose was broad; Jeremy thought it looked flattened, and his double chin was large, soft, and flabby, already glistening with perspiration. He had a magnificent mane of blond hair, not parted but combed back from his forehead in luxuriant waves that glistened dully in the glare of the ceiling lights. It curled over his collar.

Flancher was the only man in the building, besides Mutchell, who wore a coat. He also wore a wide tie with a bright geometric design, the knot of the tie pulled down to reveal his unbuttoned collar. His suit seemed expensive, flashy; it had a gray background with a large maroon plaid design throughout the material. His coat was unbuttoned, pulled back over his expansive girth that heaved now as he breathed heavily from the exertion of having walked up the steps into the building. At his wrists, large gold cuff links glittered, matching the thick gold watch on his left wrist. His tie was mounted with a gold tie pin. Jeremy had never seen anyone like him.

Flancher stood at the podium, smiling upon the whole congregation, revealing the large, even teeth that Jeremy remembered from the time Flancher had visited him and his father in the field. Flancher's gaze drifted from side to side as he drummed his fingers on the podium. At last, satisfied with what he had seen, he stepped down, grunting and holding onto the podium as he did so, and walked toward a seat beside Mutchell. He moved heavily, ponderously.

As Flancher walked along the front pew, a bald-headed, hunch-backed man suddenly stood up and extended his hand to him, smiling, bowing, and nodding his head as he did so. Flancher took the man's hand, smiled, slapped him on the shoulder, and said something that Jeremy could not hear. The man who had shaken hands with Flancher then sat down, looking over his shoulder and about the room as if to see who might have observed the friendly relationship he had with the preacher. Then he turned to face forward, folded his arms, bowed his head slightly and concentrated on the podium, a pose that he maintained until the services began. Flancher continued on his way to a seat, shaking the hand of each man that he passed. No women sat on the front row.

At last it was time to start. Jacob Mutchell rose, walked to the podium, and then staring out the windows—first on the left side of the building, and then on the right—began to address the congregation. "Uuuuh, it's real good tuh see ever'body here tuhnight. We wanta thank our visitors fer comin' our way. We gotta good crowd uv 'em tuhnight, I see." He still stared out of the windows. "We're glad tuh have ye. We wantcha tuh come back each an' ever' opportunity that prevails itse'f with ye. Uhhh, we got a great meetin' a-goin' on."

Suddenly a man several seats in front of Jeremy boomed an "Amen!" Jeremy jumped in surprise. A chorus of less enthusiastic amens followed. Jeremy watched the man in front of him for a further reaction, but none was forthcoming.

"Amen is right," said Mutchell, pleased with the response. "Praise th' Lord! Uh, Brother Flancher is a-preachin' fer us." Mutchell rocked back and forth as he spoke; he still looked out the windows on the sides of the building, occasionally pausing to look intently out one of the windows as if he had found something worthy of close scrutiny. "An' he's a-doin' a fine job fer us, too, a great job. Fine sermont this mornin', an' I know he'll do another fine job tuhnight. He's always good. Uh, we thank God fer men like Brother Flancher, an' fer bringin' 'im all this way safe an' soun' tuh preach fer us. Ain't it wunnerful?" Another chorus of amens followed, but Jeremy was not surprised this time. Mutchell continued, "We want all uv yuh tuh be shore to be here ever' service. It's just such a blessin'. We—we—uh—visitors is welcome; members is expected." Mutchell paused for effect. "Now, let's start our service with prayer. Shall we stand?" Mutchell accompanied this last request with a sweeping upward motion of his hands.

There was a great scuffling of feet as most people stood, including Jeremy as soon as he realized what everyone else was doing. Mutchell bowed his head as he began to pray, but Jeremy did not bow at first. He looked around to see what others were doing. One woman, who had elected not to stand, took advantage of the privacy to wipe her child's nose. A young boy and girl, two rows in front of Jeremy, seized this opportunity to embrace while she leaned against him, her head on his shoulder. She kissed his neck, and he squeezed her close. A tall, thin woman sitting before the piano idly turned through her songbook, at the same time fanning herself with a handkerchief. She was frowning, and she squinted as she looked at the book. The little girl on the bench directly in front of Jeremy caught his attention, and then slowly, deliberately, stuck out her tongue at him. Jeremy bowed his head, pushed back his hair, and listened to the prayer in progress.

"Uhh—an' we pray, our Heavenly Father, that yuh'll bless th' widders an' orphants, our Heavenly Father, an'—uh—that yuh'll bless Brother Flancher with a happy recollection uv those things that he's studied. Uhhhh—may his words fall on good an' honest hearts, our Heavenly Father, an' bring forth much fruit tuh yer name's honor an' glory. Lead us an' guide us, an'—uh—guide, guard, an' direct us, an' pertect us, for we ast it all in Jesus' name. Amen!"

A vigorous chorus of amens seconded the conclusion to Mutchell's prayer, and then again there was much confusion as people re-settled themselves on their benches. Jeremy noticed that during the prayer, the boy beside him had unbuttoned two more buttons on his shirt. Jeremy looked up at the mother to see her reaction, but she did not seem to notice. She stared straight ahead, still, except that she flexed the hand she had hurt on the bench.

A man stood up and announced that the congregation should sing song number 23, and the congregation launched into song. As Jeremy looked around, not singing, he noticed many others were not singing either; they were using their songbooks as fans, for the temperature had continued to rise in the building. Jeremy wiped his face with his hand and pushed back his hair from his face. He did not join in the singing.

The song seemed very long, and Jeremy was glad when it was over. He was beginning to wonder if coming to church had been such a good idea after all. *I wonder if all people do at church is just sing and pray.* He shifted about, trying to find a more comfortable position on the hard seat, and finally slumped forward, his elbows on his knees, his head in his hands.

At last, however, this song ended and the man who had led the song, walking back toward his seat even before the song was finished, announced that he would lead number 257 after prayer. He cleared his throat as he walked back to his seat, swinging his songbook carelessly.

Now as Jeremy watched, another man arose and strode to the podium. Jeremy noted with some relief that he was not carrying a songbook. He wondered what this man intended to do. "Now, I ain't a-gonna preach yuh no sermont," the man said, "though Lord knows I'd like to. Hearin' all this good singin' shore makes me wanta preach. Hallelujah!" There was a brief pause as the speaker swallowed. "But I ain't a-gonna preach yuh no sermont. I'm up here tuh lead yuh in prayer, an' that's what I'm a-gonna do. Prayin' is very important, an' leadin' prayer is a great responsibility."

At this point, Jeremy's attention was distracted from the speaker to the songbook in his hands. He turned through the book, hardly aware of the ongoing drone of the voice of the speaker as he continued to assure the audience that he did not intend to preach to them. As Jeremy turned through the book, he came at last to a title, "Are You Washed in the Blood of the Lamb?" He thought that he recognized it. He remembered listening with his mother to this song being sung on the radio, and he read the words with renewed interest.

He knew that the lamb referred to in the title was Jesus. His mother had told him that. But he still wondered why Jesus would call himself a lamb. Every time he thought of a lamb, he saw in his mind's eye a spindly, awkward, dirty animal with floppy ears, a mucus-clotted nose, and a tail ragged with filth. Jeremy concentrated on the words of the song. "Have you been to Jesus for the cleansing power? Are you washed in the blood of the lamb?" In spite of what his mother had told him about the song, he had some difficulty with the idea of washing in blood.

"Our Father in heaven, hollowed be thy name," the man at the podium began to pray. "This evenin' as we come before thee with the shades uv night a-huvverin' over us, Heavenly Father, we're thankful and grateful tuh yuh fer this opportunity tuh pray tuh yuh." On the bench directly in front of Jeremy, a young woman with four children leaned over to whisper to one of them, "You don't put yer head down, you ain't gittin' no candy when we git home." Jeremy could not tell which child she addressed, but he hoped it was the little girl who had stuck out her tongue at him.

"Be with th' doctors an' nurses," the prayer droned on. "Guide their hands. Bless our leaders an' rulers. Thank ye fer th' land whur we live, a land uv Bibles whur we can worship yuh without fear uv molestation."

Jeremy's attention wandered from the prayer to one of his favorite daydreams. In his mind he could see a beautiful garden, suffused with soft moonlight. He was in an expensive black suit with a starched white shirt. His hair was combed back loosely. As he waited, the girl came to him in her flowing off-the-shoulder white dress. She was beautiful, as she always was in his dream. She leaned back against a tree and he stood over her, not speaking, not touching her. The girl moved away, and Jeremy watched her as she glided rather than walked over the ground; then he followed her. She walked to a hammock and lay back in it, stretching full length. She looked up at him, invitingly, through half-closed eyes. He came to her and leaned over her. They were close, so very close. He was intensely aware of her. He could feel his throat constricting, and he shifted his weight on the seat. His dream was shattered by a clearing of throats and rearranging of human bodies. The prayer had ended.

9

THERE WAS ANOTHER SONG, UNEVENTFUL. And then all eyes riveted on Brother Flancher as he rose majestically from his seat, gave a hitch to his trousers, and strode toward the podium. He put out a hand to brace himself against the podium and heaved himself up onto the dais, then stood silently, patiently, waiting for the congregation to settle down. His heavy eyebrows bristled; his smooth, full face glistened with perspiration. Still facing the congregation, without having taken his eyes from them, he extracted a starched white handkerchief from one of his back pockets and mopped his face. Then he carelessly folded the handkerchief and placed it on the podium, smiling tolerantly, his eyes roving over audience all the while. At last he spoke.

"Now, all you folks know that I got a coat," he said, struggling to get his arms and shoulders out of his coat, "so I'm just a-gonna take this un off an' put it right over here on this here bench." He started to step down from the dais, but the bald-headed man who had greeted him earlier leaped to his feet to take the coat. He smiled and bowed as he offered to take the coat from Flancher, and then he made a show of folding it carefully and placing it beside him on the bench. "Thankee, Sir," said Flancher. Then he turned once more to the audience. "It's great tuh be here tuhnight," Flancher began. He paused to wipe perspiration from his face. His shirt clung to him damply. "An' I want tuh thank ye fer comin'. Ain't yuh glad yuh come?" he asked, beaming on the crowd. "If yuh are, say, 'Praise th' Lord.'" There were only a few scattered responses, and Flancher seemed disappointed. "Now that don't sound much like yer really glad. If yuh really mean it, then let's hear it!" There was a stronger response. "Now I cain't preach tuh no crowd that's half asleep. I wanta hear yuh say, 'Praise th' Lord.' Now, come on, all together. Less hear it!" Flancher shouted, rising on his toes and leaning forward over the podium. A loud chorus responded, but

48

Flancher still was not satisfied. "Ag'in!" he shouted, and then again and again until the whole building seemed to shake with the uneven chorus. Jeremy noticed that some young people had stood up and were jumping up and down, shouting, "Praise th' Lord!" at the tops of their lungs, laughing as they did so. Jeremy was not sure what he should do. Nolan had fallen asleep on his bench, his head lolling against the back of the seat, his mouth drooping open.

Flancher seemed satisfied now. He stood, a faint, triumphant smile on his lips. He lifted his handkerchief again, wiped his face, and ran the handkerchief around the inside of his collar. He hooked his finger in his tie and pulled the knot down further. He became still, peering down at the podium over which he towered. Then, jabbing his finger at the audience, he shouted, "Moses stood before th' burnin' bush!" He dragged out the words for effect. "Yes, he did. Oh, yes, he did."

"Amen!" shouted the crowd.

Flancher immediately captured Jeremy's attention. He loved the story about the burning bush. He could almost see the flames leaping from the bush, which in Jeremy's imagination was an algerita bush. When Flancher declared that the bush was not consumed by the flames, Jeremy wanted to believe every word. He knew he had never seen such a bush, and he wondered if Flancher had. "Moses didn' want tuh obey God. He tole th' Lord, 'I cain't speak. I cain't do yer will, Lord.' An' what did God say? What did th' Lord say? He tole Moses tuh shut up an' tuh quit makin' excuses, an' tuh git down tuh Egypt an' set 'is people free." Flancher was pacing, shouting. "Oh, yes, that's what he said. Praise th' Lord! Now God has tole you tuh quit sinnin', an' yer makin' excuses, ain'tcha?" He wagged his finger at the congregation. "Oh, I know yuh do. Yuh say, 'I cain't,' just like Moses did, er yuh say, 'I will tomorrer,' but th' Lord wants yuh now. An if th' Lord don't gitcha, hell will! Oh, yes. Hell will. It will!"

The word "hell" stirred Jeremy's imagination. He tried to imagine what hell was like; he wished Flancher would elaborate on the subject. Jeremy believed in hell—at least he thought he did—and he believed that sinners would go there.

"Moses had a rod," said Flancher, and then he paused and began to look around the building. "I need a rod," he said, looking about the podium. Instantly, the hand-shaker coat-folder was on his feet. Without a word, he disappeared out the door behind the podium. Flancher, seeming not to notice the man's disappearance, continued. "I need a rod like Moses had. I wanta show yuh what that rod uz like, an' what mighty things th' Lord can do in his name." Flancher raised his arms above his head, revealing dark perspiration stains under his arms. He stepped back to the podium and reached for his handkerchief, which by now was reduced to a limp cloth. Flancher's hair had loosened and was tumbling about his ears; his shirt had begun to work its way out of his trousers. He put his handkerchief back on the podium and gave his trousers a great hitch, at the same time trying to stuff his shirt back into them, and then resumed his sermon.

"Now Moses. . . " he began, but he was interrupted by a clattering commotion at the door behind him. The hand-shaker coat-folder was back and was struggling, trying to hold the door open at the same time he was trying to get a long pole through the door. He looked at Flancher and grinned broadly. "I found yuh a rod, Brother Flancher."

"Well, now," said Flancher, visibly impressed. "That's some rod." He took the proffered pole and tried to stand it on end, but it was so long that one end of it struck the ceiling of the building. "What kind uv pole is this anyway?" he asked.

Someone on the front seat spoke up: "That's a measuring stick tuh measure th' level of gas in underground tanks. I bet it come from Jim Buhler's place. He's th' onliest one in this county that ud have a rod like that."

"Well, this is some staff indeed," continued Flancher. The hand-shaker coat-folder rod-provider looked around to see the audience's reaction to the rod. He turned back to look at Flancher, well pleased with himself. He crossed his legs nonchalantly, as if providing props to preachers was an everyday business for him. He sat down, carefully re-folding Flancher's coat, and then he closed his eyes, smiling slightly.

"Now, Moses had a rod like this un," Flancher was saying. "Just an ordinary rod made uv wood, but God did great things with it. Yessir, great things. Oh, yes, he did. Moses lifted that rod up." Flancher raised the rod above his head. The perspiration stains under his arms were spreading. "An' then he threw that rod down in front uv that wicked king." And here Flancher hurled the rod to the floor with a great clatter. Jeremy jumped involuntarily. The audience gasped. The rod bounced up from the floor and landed across the laps of two men sitting on the front bench. A titter of laughter rippled through the audience, but the two men acted as if nothing had happened. They sat stiffly, continuing to watch Flancher, and they let the rod lie in their laps until Flancher picked it up. "Didn' mean tuh startle ye," he said. He threw the rod down again, more gently this time. "That rod hit th' groun', and it become a snake—a real, live, crawling snake. Yes, it did."

"Preach th' Word!" someone shouted.

Jeremy strained to see the rod. He wanted to see what had happened to it.

Flancher retrieved the staff and walked with it back and forth before the audience, now twirling it over his head like a giant baton, now striking the podium or one of the seats for emphasis, and all the time spinning the marvelous tale of Moses. For the present, Flancher had given up on using his handkerchief, and he was simply wiping away his perspiration the best he could with his hand. The right front panel of his shirttail was completely out of his trousers now. The shirt was so wet that it was transparent, and Jeremy could see the hair on Flancher's chest and stomach through his shirt.

Flancher's sermon gained momentum. Loud, fervent "Amens" could be heard from time to time. "Hallelujahs" punctuated Flancher's remarks. He bore down. He had put his rod aside for now, and he stalked before the crowd, raising and lowering his voice, jabbing his forefinger at the audience, waving his rod, pushing the crowd to a fever pitch.

Leaning over the podium, he pleaded with the audience: "Moses wuz called by God, an' you are called by God. Moses said, 'I cain't do it.' Is that what you say, sinner? Do yuh say, 'I cain't do it?' God knows better. He calls yuh like he did Moses, an' he can take you like he did Moses' rod an' do wunnerful things, but yuh gotta come tuh God. God wants yuh tuh come down here tuhnight an' give 'im yer heart. Come down here, sinner, an' let God save yuh. Who'll come? Who'll flee th' wrath uv God an' th' flames uv hell?"

Flancher looked at the audience expectantly. "Do yuh know what hell is like?" he asked. Jeremy's interest picked up. "Hell is fire an' brimstone ferever. Eternity. Ah, Brother, how long is eternity?" Flancher shook his head and stood reflectively, as if he were struggling with some profound issue. "How long is eternity? How long is that tuh suffer in flames and brimstone? Think uv a steel ball, ten-foot thick. Can yuh imagine that?"

Jeremy tried. Some of the audience nodded. Someone shouted, "Yessir."

"Now," Flancher continued, "think uv a little ole ant a-crawlin' aroun' on that ball. How long would it take fer that little ole ant tuh wear a trench an inch deep? Would it take a million years? Why, think uv it! An' then think how long would it take fer that little ole ant tuh wear a trench plumb through that steel ball? Why, it ud take a hunnerd million years, an' you know what? When that ant got through, hell woulda just got started." Jeremy was amazed. Flancher's analogy overwhelmed him. He decided he was very afraid of hell.

Flancher had become louder and increasingly emotional. His voice was hoarse, strained. "Oh, sinner, flee from this eternal hell. Cain't yuh see th' flames? Cain't yuh smell th' brimstone? Cain't you hear them flames a-cracklin'? Come tuh Jesus this very minute. Who will accept Jesus?" Flancher's eyes darted over the crowd. With his hand, he motioned for people to come to him. "Who'll come? Who'll come an' receive th' blessed Holy Ghost an' escape from hell? Who'll..."

"Aiyiieeee!" A scream split the air. Jeremy jumped, and his heart skipped a beat. The woman on the seat in front of him, the woman with the four children, was standing up, rigid, her arms stretched toward the ceiling, and she was screaming again and again. To Jeremy's surprise, the congregation did not seem frightened or even unduly concerned, for in response to her screams, they shouted, "Praise th' Lord!" The woman continued to scream; her children looked at her in amazement, and her youngest child began to cry. The husband sat impassively, staring straight ahead, not looking at the woman at all.

"Oh, Jesus!" She cried. "Oh, Jesus, Jesus, Jesus, Jesus, Jesus." Over and over again she screamed. Then she hid her face in her hands and wept openly. Jeremy looked at Flancher to see his reaction to this strange behavior, but Flancher seemed immensely pleased. He smiled and extended his arms to the woman. "Bless yuh, Sister. Bless yuh," he said. "You just come right up here. You folks there on th' bench, you let 'er by." All the people on the bench between the lady and the aisle moved about, clumsily trying to get out of her way as she stumbled over their legs in her haste to reach the aisle. She was still crying hysterically as she turned up the aisle to rush into Flancher's open arms. He welcomed her warmly, holding her to him, and then he led the woman, still sobbing brokenly, to a bench and indicated to her that she should sit there. The men who were sitting on the bench all rose and moved to other seats. Jeremy could not understand what was going on. On the bench in front of him, one of the woman's children asked her father, "Can I go be with Mama?"

"You sit still," he replied.

Flancher had hardly seated the first woman when another lady started down the aisle toward him. "Bless yuh, Sister," he said. "Praise th' Lord. Who will come tuh th' Lord? Who will come an' join these sweet sisters? Who will be saved?" He seated the second lady, and then made a motion to the woman seated at the piano. She had been waiting for just such a signal it seemed, for she immediately launched into a sad, funeral-like dirge. "Who will come?" pleaded Flancher, walking back and forth before the crowd, never taking his eyes off the audience—most of whom were standing now, some swaying to the music, clapping in rhythm.

A man in front of Jeremy stood up and began babbling something that Jeremy could not understand. He seemed to be saying, "Gitta, gitta, gitta, gitta," over and over. Flancher, in contrast to his previous responses to the two women, ignored the man, and so did everyone else. Nolan, awake now, looked at Jeremy shyly, pointed to the man, made a circling motion around his ear with his index finger, and laughed. "Crazy," he said.

By now the room was becoming a mass of confusion. There were loud shouts and groans everywhere; people old, young, middle-aged, began walking down the aisle to be welcomed by Flancher, who would embrace each of them or shake hands with them, and then show them to seats. The people who responded sat with their heads lowered, and most of them were crying. One man, who had started down the aisle toward Flancher, stopped about midway, sat down in the aisle and remained there, not moving, his eyes fixed in an empty stare. Above the sound of the crying was the constant dirge of the piano and the steady, dull hum of the slow-turning ceiling fans. Occasionally, someone would shout in ecstasy.

Jeremy was surprised at the number who responded. Everyone on his bench went except him and two boys. Nolan took advantage of his mother's absence to unbutton his shirt again. He winked at Jeremy as he did so. The little girl on the seat in front of Jeremy was tugging at her father's sleeve. "Whur'd Mama go, Daddy?" The father ignored the question, but he put his arm around the little girl and pulled her head to his chest.

Nolan tapped Jeremy on the arm. "I'll go up there if you will," he said.

Jeremy looked away. He did not know what to say.

The babbler still stood. He continued to speak in a way that Jeremy could not understand: "Gitta, gitta, gitta," and he seemed to be talking to no one in particular. He never moved; he never looked right nor left; he just continued his stream of gibberish. Others about the room were talking, as far as Jeremy could tell, to no one and in no language that he could understand. These people remained at their benches. They did not go to Flancher.

Then Jeremy became aware of an old woman who was out in the aisle, but she was not walking toward Flancher. Instead she walked toward him. As she walked, she was shouting to those whom she passed: "Ye better come up an' git saved, er th' Devil'll eat yer soul tuhnight." Jeremy watched her to see what she would do. She seemed very old, and she walked with a cane. She was hump-backed, and the front of her dress which hung about her shoulders was heavily soiled.

The hem of her slip hung below her dress, and she walked awkwardly in high-heeled shoes. As she moved along the benches, she banged on them with her cane, and she shouted at the people still sitting down. "You better git yerse'f up tuh that preacher man if yuh know what's good fer yuh. Yer goin' tuh hell, shore and certain." As she came abreast of the bench on which Jeremy sat, she spied him and came toward him.

"Are ye saved, Sonny?" she asked, giving him a toothless grin that multiplied the wrinkles in her face. She moved down the bench toward Jeremy and thrust her face into his. Jeremy became aware of a distinctly unpleasant odor. "Have ye got th' Holy Spirit, Boy?" she asked raspily. "You been saved?"

Jeremy was terrified. "I donno. I donno," he mumbled weakly.

"Come on, Sonny, an' be saved," she persisted, trying to put her arm around him. Jeremy tried to push her away, inadvertently tangling his hands in the folds of her dress. He looked around for an avenue of escape. The two boys sitting near him slid toward the aisle, away from the woman. Jeremy tried to slide the other way, but he was already against the wall. He wondered who this ugly old woman could be and what could she possibly want.

And then the music of the piano ceased, and Flancher's voice could be heard above the noise in the room. "Praise th' Lord. Praise th' Lord, brothers an' sisters. Now, let's all git quiet now. Let's all be quiet an' be seated." Jeremy noticed with relief that the old woman released her hold on his arm, but she sat down beside him. He looked at her out of the corner of his eye. She ignored Jeremy; she had fixed her eyes on Flancher. Who could she be? Why she had singled him out?

"That's it. Now, all be quiet. Let's all have a seat." Two men stepped up to the babbler and gently pushed him back into his seat. As soon as he sat down, he stopped talking. The man sitting in the middle of the aisle got up and returned to his seat. Flancher was gaining control of the crowd. He worked patiently, authoritatively. At last he had everyone's attention, and the only noise in the room, besides that of the fans, was the muffled sobbing of those who sat on the front seats where Flancher had placed them. "That's it. Thank ye, brethern, thank ye. Now all these folks has come up here a-wantin' us tuh pray fer 'em. They want God's mercy, an' they want our prayers. I'm a-gonna talk tuh each uv 'em tuh find out what's on their hearts, an' then we'll pray fer 'em."

Flancher began now to move from person to person along the benches. He embraced each person and held a whispered conversation with him or her. He would always pat the person on the back before he moved on. As he neared the end of one of the rows of respondents, he paused and talked earnestly with a woman. After awhile, he straightened and said, "Now, Sister Blum has come here tuhnight wantin' tuh be baptized with th' Holy Spirit, an' she has asked us tuh he'p 'er. So, we're a-gonna ast 'er tuh stan', an' we're a-gonna pray fer her." The woman stood, and Flancher put his hand on her head and began to pray. As he prayed, he pushed against the woman's head, hard, suddenly, and she dropped toward the floor, so quickly that Flancher was barely able to grab her and support her as she fell. Flancher went through the same procedure with the next woman, who also fell to the floor. Jeremy craned his neck to see the women, but he couldn't.

At last Flancher straightened and returned to the podium. He seemed on the verge of tears as he spoke. "All uv these has come forward tuhnight tuh give their hearts tuh God. We already prayed fer two of these sisters so's they can receive th' Holy Spirit, an' I know they did. You know they did. You watched 'em die in th' spirit right here before yer eyes. Our God is a god who answers prayer. These other good folks wants us tuh pray fer them so's they can be forgiven fer their sins. Praise th' Lord fer bringin' all these souls tuhnight. It's th' power uv th' gospel." Flancher was much calmer now than he had been during the sermon. His appearance was bedraggled; his hair fell about his face. Perspiration streaked his face. He had given up trying to keep it off, even with his hand. He carried his handkerchief rolled into a hard knot. He seemed weary, but he was smiling.

He addressed those who had responded to his invitation. "I want tuh say somethin' tuh all of yuh that has responded here tuhnight. We're gonna pray fer yuh, an' God is gonna hear, an' he's a-gonna do great things. Praise his name. But I wantcha tuh know that after we pray here together, if there is any one uv yuh who would like tuh know about a deeper, fuller prayer life like I have found, I'll be happy tuh share it with yuh. If yuh wanta know more about th' life uv th' Spirit, just stay here at the front after services is over, an' I'll tell yuh how I found th' deeper life an' all that it's meant fer me since then. I want tuh talk tuh yuh about prayer, an' all th' wunnerful thin's prayer can do fer you. You folks that is needy. If yuh need anythin', I can teach yuh how tuh pray an' expect tuh receive what yuh pray fer. Jesus said, 'Ast an' you shall receive,' an' I believe ever' word uv what he said. People tell me th' Bible ain't reasonable. Well, brethern, that's exactly why I believe it. So you stay aroun', an' I'll tell yuh how yuh can experience th' wunnerful power uv th' Lord at work in yer life. It's beautiful, an' I'd love tuh share it with ever'body."

Jeremy stole a glance at the old woman beside him and saw that she was nodding her head, smiling her approval.

"Now, let us pray," said Flancher.

His prayer was long. Occasional sobs could be heard throughout the building. Jeremy had never seen anything like this. He could not hear everything said, but he did understand the word "Jesus," and he heard it over and over. At last, Flancher concluded his prayer. A chorus of hallelujahs resounded throughout the building, along with happy shouts of, "Oh, thank you, Jesus, thank you." The congregation then arranged themselves on their benches as Flancher walked, wearily now, to a seat and slumped onto it.

Jacob Mutchell rose again and stepped to the podium. "Well—uh— we all had a great service here tuhnight. An' I wantcha tuh know that we're a-gonna have a bunch uv special nights. One night, we're a-gonna have ice cream, an' a night uv testifyin', an' then one night we're a-gonna have a special healing service. We want yuh tuh come back fer all these services and—uh—be with us. Is there any closin' announcement?" He looked around, but no one said anything. "Well, if they ain't, then—uh—let's have a dismissal prayer. Uhh, Brother Hawke, will you dismiss us?" The dismissal prayer was short.

10

JEREMY COULD EASILY FIND HIS WAY BACK toward his house, but alone now, his experience at church began to dim, and he became uneasy. What if he met Hazel on the road home? He knew that she wandered the countryside, and he was constantly on the lookout for her.

He had first heard of Hazel several months before. He had been sitting in the living room reading, and he had become aware that his parents were talking about someone named Hazel. "She oughtta be put away," Lem was saying. "She musta scared them Wilsons half tuh death a-comin' intuh their house in th' middle uv th' night thataway."

"Well, accordin' tuh Bess Wilson, it uz quite a scare. Said she woke up, an' there uz Hazel, just a-leanin' over 'er an 'a-starin' at 'er. An' you know, Lem, Bess an' 'er husband ain't been in good health fer years now."

"What I don't unnerstan' is why they just leave Hazel out there alone on that place. She ain't got no husband er nobody."

"Who's Hazel?" Jeremy had interrupted.

"Oh, she's just a pore ole woman who ain't right in th' mind." His mother tried to play down the significance of the conversation.

"Will she come intuh our house?"

"I don't think so. She lives a long way from here."

Lem was not so comforting. "Well, she may live a long way off, but I heard folks on th' other side uv Dorman sayin' that they seen 'er all th' way over there. She gits aroun' fer an ole lady. She needs tuh be locked up."

"What does she do when she comes intuh yer house?"

His mother started to speak, but Lem interrupted. "She just comes in an' goes all through th' house. Bill Coleman uz a-tellin' me that he thinks she may be a witch, that she goes aroun' a-tryin' tuh put a curse on folks while they're asleep."

Jeremy's interest increased. "How does she do that?"

"Now, Lem," his mother said. "Don't you go a-scarin' th' boy. You know how sensitive he is. He won't be able tuh sleep tuhnight."

"Hell, he may as well know th' truth. She comes in an' gits right down over somebody that's a-sleepin', an' she puts a curse on 'em. Least that's what Bill Coleman thinks."

"Is she th' one that put th' curse on black people?"

"Oh, Jeremy," his mother remonstrated. "No, she never did that. She don't put curses on nobody."

Now, alone in the dark field, Jeremy began to worry. I wonder what she looks like, he said to himself. Then, suddenly, he was seized with an inspiration. He stopped in his tracks. "I bet that uz Hazel that come an' sat down by me in church. I bet she uz a-tryin' tuh put a curse on me then." He turned around completely, twice, peering into the darkness. "Man, if that uz her, then she may be a-follerin' me right now." He quickened his pace toward home.

When he arrived home the house was dark, and he slipped quietly into his room and without lighting his kerosene lamp prepared for bed, but he had difficulty going to sleep. He went over and over the events of the evening, Flancher's sermon, and especially the old woman who he was sure must be Hazel.

He thought about what Flancher had said about prayer. He had heard of prayer all his life, but he had never known either of his parents to pray, nor even to discuss it. And then he thought about his wishes. He had never had any luck wishing. How many times had he wished for a bicycle? If Flancher was right, it seemed that he should be able to pray for things. Such a thought helped to lift his spirits and to forget Hazel. *Maybe I should start praying instead of wishing*, he thought.

Still, it was difficult for him to go to sleep. He kept hearing noises outside his window, and he got up to look outside to see if he could see Hazel, but the night was dark now. He listened for a long time, but not hearing any sounds, he went back to bed and tried to summon up his favorite dream about him and the beautiful girl in the garden, but tonight the dream would not come. In his mind he kept hearing Flancher calling people to repent, and he still could hear the shouts from the audience. He thought of the old crone who had demanded to know if he was saved, and how she had sat down beside him. He remembered her foul breath, her withered face. "I know it uz Hazel," he said. And then, "She must be a witch, shore 'nuff." He lay on his bed, trying to go to sleep, but he was sure that he heard a noise outside, and he got up once more and walked over to his window. He stood for a long time and stared out into the darkness.

11

FROM AN UNEASY SLEEP, JEREMY AWOKE the next morning to his mother's call: "Come gitcher breakfast, Jeremy. Yer gonna be late." He got up and began to dress. His mind returned to the service of the night before. There were so many things about the service that he had not understood, so many questions that he wanted to ask. He walked in to breakfast, hoping that his parents would be in a good mood. He knew that he had gone to church without his father's permission, and he feared some reaction from him. He hoped that he would find his mother receptive, because he wanted to ask her some questions—questions that he would not ask his father.

He sat down to his usual breakfast, dry cereal and milk, noting that his father had already left the kitchen. He was pleased, however, to see his mother sit down with him and pour herself a cup of coffee. He took this as a good sign that he would have an opportunity to ask her some of the questions that were on his mind. The fact that his father was not in the room made him feel even better about raising the questions.

"Maw, have you ever been tuh th' Tabernacle of the Holy Spirit?

"Cain't say that I have. Why?"

"Well, I uz just a-wonderin'."

"That's whur yuh went tuh church las' night, ain't it?"

"Yeah. Maw, what do alla them kneelin' people do?"

"I don't rightly know, Jeremy."

"But you said that yuh went tuh church."

"Jeremy, that church yuh went to las' night wuz a differ'nt kind uv church. Them people is Holy Rollers, an' they do strange things. They got all kinds uv funny beliefs. That's one reason yer paw an' me didn' want yuh a-goin' down there. They believe that you git th' Holy Spirit an' that they kin perform all kinds uv miracles an' speak with tongues, an' heal people, an' alla that."

"What's a Holy Roller? Why do yuh call 'em Holy Rollers?"

"Why, I guess it's 'cause they jump aroun' a lot an' roll on th' floor an' such stuff. Leastaways I've heard that they do that."

"Did you an' Paw ever go tuh a Holy Roller church?"

"No," she answered quickly. "My paw tole me that nobody received th' Holy Spirit these days, an' I believed him then, an' I still do."

"But, Maw, what about alla those people las' night?"

"What about 'em?"

"Brother Flancher said ever'body could git th' Holy Spirit. An' they wuz lots uv people that acted like they did."

"They wuz misled, Jeremy. They is lots uv false prophets a-goin' aroun' these days. Yuh gotta be keerful uv 'em."

This was a new idea for Jeremy. "You think Brother Flancher is a false prophet?"

"I wouldn' be a bit surprised. Not a bit. 'Specially if he says people are a-gittin' th' Holy Spirit these days. Ain't nobody baptized with th' Holy Spirit these days. It's all in th' Bible. I cain't show yuh th' chapter an' verse, but my paw could, if he uz here."

"But, Maw, Brother Flancher said ever'body oughtta git it, an' he's a preacher, an' he's a good un."

"You cain't trust ever' preacher, Jeremy."

"But Maw, a woman there las' night got th' holy laugh. I seen 'er just a-laughin' all th' way outta th' church, an' I heard people a-sayin' that she had th' holy laugh. People said it uz th' Holy Spirit a-workin' on her."

"Now, Jeremy, how do yuh know she got any holy laugh?"

"Th' people uz a'talkin' about it."

His mother stood, indicating that the conversation was over. "If I uz you, I wouldn' mention no holy laugh tuh yer paw. You finish yer cereal if yuh want it, an' then you hurry out tuh work. He'll be a-waitin' fer yuh." She began clearing the table. "An' you remember what I said. Them people uz misled."

Jeremy realized the conversation was over. He walked out into the yard to find his father, but his conversation with his mother stuck with him. Why did she dismiss the holy laugh? With his own eyes, he had seen the woman laughing. And surely Flancher, a preacher, could recognize the Holy Spirit when he saw it. Jeremy decided that the whole idea of church and religion was very complex.

As he and his father walked to the field that morning, his father said, "Hear yuh went tuh church las' night."

He looked at his father, defensive. He recalled what his father had said about his reading the Bible, and he still remembered what his mother had said about the church and her warning not to ask Lem about the holy laugh. He wondered what his father would say.

"Yes, Sir."

They walked along in silence for awhile. In fact, Jeremy thought that his father had forgotten the subject. Then Lem said, "Well, wha'd yuh think uv it?"

"Oh, it uz fine, I guess."

There was another long silence. Then Jeremy said, "Maw says people don't git th' Holy Spirit no more."

"She's right as rain about that," Lem replied, but that was all he said. He seemed to have lost interest in the topic. Jeremy sensed that his father had said all he intended to say, and so he remained quiet.

Throughout that long, hot day, Jeremy pondered. Should he believe all that Flancher had said? He could remember Mrs. Russell at school always asking on Monday mornings how many of the students had gone to church the day before. Usually she would make a contest of it by asking for a show of hands on each row. The row on which the most hands were raised would win. There was no prize. Jeremy was always embarrassed because he had never been to church, and he wanted to be able to raise his hand. At last he convinced himself that listening to portions of religious programs on the radio on Sunday with his mother was the same as going to church, and he began raising his hand every Monday.

Mrs. Russell insisted that the students should listen to the preacher and do what he told them to do. Now his mother had told him that perhaps he should not listen to Flancher. He wanted to believe his mother, but she confused him. She had talked about how important it was to go to church and to be saved, and now she was critical of the church.

Jeremy knew it would be difficult to go to church during the week. He and Lem worked late every evening, and he knew that when he got home, he would have his chores to do. On the other hand, there were some times when Lem would go into town on an errand, and while he more often than not left Jeremy in the field to work, sometimes he would excuse him for the day. And, Jeremy reflected, there was always the remote possibility of rain. He scanned the skies, but all he could see was the pale blue sky stretching in cloudless grandeur from one horizon to another and directly overhead the sun shining unmercifully bright. He and Lem did not get home early enough that night for Jeremy to make any plans for church; he finished his chores by lantern light.

In his room that night after his folks were in bed, Jeremy lit his lamp and opened his Bible, and there on the flyleaf were the words: "And the Spirit and the Bride say, 'Come.'" Why, here in the Bible he could read about the Spirit that Flancher talked about. So, there is a Spirit, he said to himself. Flancher was right! He wondered if his mother had ever read those words.

He kept trying to make sense of the Holy Spirit. He decided that if there were a Holy Spirit, and the Bible plainly said so, then there might be something like the holy laugh also.

"How 'bout that?" he asked out loud. He stood and walked about in his excitement. Then he thought, could I get the holy laugh? Maybe somebody could only get it in church. Could I get it right now, right here? He began to hope that he would start laughing. Maybe if you want the holy laugh, you just get it, he thought. So, he tried very hard to want to laugh, but nothing happened. He decided that perhaps he should encourage the laugh, but he didn't know how. He tried to remember jokes he had heard, but none of them seemed particularly funny right then. He remembered Patches chasing his tail. In his mind, he watched the dog, spinning about, always reaching for his tail, always just failing to reach it. For some reason the image stuck in his mind, but it did not make him laugh.

He concluded that he would have to make himself laugh, and he tried, but his laugh sounded unnatural there in the quiet darkness of his room. "Dang it," he said in frustration, "how does a guy git th' laugh?" He tried again to force a laugh, but although he was louder this time he was no more successful. At last he stood up and, filling his lungs with air, let out a loud laugh.

"Jeremy!" his father thundered from the next room.

Jeremy quickly became silent and sat down on his bed.

"Jeremy!"

"Sir?"

"What th' hell er you a-doin' in there?"

"I ain't a-doin' nothin', Paw," he replied, undressing and extinguishing his lamp as he spoke.

"Well, you shut up in there an' go tuh sleep so we can. You hear me, Boy?"

But Jeremy was already in bed.

12

TUESDAY WAS SPENT VERY MUCH LIKE MONDAY. Work days were always the same.

Jeremy thought all day about his recent experiences with Flancher and the church, and he hoped that something would happen so that he could go to church that evening. No clouds appeared, and his father worked steadily throughout the day.

But then as Lem and Jeremy arrived at the house that evening, Jeremy was surprised to see a car which he recognized as the McMillan's car sitting in front of his house. Leland, a neighbor and one of his best friends, was leaning against the car, and his mother, Mrs. McMillan, was at the kitchen door talking to Jeremy's mother. He joined Leland at the car while Lem walked into the house.

"Hi, Leland."

"Hi," replied Leland. It was obvious that he had cleaned up. His hair was slicked back and oily, and he wore a soft white shirt and khaki trousers.

"What 'er you a-doin' here?"

"Aw, my maw is a-takin' me tuh that dumb ole church, an' she thought how nice it ud be if I took some uv my friends, so she wanted tuh come by here an' ast yer maw if you could go." He turned his head aside and spat in disgust. "I hope yuh don't hafta go."

"Oh," replied Jeremy noncommittally. Actually, he liked the idea of going to church, but because he could tell that Leland did not, he tried to hide his true feelings.

"Always a-goin' tuh church," Leland moaned.

"Jeremy!" It was Mrs. Stroop calling. Jeremy turned to his mother and a smiling Mrs. McMillan standing in the door. Mrs. McMillan, a large, vibrant woman, wore a bright blue dress with a white lace collar that extended over her shoulders. To her left shoulder she had pinned an artificial flower, and she was holding a white Bible in her hands. Heavily made up with bright red lipstick and rouge, she contrasted sharply with Mrs. Stroop, who was wearing the same drab "feed-sack" dress that she had worn for the last two days. Mrs. Stroop was bare-footed; Mrs. McMillan was wearing high heels. "Come here, Son," said Mrs. Stroop.

"Do yuh wanta go tuh church tuhnight?" she asked as Jeremy joined the two ladies. "Miz McMillan is offerin' tuh take yuh, if yuh wanta go."

"Yeah, I'll go." Jeremy tried to conceal his enthusiasm. "Lemme go git ready."

"You can go," continued his mother. "There ain't no chores yuh need tuh do tonight."

As Jeremy disappeared into his room to change he heard his mother tell Mrs. Mcmillan how nice it was for her to come by to pick up Jeremy for church.

Taking advantage of the fact that he knew Mrs. McMillan would be in a hurry, Jeremy skipped washing off. Bathing would have been out of the question, for that would have required bringing the No. 2 washtub into the kitchen and going through the bathing ritual. Jeremy simply changed clothes and rejoined the two ladies.

"Are yuh ready, Jeremy?" Mrs. McMillan asked pleasantly.

"Yes'm."

"Jeremy, did you clean up?"

"Yeah, Maw, I did."

"An' put on clean clothes?"

"Yes, Maw."

"Well, all right. You go on." She looked at him skeptically, "But you behave."

"Good," said a smiling Mrs. McMillan. "Let's go, then." She embarrassed Jeremy, for she put her arm around him as they walked down the stone walk, through the gate of the fence, and out to the car.

"You remember what I said, Son, an' you behave," shouted Mrs. Stroop from the door. "You make 'im behave, Miz McMillan."

"He'll do fine, won't yuh, Jeremy?" said Mrs. McMillan, giving him a hug. Then turning back to Jeremy's mother, she said, "An' thanks ever so much fer lettin' th' boy go. I just know it'll be good fer 'im." Then she looked pointedly at Leland and said, "And it'll be good fer Leland, too." Leland turned aside and scowled.

Jeremy clambered into the back seat beside Leland, who was still disgusted with the evening's prospects, while Mrs. McMillan got into the driver's seat and started the car. "We're off," she declared gaily. The odor of her perfume filled the car.

The McMillans and Jeremy arrived late at the church building. The front lawn was filled with cars and pickups, but all the people had already gone inside. "Oh, I just knew that we were goin' tuh be late," complained Mrs. McMillan cheerfully as she tried to park her car between first one and then another pair of vehicles.

"Wish we'da been a lot later," grumbled Leland under his breath.

Mrs. McMillan looked at him through the rearview mirror. "What did you say, Son?"

"Nothin'. I never said nothin'." He looked at Jeremy and made a face.

Inside, the building was almost full; the first two rows were once again taken up with people kneeling with their faces buried on their arms. Jeremy leaned over to ask Leland, "What er them people a-doin'?" He indicated the kneelers.

"They're a-prayin'. They're always a-prayin'."

"Why er they a-prayin'?"

"Hell, I don't know. They just always do."

There were two vacant seats about halfway to the front and over against the wall. Jeremy and Leland elected to sit there, but Mrs. McMillan walked up two more rows of seats to sit down. As she left the two boys, she said, "Now, I don't know about lettin' you two boys sit here by yerselves. You make sure that you behave." She smiled sweetly upon them.

Jeremy sat down just as a man on the front seat stepped to the podium to lead the congregation in prayer. Jeremy was vaguely aware that although the man leading the prayer was not one of the two men who had prayed on Sunday night, most of the words of the prayer sounded the same.

After the prayer, the crowd labored through a song, and at last Flancher rose to speak. He was not wearing a coat tonight. The knot in his tie was once again pulled down from his throat, and he was carrying another starched white handkerchief in his hand. Perspiration already stood out on his face. "God goes higher," he said. "He takes yuh higher. Hallelujah! Somebody say, 'Glory!'" A resounding chorus responded. Flancher smiled upon the audience, his eyes sweeping the congregation.

Then Flancher began his sermon, speaking slowly, quietly. "Hell is forever an' ever, Brother. Don't go there, oh, don't you go there. Think uv them leapin' flames, that eternal sufferin', an' don't you go there." Jeremy listened intently. He certainly did not want to go to hell.

The image of the leaping flames was peculiarly disturbing. Jeremy could remember watching his father burn brush on the farm. He could remember watching as the flames would leap high into the air, emitting billowing clouds of smoke. He shivered slightly.

Now, Flancher leaned forward and put his right hand on his knee for emphasis. "You be prepared tuh meet yer God, an' don't wait too late." Flancher stopped. He dropped his head and appeared deep in thought. For a moment Jeremy thought he was through preaching, but then Flancher slowly raised his head. He mopped his face and hands with his bedraggled handkerchief, and then solemnly began: "I remember my daddy." He paused again and swallowed hard. "I remember my daddy a-dyin'."

Leland leaned over to Jeremy. "He preaches about 'is daddy a-dyin' ever' time."

"He wuz down in Three Rivers, Texas, then, an' I went tuh see 'im. It uz three year ago this summer. I'd been a-preachin' in Oklahoma, an' I got word that he uz a-dyin', an' I went tuh see 'im. I remember walkin' intuh th' house. Ah, brethern, that house brought back such memories tuh me. Memories uv happier days when my fam'ly wuz all alive an' well." Again Flancher paused. He pressed his fingers against his eyes and looked away from the congregation and out of the windows. He lifted his handkerchief and wiped his eyes. He swallowed hard and began again: "I remember walkin' intuh th' house an' alla them memories, an' a-goin' back in that dark, back bedroom where my daddy always slept. How many times I had been back there in that bedroom." Flancher shook his head sadly. "An' there he wuz, my big ole fat daddy a-layin' there on th' bed a-dyin'." He stopped again. Somewhere in the crowd, someone began to cry. Flancher's face was fiery red, and tears began to trickle down his face. "A-dyin'. My daddy uz a-dyin'."

He spoke with great difficulty, his voice trembling. "There he lay, my pore ole daddy, an' he said—he said—'Cleo.' That's what he always called me, Cleo." Flancher's voice broke. "An' I said, 'Here I am, Daddy.' An' he said, 'Cleo, oh, Cleo, take my han'. I'm a-dyin'. I'm a-dyin'. I know I am, an' I'm afeard uv hell.'" More people were crying, and Flancher paused to gain control of himself.

"My daddy said tuh me, 'Cleo, will yuh pray fer me? I don't wanta go tuh hell.' An', oh, brothers and sisters, there in that dark, hot room, I knelt down by my daddy's bed, an' I took his sweet han' in mine." Flancher's lips trembled; he was crying openly. "I took his sweet han' in mine, an' I kissed it. Oh, how I wish I could take it tuhnight. What I'd give tuh hold that sweet han' tuhnight." Someone behind Jeremy began crying. Solemn amens sounded. "Jus' tuh see my daddy tuhnight." Flancher shook with sobs. The tension in the room rose. The fans clanked overhead. "I knelt down there." Flancher shook his head, paused, blew his nose into his handkerchief, and continued. "An' I prayed. I prayed like I never prayed before. Oh, how I prayed. An' while I prayed, I heard my daddy a-sayin', 'O thank ye, Jesus. Thank ye. I see th' light.'" Flancher had gained control of himself now, and his voice was rising. "I see th' light. That's what he said. Praise th' Lord! I see th' light!" Flancher shouted. Then for emphasis, he shouted even louder, "My Daddy said, 'I see th' light! I see th' angels a-comin' tuh git me. I'm a-goin' home tuh glory. Hallelujah!'"

"Say 'Hallelujah!', brethern."

The audience cried jubilantly, "Hallelujah!"

"Say it ag'in!"

Another roar: "Hallelujah!"

"Praise God!" someone screamed. "Praise th' Lord!" shouted another.

"My daddy wuz afraid uv hell," Flancher continued. "My brethern an' sistern, he uz afraid uv hell, but I sat there by 'im, an' I held 'is han' in mine, an' he died there. He died there, a-holdin' my han', but praise th' Lord, he uz saved. He uz saved! I want you tuh be afraid uv hell an' be saved like my daddy wuz. Come tuh Jesus now an' be saved." Even as he spoke these last words, several people had already moved out into the aisle and were making their way to meet Flancher. The whole congregation was on its feet. Many swayed as they held their arms above their heads. Some, still crying, reached out to embrace their neighbors. Women cried in each other's arms.

Somewhere, Jeremy heard someone cry out, "I see Jesus. I see Jesus. Oh, thank God. Oh, lovely, lovely Jesus. Praise God! Oh, dear God! Praise God!" He looked around trying to locate the person who made this claim, but he could not be sure. He wondered if someone really did see Jesus, and he twisted his head, looking up to see if he could spot anything that looked like Jesus.

The man beside Jeremy jostled him as he rose to his feet. He began to babble: "Owalla, owalla, geo, geo, ho, ho, ho." Jeremy looked at him in amazement. What could he be saying? He tried to move away from the man.

"It's okay," said a woman beside the man. She put her hand on Jeremy's shoulder. "He's just a-speakin' in tongues. It's wunnerful." Jeremy looked at the woman, and then back at the man who continued to babble, never looking at anyone.

Eventually the congregation quieted, and Flancher began talking to those who had come forward. It seemed to Jeremy that there were more people on the front benches than there had been on Sunday night, and it was a long time before Flancher finished talking to each one, and then he rose and turned toward the audience. "I got such wunnerful news," he said. "Nora Hickam has come tuh us, askin' tuh be baptized. Ain't that wunnerful? Here she is."

Nora stood up, not quite erect, turned slightly, and smiled at the congregation. Then she sat back down. At this point, Flancher leaned over to whisper to Mutchell. After a few moments, he straightened and said, "I just spoke tuh Brother Mutchell, an' he said that it's okay tuh use his stock tank fer th' baptizin', so just as soon as this service is over, we're all a-goin' over there, just across th' road tuh Brother Mutchell's place, and we'll have th' baptizin' there."

Flancher turned and walked wearily toward his seat.

Mutchell rose to make the concluding announcements. "We're just delighted that this precious soul has come forward tuh be buried with her Lord in baptism. An' we'll baptize 'er right after th' service is over. I think all uv yuh know whur I live, an' yuh know whur my stock tank is at. Some uv yuh prob'ly been a-fishin' there. If yuh don't know th' way, just foller somebody that does. Praise th' Lord!"

Someone behind Jeremy whispered, "If yuh don't know th' way, just foller yer nose."

"Tuhnight uz shore good, wuzn't it?" The congregation agreed enthusiastically. "But brethern, our meetin' has just started," Mutchell continued. "We're a-gonna have ice cream one night. We want all uv you tuh come that night, and—uh—bring yer ice cream freezers. Filled, uv course." Mutchell laughed. "An' we're also a-gonna have some other special services." He stared out the windows on the side of the building. "One night, we're a-gonna have a very special healin' service." The audience shouted its approval.

Mutchell nodded approvingly. "Are there any other announcements?"

There were none. "Okay, then—uh—we'll be dismissed. Oh, oh, I almost fergot. This whole meetin' has been such a success that—uh— we decided tuh maybe extend it fer—uh—a few days. We'll talk about that more, though. Is there anything else? If not, let's bow, an' ast Brother Howard tuh dismiss us."

Jeremy and Leland walked outside toward the McMillan's car. "Sheeee! Church goes on ferever," groused Leland. "An' didn' I tell yuh that ole Flancher could talk forever about his big ole fat daddy? He done that when he uz here las' year fer a meetin'. Same story. Who gives a damn about his ole man?"

"Now, Leland," complained Mrs. Mc Millan. "You shouldn't talk that way about the deceased."

Mrs. McMillan drove the short distance to Mutchell's stock tank. Jeremy was already aware of the distinct stench from the pigpens as they drove through the gate to Mutchell's place. As Mrs. McMillan approached the pond, a man was directing traffic, arranging the cars so that they formed a half-circle around one side of the stock tank. He walked over to Mrs. McMillan. "Would yuh leave yer lights on, ma'am? We need some light fer th' baptizin'."

"Certainly." Mrs. McMillan smiled.

"Can me an' Jeremy git out, Maw?" asked Leland.

"Why, yes, I think that would be fine. Just don't git in nobody's way."

Jeremy was glad to get out. He enjoyed the smell of the water and the soft rippling sound of it washing up on the shore. Here near the water, the odor of the pigs was not as strong.

As Jeremy watched, Flancher appeared in the car lights. He had removed his tie and his shoes. He stood on the bank with his pants legs rolled up to his knees. He carried a fresh handkerchief in his left hand.

The lady to be baptized stood with him. She was wrapped in a quilt.

"Just wait a minute, Brother Flancher," said a man whom Jeremy did not recognize. "We'll be through in a minute." Then he and three other men, all with their shoes off and their pants legs rolled up, waded out into the water. They were carrying long, slender saplings, and as they entered the water, they began to beat its surface vigorously.

"What er they a-doin'?" Jeremy asked Leland.

"They're a-switchin' th' water," said a voice behind them. "Sometimes they's cottonmouth moccasins in th' water, an' we don't want nobody bit."

Jeremy looked closely at the water, shining in the glow of the lights of the cars. He could not see any snakes, but he decided that he was glad he was not being baptized.

The baptism over, Jeremy and Leland returned to the car and climbed in without comment. Jeremy remained quiet all the way home. Once again, he had been impressed with Flancher. And there had been the incident of the man "speaking in tongues." There had also been the baptism, but it had been lacking in excitement as far as Jeremy was concerned.

Jeremy did wish he could see Jesus, tonight more than ever, for he had read just the night before in his Bible about the Son of God coming to earth with trumpet blasts and thousands of angels, and he thought such a sight would be wonderful. And there had been the man in church who claimed to be seeing Jesus. Jeremy tried hard to picture in his mind what Jesus would look like.

He was still thinking about seeing Jesus when Mrs. McMillan pulled up in front of his house. "Yer awful quiet tonight, Jeremy. Don't yuh feel well?" Mrs. McMillan asked.

"Oh, no. I'm fine. Thankee. Thankee fer takin' me tuh church. I'll see yuh, Leland."

"Maybe yer thinkin' about th' baptizin'. Maybe yer thinkin' about yer own soul," she said gently.

Jeremy looked at Leland. "Oh, no. I don't know. Thankee."

Jeremy got out of the car and stood still as Mrs. McMillan and Leland pulled away. He did not go immediately into the house. There was a full moon and a cloudless sky, and the moon shone bright enough to create shadows. The atmosphere put Jeremy into a thoughtful mood. He liked to be outside on nights such as this one. He decided to walk around for a while, and walked away from the house. Patches awoke from his sleep under the Stroop car and trotted out to meet him, but Jeremy pushed him away. Somehow he wanted to be alone in the solemnity of the evening. He hoped that he would not see Hazel.

There was not a breath of breeze. He savored the night. Somewhere far away, he heard the cooing of a mourning dove. He listened to the swooping drone of a bull-bat, soaring against the evening sky, and he was at peace with himself.

And then he saw it. At first Jeremy could not believe his eyes, but when he looked again he was sure that he saw Jesus descending! Jesus was already low on the horizon, just above the tips of the mesquite trees to the northwest of the house. He could not be more than a few hundred yards away. Jeremy stood in open-mouthed amazement. He did not know what to do. He lifted his arms high in the air; then he fell to his knees, keeping his eyes on the figure of Jesus. He remained on his knees. What should he do? Should he shout? Should he pray?

His heart beat rapidly. Then, gradually, he sensed that something was not right. The figure of Jesus was not moving. Why was that? Why didn't he come on down to earth? At the same time, Jeremy became aware that there were no clouds accompanying Jesus, nor were there angels to be seen, and where were the trumpet blasts?

He looked around. He remembered he had read that when Jesus came back to the earth, there would be dead people raised. He had decided then that he did not want to see a dead person, and he hoped now that he would not see one. Was Hazel perhaps one of those? What would he do if he saw a dead person? He turned completely around, searching for dead people revived to life, but he couldn't see any. He turned back to the figure just above the trees and watched closely, not taking his eyes off Jesus—but as he watched, he gradually realized that what he saw was not Jesus. It became increasingly clear that the figure was the silhouette of the farm windmill, protruding just above the trees in the dim moonlight. He rose quickly from the ground and dusted off his knees. He looked back at the figure once more just to make sure; then hurried into the house.

13

THROUGH FRIDAY, JEREMY AND LEM WORKED LATE each evening. Lem was hurrying to finish the project they were working on.

Saturday morning dawned hot and sultry. Jeremy knew there would be work to do until early afternoon, but the family always went into town to buy groceries on Saturday, and Jeremy looked forward to the respite.

Depending on Lem's mood, Jeremy would start asking early in the afternoon how much longer they had to work, but he tried to ask in such a way as to make his father think he was only concerned that they quit in plenty of time to go to town, to buy groceries, and to get back home before dark.

"Paw, you ain't forgot that we got tuh go an git groc'ries, have yuh?"

"No, Boy, I ain't forgot."

"Well, don't yuh think that we ought tuh start purty quick? You remember that ole car uz hard tuh start th' las' time we went tuh town." Then Jeremy added hopefully, "An' I still got tuh do my chores."

"I'll worry 'bout that damn car, Boy. You just worry 'bout keepin' up."

If his father did not seem in a good mood, then Jeremy would not say anything, and the first indication he would have that the work day was over would be when at the end of a row, his father would abruptly turn toward home.

Once Lem made up his mind that it was time to quit work and go to town, he and Jeremy would not even change clothes. Mrs. Stroop would always be ready to go, and the family would climb into the car.

The trip was over a rocky dirt road, covered in places with a thin layer of caliche. During the dry weather of summer, there would be no problem making the trip, except for the choking clouds of dust that arose. When two cars passed each other, the combined dust would obscure each driver's vision and make breathing almost impossible. One solution was to roll up the windows of the car, but the temperature in the enclosed car would quickly become unbearable.

As the dust swirled, Mrs. Stroop would fan herself with her handkerchief and worry, "Oh. Lem, be keerful. I cain't see nothin'."

"You don't need tuh see nothin'. You ain't doin' th' damn drivin'."

"But I'm skeered. What if we git in a wreck?"

"Wouldn' be no fear uv no wreck if all these bastards ud stay on their side uv th' damn road," Lem would reply, leaning forward and peering intently through the dust.

"Look out! Look out, Lem! See that car ahead uv us?"

"Why, uv course I do. I ain't blind."

"But th' driver has got 'is arm outta th' winder. He intends tuh turn."

"That driver a-havin 'is arm outta th' winder only means one damn thing. Th' winder is down."

Olga stared out her window. "Sometimes I just itch tuh say hell," she said.

At last, Lem would park the car in front of Dorman's general store. A sign over the door said AYERS STORE, and it was here that Lem and Olga would do their shopping. As the family entered the screened doors of the store, Jeremy noticed the large sign pasted to one of the doors. It advertised a dance at Peach Springs with music by Mike Hollis and the Rhythm Range Riders.

On this Saturday afternoon, Jeremy followed his parents into the store, where he selected an ice cream bar. He paid for it, and then he walked outside. He preferred to eat his ice cream outside in the shade of the building. Jeremy walked back and forth on the wooden sidewalk, enjoying his freedom. He heard someone call his name and he looked up, across the street, toward Gray's Blacksmith Shop, a rusty metal building practically obscured by weeds and piles of rusty junk. There in the doorway of the shop, he spied Jackie Gray, son of the owner of the shop.

Jackie was an older boy, much larger than Jeremy although they were in the same grade. Jeremy admired Jackie's muscles. His shirts always fit tightly across his shoulders. He had pale blue eyes and unruly blond hair which never seemed combed. He was always smiling, even when his teachers tried to reprimand him. Jeremy had seen him sent out of class to the principal's office several times by frustrated teachers, but Jackie always left smiling and returned smiling.

"Come on over, Stroop," shouted Jackie, and Jeremy walked across the street and greeted him. "How yuh been?"

"I'm okay," Jackie smiled. "You?"

"Yeah."

"What er you a-doin' in town?"

"Aw, my dad had tuh come intuh town, an' I come with 'im. Whatcha been a-doin'?"

"I been workin', but I ain't just been a-workin'."

"Oh."

"Hell, no. I find ways tuh enjoy myse'f."

"Yeah?"

"Damn straight. You know Sally Leyendecker?"

"Sally who?"

"Sally Leyendecker. You know 'er. She sits right across frum you in ole lady Russell's room. I know yuh noticed 'er. You couldn' he'p but notice 'er, th' way she's stacked."

Jeremy did know Sally. He said, "Oh, yeah, she's th' one that's always failin' her spellin' tests."

Sally was an older girl with long, dirty blond hair that hung to her waist. Jeremy could see her now, slouching in her seat, her dress carelessly draped above her knees. Her breasts were much more developed than those of the other girls in the room. All the boys had noticed her breasts and had made them the focus of more than one conversation.

"Damn," H.C. had said one day, "you guys see ole Sally's tits tuhday? They jiggled ever' time she took a step."

"Well, you know th' sayin': LSMFT."

All the boys had laughed except Jeremy. He did not know what LSMFT meant. He had asked one of the boys what the letters meant, and the boy had been incredulous. "Stroop, don't yuh know nuthin'? LSMFT means "loose straps means floppy tits." Man, whur wuz you raised?"

All the boys standing nearby had laughed and shook their heads.

Sally was a quiet girl who seldom came to school. When she came, she rode the bus with Jeremy, but the two had never spoken.

"Yeah, I know 'er," Jeremy said.

"Boy, you shoulda been with me an' ole Vincent last Sattidy."

Jeremy was having trouble keeping up with the conversation.

"Why?"

"Me an' ole Vincent run intuh Sally here in town."

"Oh."

Jackie giggled. "We talked 'er intuh goin' out tuh Owl Creek Bridge with us. Hot damn!" Jackie hugged himself and smiled broadly.

Jeremy knew the bridge. It was an old wooden structure that crossed the San Felipe River. He had heard Lem say more than once that the bridge should be condemned because it was not sturdy enough for automobile traffic, and he had heard some of the younger boys talk about going there to shoot gar fish from the bridge and to smoke. Older boys talked about the bridge, but as they talked, they would smile and shove each other.

"How'd yuh git 'er tuh do that?"

Jackie smiled. "It wuzn't very hard. Me an' Vincent found 'er a-sittin' down at Appleton's gas station. Her ole man wuz inside, I guess. We didn' see 'im. We just went up an' started talkin'. She wuzn't none too fren'ly at first, but like Vincent said, we wuzn't exactly lookin' fer conversation." Jackie slappd Jeremy on the shoulder and winked.

"She just had on a tee shirt an' some shorts. She looked purty good." Jackie cupped his hands and made an uplifting motion on his chest.

"Vincent bought 'er some candy, an' we started a-talkin', an' ole Vincent kep' on a-flirtin' with 'er, an' after awhile she got a little more fren'ly. Then Vincent ast 'er if she ud like some beer, an' she said she would, so Vincent an' me took 'er over tuh his car, an' he tole her that if she ud go tuh Owl Creek Bridge with us, she could have all th' beer she wanted. He showed 'er th' beer. He musta had almost a full case in that there car uv his. An' then she got in, an' said, 'Less go,' an' by God, we went." Jackie laughed and adjusted the front of hiz trousers with an exaggerated motion.

"Damn, did we ever go. Whoeee! Lemme tell yuh. Sally ain't no quiet girl oncet yuh git 'er full uv beer. I think maybe she hadn' drunk much beer before, 'cause that beer took a-hold uv 'er purty quick, an' she shore warmed up tuh us. Vincent wuz a-drivin', an' I uz in th' back seat with Sally, an' I started a-feelin' 'er up, an' she never stopped me a-tall." Jackie laughed. "My ole man always tole me, git a couple uv beers in a gal, an' you got yer hand high on 'er laig."

He paused. "Boy, me an' Vincent had a good time with that little gal. She may not be so good at spellin', but she is plenty good in th' back seat uv a car."

He gave his last comment some time for consideration. Then he said, "Since I uz in th' back seat I went first, an' then I got in th' front seat, an' Vincent got in th' back seat with 'er. Damn, I thought he ud never git thoo." He laughed again. Then he became sober.

"I got a little uneasy there fer a minute," he said, shaking his head, not smiling. "Ole Vincent just went sort uv crazy, I think. He started wantin' 'er tuh lick 'is armpits, an' she kep' on a-sayin', 'No! No! Stop it!'"

"Vincent just sort uv seemed tuh lose it there fer a minute. He slapped 'er purty good a time er two. I uz a-sittin' in th' front seat, but I heard 'er just keep on a-sayin', 'Stop, stop,' all muffled like, 'cause ole Vincent uz all over 'er, an' he just wouldn' stop. Fin'ly, Vincent got thoo, an' he come aroun' an' got in th' front seat with me. He reached inside his shirt and pulled out the strap uv 'er bra, an' winked at me. I looked back intuh th' back seat, an' she uz a-runnin' her han' between th' car seat an' its back, a-lookin' fer her bra, I guess. Then she looked aroun' down on th' floorboard, but uv course she couldn' fin' it cause Vincent had it. Then he turned aroun' tuh face 'er, an' pulled her bra out uv his shirt, an' dangled it in front uv 'er, an' she grabbed fer it, but he jerked it back real quick, an' damn, she really got mad. She started a-bouncin' aroun' in that back seat an' a-poundin' on him, an' I don't know what she uz a-sayin' 'cause she uz a-screamin' at th' top uv her lungs, an' her words wuzn't none too clear. I did pick up a bunch uv cuss words clear enuff."

"Vincent listened to 'er fer awhile, an' then he leaned over th' seat an' tole 'er tuh shut up, said he planned tuh keep 'er damn bra, an' they wuzn't nothin' she could do about it. Said he always liked tuh keep a souvenir uv ever' girl he poked. She uz some mad. She tried tuh git out uv th' car, but Vincent pushed 'er back in th' seat, an' she just sort uv sat there fer a minute er two, just a-starin' at 'im."

Jackie shook his head. "Later, on th' way home, she uz still purty mad at Vincent. She called 'im a whole bunch uv names, some I ain't shore I had heard before, an' then she just started all over ag'in. But hell, it didn' bother him none. Then she tole 'im that she liked me better than she did him, said that he uz too rough, an' Vincent didn' like that much. He tole 'er tuh shut up er he'd git 'er in th' back seat ag'in. She shut up then, an it uz all right till we got back tuh town, an' then she ast fer her bra ag'in. Vincent tole 'er ag'in that he kept souvenirs, an' damn, she got mad all over ag'in. She started a-screamin' an' a-goin' on an' on. I uz afraid that somebody might hear 'er. She jumped outta th' car, her tits just a-jigglin' on account uv she didn' have no bra on a-tall yuh see, an' by God, she slammed that door an' took off across th' street, an' then just as she got on th' other side uv th' street, she whirled aroun', an' she started a-givin' Vincent th' finger. I mean she stood there just a-jabbin' 'er finger in th' air, all th' time a-cussin' a blue streak, but Vincent, he just laughed. Hell, he didn' care. Damn, she uz one mad woman. But it uz a lot uv fun. We shore didn' have much beer lef' when we got home, though."

Jackie was full of such stories, and Jeremy loved to hear them. He wished he had stories to tell Jackie, but he had no experience to share with the older boy.

"You ain't never had none uv that, have ye?" Jackie asked. "You ain't never took no girl out tuh Owl Creek Bridge, have yuh?"

Jeremy shuffled his feet.

"Hell, I bet you ain't even whacked off, Stroop. Yer just a damn kid."

The shift in the conversation frustrated Jeremy. He could not think of anything to say. He was glad to hear Lem calling him from across the street.

He joined his father in Ayers Store, talking to the store owner and another man he did not know. His father was saying that it had been very hot lately.

"Tell me about it," said the man that Jeremy did not know. "Yestiddy I seen a dog a-chasin' a rabbit, and they uz so hot they uz both a-walkin'."

All three men enjoyed the joke.

Jeremy started to walk to the car, but as he turned away the stranger said, "Yeah, as I uz a-sayin', Sheriff Pickard went out an' got 'im tuhday. Found 'im just a-walkin' along th' road. I uz always afraid uv this, Lem. He's always had a problem with 'is liquor, ain't he?"

"That's so," replied Lem.

Jeremy stopped to hear more.

The stranger continued. "Still it's a shame. I know it must be hard fer you, him a-bein' yer brother an' all. An' yuh know, Darl is a good worker when he's sober. He's one uv th' best men in th' county when it comes tuh operatin' heavy road machinery. He kin git a job just about anywheres. He just cain't keep one. Seems like he works fer a while, gits a little money, an' then he goes off on one uv his binges, an' that's that."

Jeremy realized that the man was talking about Darl Stroop, Lem's brother, the town drunkard.

At last his parents came out of the store, each laden with sacks of groceries. Mr. Ayers followed, carrying a sack of groceries in one hand and a large block of ice suspended from ice tongs in the other.

"Open th' door, Boy," ordered Lem, and Jeremy hurried to do so. He stood watching, holding the rear door of the car open as the Stroops loaded their groceries, and Mr. Ayers put the ice on the rear floorboard. To slow the melting of the ice, Lem wrapped the ice in a quilt that he had brought from home. Then he arranged the sacks of groceries in the back seat, leaving room for Jeremy to sit. "Thanks fer comin' by, folks," said Mr. Ayers as he wiped perspiration from his forehead, waved good-bye, and turned back into his store. Jeremy placed his bare feet on the quilt which wrapped the ice.

"See yuh nex' week, I guess," Lem called after him.

On the trip home, the ice began to melt, and the saturated quilt felt good against Jeremy's feet.

"Paw, what uz that guy a-sayin' about Uncle Darl?" Jeremy asked.

"Nothin' much." Lem was noncommittal.

Jeremy's mother turned to look at Lem. "Is Darl in trouble ag'in?"

"Sheriff picked 'im up."

"He been a-beatin' Billie ag'in?"

"Hell, how should I know, Olga? I didn' ast."

"I bet he did. I don't see why that woman stays with 'im. I know he's yer brother, Lem, but he's just no good. He's so violent when he's drunk. An' it ain't just Billie, though Lord knows she's suffered enuff. You remember that time when he hit yer paw over th' head with that wrench? We thought he'd killed 'im there fer a minute."

"He's got 'is good points."

"I guess so, but I saw Billie th' las' time he beat 'er, an' I felt so sorry fer 'er. Her face uz all black an' blue, an' 'er eyes uz all swole shut, an' she had that big ugly bruise on 'er arm. I swear, Lem. I couldn' look at 'er without cryin'."

Lem made no reply.

"I guess," Olga continued, "he comes by it honest. You know, Lem, that you an' Darl's paw drunk hisse'f tuh death. I remember when he got so sick th' las' time. They took 'im tuh th' doctor, an th' doctor tole us that there wuzn't no hope. Alcohol had et up 'is liver."

Lem nodded again.

"Yeah," Olga said. "I 'member Brother Lightfoot, th' preacher that baptized me, went up tuh see 'im tuh git 'im tuh repent, but he tole Brother Lightfoot they wuzn't no use. Said what he uz a-sufferin' wuz already his hell right here on earth, that he uz already a-payin' fer th' life he'd lived, an' there warn't no use in any 'leventh hour repentin'. I guess I sorta agreed with that. I never did put too much stock in these people who live sinful lives, all high and mighty, and then repent on their death beds."

Lem said nothing. He flexed his hands on the wheel.

Olga continued. "Some uv th' men frum church went up tuh sit with 'im after he got so bad, an' they said it uz plumb pitiful. Said it took sev'ral uv 'em just tuh hold 'im on th' bed, said he kep' on a-tryin' tuh git up out uv bed and jump outta th' winder. His room uz way up on th' seventh floor. Said he wanted tuh kill hisse'f. One uv th' men a-sittin' with 'im tole th' doctor about it, an' th' doctor said he wuzn't surprised. Said when someone got sick like yer paw wuz, no pain killer ud work."

There was a long silence, then Olga said, "I saw Miz Coward in town at Ayers Store."

"So," said Lem. "What did she have on her mind?"

"Oh, not a whole lot. She's been a-havin' lotsa troubles lately, I guess."

Lem did not respond.

"You know that son uv theirs. What's 'is name?"

"Damn if I know."

"Oh, sure yuh do. He worked over here las' fall a-pickin' cotton."

"I don't remember 'is name. He uz just another cotton picker tuh me. An' if he uz like th' rest that uz here las' fall, he wuzn't worth a damn."

"Oh, I remember. His name uz Charley Coward."

Lem stared ahead.

Mrs. Stroop was not discouraged. "They had tuh take 'im tuh th' doctor. He uz in real bad shape."

Now Jeremy joined the conversation. Illnesses intrigued him. "What uz wrong with 'im, Maw?"

Mrs. Stroop welcomed the interest. "Well, Miz Coward said that first he had this fever, an' then he started a-gittin' these headaches. Real bad. Said they uz so bad he ud hafta go tuh bed. Then he started complainin' 'bout this pain in th' back uv 'is neck an' 'is ear, an' she said that when she felt behin' his ear it uz all soft an' mushy. Said Charley screamed when she touched 'is head there behin' his ear."

Jeremy was intensely interested. "What did they do?"

"Well," continued Mrs. Stroop. "They took 'im tuh th' doctor, an' th' doctor said he had a massatoit bone."

Lem roused himself to ask, "What th' hell is a massatoit bone?"

"She said that Charley's massatoit bone got real touchy, an' th' doctor said that they ud hafta operate er th' infection might kill 'im. So they operated, an' Miz Coward says he's doin' purty good now. He still has dizzy spells, an' he gits real tired."

Jeremy was silent for a while, and then he said, "I never heard uv no massatoit bone, Maw."

"Well, I heard uv it a time er two." She straightened her skirt over her legs.

Again a moment of silence. Then Jeremy said, "Can anybody git a massatoit bone, Maw?"

"Why, I suppose they could. Why?"

"I uz just a-wonderin'."

"Now, Jeremy, don't you git no silly idees. Yuu ain't got no massatoit bone."

Jeremy sat silently.

"You don't be a-worryin' 'bout no massatoit bone. I swear, I shouldna tole yuh about it. Ever' time you hear 'bout somebody a-bein' sick you decide you got th' same thing wrong with you."

"But, Maw, sometimes I git headaches, an' . . . ."

"Jeremy, that's enuff. You ain't got no massatoit bone."

Jeremy decided that he had a slight headache, and he thought that he felt especially warm. He touched the bone behind his left ear; it seemed tender to his touch.

14

JEREMY SLEPT LATE THE FOLLOWING SUNDAY MORNING, so late that his mother finally woke him, telling him it was almost noon. He got out of bed, dressed, and stumbled outside without breakfast. Sleeping as he did on Sundays dulled him. As he stepped outside, Patches met him with his usual excited leaps. He would lunge against Jeremy, then tear around him in a circle, which would end when he jumped against Jeremy again. He repeated the ritual over and over, his tail wagging furiously. "Git down, dawg," laughed the boy, but he sat down on the large rock doorstep and caught the squirming dog in his arms and held him close, laughing as Patches tried to lick his face.

Jeremy loved Patches. He had always had a dog as long as he could remember. First, there had been Snowball, and then Ring, and now there was Patches. Jeremy did not care for any of the other animals on the farm. He especially hated sheep, and he held cats in high disdain as well. Cats multiplied profusely on the farm. Most of them lived down at the barn and, in fact, had returned to an almost feral state. Once, when several cats in succession had given birth under the house, Lem had announced that there were simply "too damn many cats." He had collected a litter and its mother, put them into a gunny sack, taken them to one of the stock tanks and had thrown the sack into the water. Jeremy had gone with him. "Good damn riddance," he had heard Lem say as he turned away from the water's edge. Jeremy had stood and watched the sack sag down into the water, finally emitting a few air bubbles as it sank to the bottom.

Jeremy loved to persecute the cats himself, and knowing how his father felt about them, he had felt secure in tormenting them. He had heard, for example, that cats always landed on their feet and had decided to test this theory. He caught one of the tamer cats, and then climbed up in a wagon and dropped it. It landed on its feet. He then caught the cat, climbed up in the wagon, and holding the cat upside down, dropped it again. Once again it landed on its feet. He picked up the cat a third time, and this time, standing on the ground, he held the cat upside down and then dropped it. Once again it landed on its feet. Jeremy thought about kneeling down and throwing the cat toward the ground to see if it could land on its feet from that height, but he was unable to catch the cat again in order to continue his experiment.

He had also experimented with cats to learn whether or not they could swim. He had caught a cat and taken it to the stock tank. Then, holding the cat, he waded out into the water until he was in water up to his waist, some twenty feet from shore. Then he pitched the cat into the water. He had been surprised at how quickly the cat had learned to swim.

Once when his friend, Leland, had been visiting, he had said, "You got too many damn cats, Stroop."

"We got a bunch."

"But cats is dangerous. They can kill yuh."

"Aw, how can they do that?"

"Any cat can kill yuh. My paw tole me all about it. Cats'll steal yer breath."

"How do they do that?"

"Well, they can. Paw tole me that they'll come intuh yer house at night, an' then they'll git up in th' bed with yuh, an' they'll lay on yer chest, an' they'll steal yer breath."

"Steal yer breath?"

"Right outta yer mouth. Paw tole me that a cat near 'bout stole my breath when I uz just a kid. Said he come in tuh check on me, an' there uz this cat, just a-layin' right there on my chest a-gittin' ready tuh steal my breath."

"Wha'd yer paw do?"

"Knocked th' livin' hell out uv that cat. Listen, Stroop, cats'll come intuh yer house an' kill yuh. Me, I always go tuh sleep on my stomach, so no cat can come in an' steal my breath away. You oughtta do that too."

Jeremy was not much concerned.

There had been only one cat that Jeremy had respected enough even to name. It was a black cat which Jeremy called Tom. It was a huge cat, and it was seldom around. Occasionally, it would re-appear for a few days, and then it would disappear again, "tom-cattin' aroun'," according to Lem. It appeared one day after one of its mysterious jaunts, its head swollen and bleeding, one of its eyes tightly closed.

"What's wrong with 'im, Paw?" Jeremy had asked.

"Looks like tuh me he got in a fight with a rattlesnake," replied Lem, "An' th' rattlesnake won."

Tom had stayed around for a couple of days without getting noticeably better, and then he had disappeared, never to be seen again.

Jeremy's mother had never liked Tom. He was black, and she had strong superstitions about black cats. Jeremy had learned the depth of her superstition the only time he could remember the family planning to go to church. A neighbor had invited them to Dorman to the First Baptist Church, and they had gotten up early, dressed, loaded into the car and begun their trip. Jeremy had been sitting in the back seat, watching the road. A black cat had appeared out of the bushes on the right side of the road and darted across.

"Hey, Paw, didja see that black cat?" asked Jeremy.

Only silence greeted his remark. Lem shifted on the seat and leaned forward over the wheel.

Then Mrs. Stroop said, "Lem."

Lem said nothing. He glared at the road and increased the speed of the car.

"Now, Lem."

Lem flexed his hands on the wheel. He still did not look at his wife.

"You turn this car aroun', Lem. You know how I feel."

"That damn cat a-crossin' our road don't mean nothin'." Lem concentrated fiercely on the road before him.

"Lem." Mrs. Stroop was quietly determined.

"Damnation," snarled Lem, but he slammed down the brake on the car and brought it to a screeching stop, the locked wheels skidding on the gravelly road. Jeremy slid off of the back seat and was slammed against the back of Lem's seat. Lem sat still, his eyes fixed upon the road ahead for a moment. Then he began to turn around in the road, the wheels of the car violently spewing gravel from under them. Jeremy was thrown against the door of the car.

"Why er we a-turnin' aroun', Paw?" asked Jeremy, straightening himself with difficulty in the swerving car.

"Ast yer maw," snarled Lem.

"Maw, why er we a-turnin' aroun'?"

"A black cat a-crossin' th' road is bad luck, Jeremy."

Lem had jerked the car around awkwardly, slammed the accelerator to the floor and headed for home. Nobody said a word.

15

WITH A FREE DAY BEFORE HIM, Jeremy wandered toward the barn. As he made his way, he felt nature's urge and turned aside toward the outhouse. It was what Lem called a "one-holer." Out in the pasture, or even behind the barn, Jeremy would simply have squatted, but he knew that this close to the house his father would not tolerate his not going to the privy. He approached the outhouse with some uneasiness, though, especially in the summer.

Once he stepped inside the door, he always inspected the privy. In summertime, yellow jackets built their nests in the ceiling of the outhouse, and Jeremy had great respect for them and their stings. Once when he had been gathering corn with Lem they had come to an area in the field where some of the stalks had dropped to the ground, and as Jeremy walked along, he had stepped on a nest of yellow jackets on one of the fallen stalks. Immediately the wasps had swarmed him. Some had flown up inside his pants leg and had begun stinging; others buzzed around his head, stinging him on his face and neck. Jeremy had screamed and danced around trying to escape the stings. As soon as Lem realized what was happening, he seized Jeremy and pressed him to the ground. Jeremy fought his father, trying to get up, trying to escape the wasps, but Lem held him down. "Be still, Boy. I know yer hurt, but just be still so's I kin h'ep yuh."

Lem had taken Jeremy's pants off so he could get to the stings. Then he had taken some tobacco from his pocket, put it into his mouth, chewed it into a paste-like consistency and coated the stings on Jeremy's legs and face with the tobacco poultice. Jeremy never knew whether or not the tobacco had helped. He had become very ill and had spent the next two days in bed.

Ever since that incident, Jeremy always inspected the privy carefully each time he entered it. Usually, the wasp nests would be small with only one or two wasps on them. Lem would destroy the nests before the wasps had time to produce their young. Occasionally, when Jeremy was sitting on the hole, one of the wasps would drop down from the nest and buzz close to him, but after its initial drop it would rise and fly out of the privy through a crack between the door and its facing. Jeremy also sometimes found "mud-dobbers" in the privy, but these did not concern him They were solitary creatures, and as far as he knew, they never stung anyone. They devoted all their attention to their curious mud houses.

Jeremy worried more about black widow spiders. He had heard tales about black widows building their nests in outhouses, and he had seen them, small, jet-black spiders with a red hour-glass design on their abdomens. He was always afraid that one of the spiders would crawl onto him and bite him as he sat over the hole.

Jeremy picked up the Sears catalog which lay beside him, the source of paper in the outhouse. And there on the cover, as always, was the gleaming red bicycle. Jeremy had stared at the bicycle many times, and he had wished fervently for it, or one like it. But recently, after listening to Flancher preach, he had begun to think that perhaps there was a better way to get the bicycle than just to wish for it. Flancher had preached about how prayers could be, would be, answered. He remembered Flancher saying over and over, "Ast in faith, nothin' doubtin', and see what God will give yuh." But Jeremy was not sure how one should pray. He had intended to ask his mother about it but had never found the right time.

Jeremy had another attraction to the Sears catalog. He had discovered the lingerie section. As Jeremy sat over the hole, he would study the girls in their flimsy nightwear or in their underwear, and the pictures excited him. Every one of the poses was seductive to him. Recently the pictures had inspired powerful urges in him, and he felt guilty about what he experienced while looking at the pictures.

When it came time for Jeremy to clean himself, he never used any of the lingerie pages. He would save them for next time. Before he left the privy, he would turn to another section in the catalog so his father or mother would not use any of his favorite pages.

Having adjusted the pages in the catalog, and having stood up and turned around to take one more look into the hole to see if there were any black widows, Jeremy would hurry out into the sunlight.

16

WHEN JEREMY CAME TO THE BREAKFAST TABLE the next morning, he found his father had not yet finished eating. Lem watched Jeremy take his place at the table, and as soon as the boy was seated, he began.

"Well, how have you an' th' Holy Rollers been gittin' along?" he asked, his mouth full of biscuit and gravy.

Jeremy shrugged his shoulders. "Oh, all right."

"Anybody been a-gittin' th' Holy Ghost?"

"I donno. I guess."

Lem snorted. "Hmmmm. I just bet they did. Did you?"

"Huh?" Jeremy was surprised. "Who? Me? No, no, I didn'." Then, trying to distract his father, he said, "But Miz McMillan went up tuh th' front. She responded tuh Brother Flancher."

"Musta had a new dress, er maybe she just got one uv them new home permanents."

"Now, Lem," remonstrated Mrs. Stroop. "I wish yuh wouldn' talk about Miz McMillan thataway. She's a good woman. You know she brought food over here when yer sister died, an' she's real good about visitin' th' sick an' takin' care uv folks that is less fortunate."

"I ain't sayin nothin' about them thangs," said Lem. "She's just like all uv them other wimmen that go tuh that church, an' you know it. She just goes tuh show off 'er dress."

There was silence, and then Lem said to Jeremy, "You shore you didn' git th' Holy Ghost?" Lem watched Jeremy's face.

"No, sir. I didn'."

"Yuh better be damn shore yuh didn't. An' I better not ever hear uv no such nonsense. You unnerstan'? Ain't no such thing as no damn Holy Ghost nohow."

"But, Paw, Brother Flancher says that yuh gotta be baptized with th' Holy Ghost."

"Dammit! I don't keer what he said. You hush that nonsense. They ain't no Holy Ghost."

"Yes, Sir."

Lem attacked his biscuits and gravy again. "Spend too much time down there at that church, tuh my way uv thinkin'," he said to no one in particular. "Either there er down tuh th' barn."

"I guess I cain't go tuhnight," Jeremy said.

"Now, yer damn shore right about that," Lem nodded. "You shore as hell ain't. Yer gonna put in a day's work, an' when yer through in th' fiel', yer gonna do yer chores, all uv 'em, when yuh git in."

Lem tore a biscuit in half and used one piece of it to wipe the remaining gravy from his plate. He put the gravy-soaked biscuit into his mouth and washed it down with the remainder of his coffee. Then, rising from the table he said, "Hurry, Boy. We got work tuh do tuhday. It's a damn shore thing that th' Holy Ghost ain't a-gonna do our work fer us." He paused and looked directly at Jeremy. "An' another thing. I wantcha tuh keep yer min' on workin' tuhday. I better not fin' yuh a-wanderin' off behin' me. Lately yuh been slow as a two-legged mule."

"I ain't done nothin'," said Jeremy as he added a third heaping spoonful of sugar to his cereal.

"Here, now. That's enough sugar," said his mother, pushing the sugar bowl out of his reach. "I'm not sure yuh oughtta go down tuh that church anymore, Jeremy."

"Aw, Maw. One night they're a-gonna have homemade ice cream. Just lemme go that night."

"I donno. Yer paw is upset."

"Come on, Maw. Please."

"We'll see, Jeremy. We'll see."

He ceased his begging, but he sensed that his mother was weakening, and he hoped to get to go to church again. The ice-cream supper attracted him, and he was intrigued by what Mutchell had called a special healing service. Jeremy wanted to see that service as much as he wanted the ice cream.

The day passed uneventfully. The sun bore down from a cloudless sky; the sand burned Jeremy's feet, and the water breaks were few. Jeremy worked beside his father. He was resigned to staying home that night, although he would have liked to go to church. He admitted to himself that the last service had not been very exciting: the same number of the same songs, songs that Jeremy could neither sing nor understand. There had also been the same number of long prayers, with phrases repeated so that Jeremy could anticipate them. But Flancher's sermons were different. Jeremy did not understand everything Flancher said, but he was delighted by the stories Flancher could tell and by the way he delivered his sermons. He had somehow become even bigger than when Jeremy first saw him.

Jeremy tried to get in the mood for one of his silent daydreams, but he could only think about Flancher, about the church, and about hell. Having listened to Flancher he was convinced now that he was a sinner, and that he should repent. He thought at this point that somehow repentance meant responding to Flancher when he asked for people to come to the front of the building so he could pray for them. Jeremy had watched many people do that, but he realized that not everyone went down the aisle to Flancher. Jeremy thought of the babbler who just stood and talked incoherently until someone came to him and pushed him back into his seat. And there was the old crone—Jeremy still wondered if it were Hazel—the one who wandered around from pew to pew, the one who had asked him if he had been saved.

The prospect of walking down that aisle bothered Jeremy. On the other hand, he thought, what if I put if off too long? He remembered Flancher's many references to hell, and his sermon about his dying father.

The workday ended, but the heat was still oppressive. After supper, Jeremy went down to the outbuildings to do his chores. He was at the barn feeding the one-eyed horse when he heard his father's call: "Jeremy! Jeremy! Dammit, Boy! Git out here quick!"

He dropped his feed bucket and rushed for the door. He was almost knocked down by his father, running into the barn.

"Git some towsacks, Boy. Hurry!" Lem disappeared into the recesses of the barn. Jeremy followed his father, not knowing what to expect. Inside the barn, Lem hurled empty sacks at him. "Take these an' run, git in th' car, Boy. Th' fiel's on fire!" Confused, Jeremy stood among the sacks his father had thrown at him. "Dammit! Don't jus' stan' there. Move! Th' damn fiel's on fire. Didn' yuh hear me?" And so saying, Lem gathered an armful of sacks and charged past the dazed Jeremy.

Lem stopped in desperation. "Come on, Boy. Will you git a move on?"

Outside, on the way to the car, Jeremy could see smoke rising from a field to the east. "Hurry, Boy, hurry!" Lem shoved Jeremy toward the car.

They both threw their sacks into the back seat while they climbed into the front. Lem started the car with a roar of its engine, and they sped toward the field. "Man, I wish we had some water," Lem was saying, "but we ain't, an' so we'll just hafta do our best. The fire ain't spreadin' too fast yet." He watched the flames, which were visible now. "Th' wind ain't bad, an' what wind they is will drive the fire toward th' creek. I don't think th' fire can jump th' creek, but they's some shocks uv feed in that fiel' that I'd like tuh save." Lem was talking to himself, never taking his eyes off the burning field. "We'll just do what we can."

He brought the car to a sliding halt, hopping out almost before it had come to a complete stop. "Throw me some uv them sacks," he demanded, watching the flames spreading through the short brown stubble. A light breeze was moving the flames along the ground. As Jeremy threw the sacks to his father, he selected some for himself and prepared to fight the fire. He picked out a large shock that was in full blaze, its flames leaping higher than his head, and he moved toward it. Feeling the intense heat, he stopped and backed away. The fire scared him. He looked at his father, and then started forward again, but his father called him back. "Ain't nothin' yuh can do about that shock. It's awready on fire. Just try tuh keep th' fire from reachin' as many uv th' others as yuh can." Lem was flailing at the fire around a shock as he spoke.

Jeremy rushed among the shocks, trying to keep the flames beaten away from them. By now the sun had set, and he found himself in an eerie world—now obscured by swirling smoke, now lit by blazing, sulphurous flames. Occasionally one of the shocks would ignite with a roar, and the flames would shoot high into the air, emitting a rush of searing heat.

Jeremy continued to move among the shocks. It seemed to him that the fire was spreading rapidly, and he tried to hurry. He moved deeper and deeper into the field and gradually became aware that he was surrounded by burning shocks. Everywhere the ground was on fire. He was engulfed in the searing heat. Shocks exploded in flames all around him. He could not see Lem anywhere; it had become difficult to breathe, and he had lost his sense of direction. For an instant he panicked. Everywhere he looked about him in the twilight, there were flames and smoke.

He could hardly see, and he gasped for breath. His upper body was soaked with perspiration. He approached a shock untouched by flame and tried to beat away the fire approaching it, but somehow the fire jumped the gap from the fire-line to the shock, and it exploded in his face. A shower of bright, glowing sparks filled the air. He screamed.

A blistering heat surging from the shock almost knocked Jeremy off his feet; the burning hot cinders scorched his naked back and shoulders, and he could smell his singed hair. Simultaneously, he felt intense pain in his left hand. He looked down to see that the towsack he held in his hand had caught fire, and the flames were licking his hand and arm. He dropped the bag and cried in pain. He reeled away, holding his arm, and almost stumbled into another burning shock. "I gotta git out uv here! I gotta git away!" Frightened to distraction, he began to pick his way among the flames that seemed to be everywhere. "Paw!" he screamed. "Paw, whur are yuh?"

He began to dodge among the shocks and although he burned his bare feet on the smoldering stubble, he finally escaped the fire and stood on cool ground. He watched the flames and smoke swirling in the field. That must be what hell is like, he thought. He moved further away from the heat, but he could not free himself of the thought. "Man," he said aloud. "I shore don't wanta go tuh hell."

He was surprised by the appearance of his father. Jeremy moved as if to go back among the shocks, afraid of what his father would say when he saw that he was not fighting the fire, but Lem stopped him. "May as well let it go, Boy. It's outta control here, but it cain't cross th' creek. Besides, without water there ain't much we can do. We'll just watch it 'til it burns itse'f out. I'm shore glad th' fire started in this little fiel' against th' creek. It ud a-been hell if it hadda started in one of them big fiel's up on th' hill." Lem stood, watching the flames. "Shore hate tuh have tuh tell Mr. Soules 'bout this fire. Lost a lot uv good hay here tuhnight."

Jeremy stood beside his father. He still could not dismiss the fear that he had felt when he had found himself surrounded by the fire. The pain in his hand was excruciating.

"Paw, my hand shore hurts." He held up his arm for his father to examine.

"Yeah, Son. I'm afraid that yuh got some deep burns on that arm. Better have yer maw look at it an' doctor it before yuh go tuh bed tuhnight."

"Paw, did you ever see a fire like that?" Jeremy tried to hold his hand and arm so they wouldn't hurt.

"Oh, that uz a little fire, I guess. I seen a coupla range fires that uz lots worse than that un."

"Here on this place?"

"Oh, no. It uz before we moved here. It uz out in New Mexico. Hell, a fire gits started out there, an' it can go on ferever. They ain't much water out there tuh stop a fire, an' there ain't nothin' but th' wide open spaces. That fire gits started, an' th' wind gits up, an' you can have a wind uv fifty er sixty miles an hour before yuh know it. An' once th' wind gits up like that, there ain't no stoppin' that fire. Hell, I uz out there fer six months once, an' it never rained a drop th' whole time. Then we had this big lightnin' storm, an' one uv th' strikes started a fire, an' we musta fought it fer days."

They stood and watched the fire. Now there was a broad black band between them and the active fireline. Small fires still flickered in the midst of the burned stubble. Shocks still occasionally flamed high into the air.

"This un uz big enough fer me," said Jeremy.

"I seen a housefire that uz a helluva lot worse than this," said Lem, his eyes fixed on the fire. "A helluva lot worse."

Jeremy, still nursing his hand, looked up at Lem.

"You seen a house burn up?"

"Yep, it uz a bad un."

"I ain't never seen a housefire."

"This un got bad real quick," Lem said, and then he was quiet for a moment. "They uz a woman an' her little girl in th' house, an' th' damn roof caved in on 'em before they could git out."

"Did it kill 'em?" Jeremy had momentarily forgotten his arm.

"Th' roof fallin' down didn'. But it fell on top uv 'em an' trapped 'em, right there in their kitchen. They uz both pinned down. They uz timbers that had fell down on their laigs, an' they couldn't move. It uz pitiful."

"Wow! Wha'd yuh do?"

"Wuzn't nothin' nobody could do. Th' fire uz all around 'em, an' it uz too hot tuh git to 'em. Coupla guys tried, but they just couldn' do it. That damn fire uz just too hot."

They were both quiet a moment, then Lem said, "I still remember that woman. She knew she couldn' move, an' she knew her little girl couldn'. An' she could see th' fire a-gittin' closer an' closer. It uz awful.They uz both a-screamin' an' a-slobberin' something awful, an' th' people uz just a-runnin' aroun', a-tryin' tuh fin' somethin' they could do. Th' woman kep' a-screamin', 'He'p us! He'p us! God, cain't somebody he'p us!'"

Lem shook his head. "I guess she fin'ly seen that no one uz a-gonna he'p 'er, an' she picked up a big iron fryin' pan a-layin' there on th' floor by 'er, an' she hit that little girl upside 'er head, ka-whop."

Jeremy jumped instinctively.

"God, she hit 'er. Blood busted out ever'whur. My God, that little girl screamed."

"Why'd she hit th' girl?" Jeremy was perplexed.

Lem ignored Jeremy; he was caught up in his story. "That mother uz just a-bawlin', but she hit that little girl ag'in, right in th' face.

Swung that damn fryin' pan with both hands, an' just kep' a-screamin', an' that little girl's face just a bloody mess." Lem seemed momentarily overcome. "'I don't want 'er tuh feel th' pain uv th' fire,' th' mother kep' on a-sayin. 'Oh, God, fergive me. I don't want 'er tuh feel th' pain uv th' fire.'" Lem was silent a moment. Then he said:. "She hit 'er ag'in, an' th' little girl passed out, I guess. Just went limp there on th' floor. Th' woman looked at 'er fer a minute, and then she just dropped that fryin' pan, an' slumped down on th' floor an' gathered that little girl in 'er a-arms, a-strokin' 'er, an' a-tryin' tuh perteckt 'er, an' just a-sayin' over an' over, 'It's all right now. It's all right. You won't feel no flames now. I luv yuh. I luv yuh.' An' then th' flames come."

Jeremy looked out on the burning field. As he watched, a shock burst into flames, and he moved closer to his father.

"Paw," he asked. "Do you believe in hell?"

His father looked at him quizzically, and then he looked back at the fire. "Does sort uv remind yuh uv hell, don't it?"

By the time Jeremy and his father reached the house, Jeremy's arm and feet were throbbing. He limped into the house. Olga met them at the door. She had seen the fire from her window.

"What on earth, Lem?"

"It's okay, Olga. They uz a fire down on that little fiel' on th' creek, but it's all out now. We lost some good hay."

Olga looked closely at Jeremy. "Jeremy, what happened to you?"

"I got burnt, Maw."

"My goodness. C'mere. Lemme look at yuh."

"I'm okay, Maw."

"Come here. You ain't okay. Any fool can see that. Lemme see." She took Jeremy's left arm and looked closely at it. "Oh, Jeremy. That arm looks real bad. You got some deep splotches." She continued her close examination. "I cain't see no blisters, at least not yet." She continued to examine the arm.

"My feet is all burned, too," said Jeremy.

"Yeah," said Lem. "He got too close tuh some uv them shocks and burnt his feet. Shoulda been a-wearin' shoes. I git after 'im alla th' time about that."

Olga ignored Lem's remarks. "Here. Siddown," she said to Jeremy. "Lemme look at yer feet." Olga knelt before him.

Jeremy was glad to get off his feet.

His mother gently rubbed his feet. "Yeah, you shore burned 'em, but I don't think they're as bad as yer arm. I'm worried about it."

His mother stood to her feet. "You just sit right there. I'm a-gonna git my aloe, an' I'll rub yuh good with it. It'll make yuh feel better, an' it'll he'p yuh tuh heal."

She left the room for a few minutes and returned with the aloe. "Now this won't hurt," she said. She began to rub the aloe over Jeremy's burned arm. It felt good to him. "Now," his mother said, "I'm a-gonna wrap this soft cloth aroun' yer arm. It'll h'ep tuh pertect it, an it'll keep th' aloe on yer arm."

She wrapped the arm carefully. At last, she surveyed her work and said, "Okay. That'll do fer now. Here, hold up yer feet tuh me. I'm a-gonna doctor them, too."

Jeremy welcomed his mother's ministrations. Her gentle hands and the cool aloe felt good.

"Okay," said his mother at last. "That's th' best I can do right now. How do yuh feel?"

"I'm better, but my arm still hurts."

His mother continued her critical gaze. "I expect it'll hurt fer some time, but we've done all we can fer now. You go on tuh bed, an' if yuh wake up in th' night, you call me."

Jeremy stood up, slowly.

"Can you make it all right?" his mother asked.

"I think so."

His mother watched him all the way across the room. "You call me, if yuh need me, Son."

"Yes'm."

He tried without success to sleep. He was tired, and his burned feet and left arm throbbed. Eventually, he fell into a terrifying nightmare in which he was a sinner condemned by God to a hell that was not a lake of fire but a huge, burning grain field, filled with exploding shocks of grain. In his dream the shocks were several stories high. Sulphurous clouds arose into a black night, and the heat from them was unbearable. When one of these shocks would explode, the helpless bodies of screaming sinners would be violently thrust into the air. Above the roar of the flames, he could hear the shrieks and groans of men and women; he could smell the stench of burning flesh, and he could see flames playing upon the human bodies. And yet the sinners were never consumed, and their bodies were inevitably drawn into the maelstrom, only to be repelled again and again.

In his dream, he was aware that he was slowly being drawn closer and closer to the roiling flames, and suddenly he discovered the old hag from church—Hazel, he was sure—smiling horribly, beckoning him toward the flames. "Come on, Sonny. I tole yuh that you oughtta

repent, an' you didn'. Welcome now tuh th' Devil's pit ferevermore."
She gathered her filthy, shabby dress around her and threw back her
head in a hideous laugh. She continued to laugh and to point at Jeremy
until her figure became obscured by the smoke.

"What's wrong, Son?"

He looked up and was sure that he saw Hazel leaning over him.
Only gradually did he realize that it was his mother.

"Jeremy. Wake up. Wake up."

"Ooooo," moaned Jeremy.

"Son, wake up. Yuh had a nightmare. It's okay."

Fully awake, he sat up in bed. He raised his left arm, and it
throbbed painfully.

"Are yuh okay, Son?"

He nodded dully. "My arm shore hurts."

His mother put her hand on his brow. "Yer a-sweatin' like all git
out. Now just lay down and relax. It uz just a nightmare."

She stood beside his bed for a few moments. "Are yuh all right,
Son?"

Jeremy lay back on his bed. He nodded dully.

"Are yuh sure?"

He nodded again.

"Can I git yuh anything?"

He shook his head.

His mother watched him closely. Then she turned away. She
stopped at the door of his room and looked back at him. "Call me if yuh
need me." She stood for another minute, and then she returned to her
room.

Jeremy lay back upon the bed, carefully cradling his burned arm.
"Oh, God. I don't wanta go tuh hell." He lay on his back and gently
placed his arm on the top of his sheet. It was a long time before he fell
asleep again.

17

JEREMY AWOKE ILL THE NEXT MORNING, too sick to work. His left arm had deep red splotches on it. His feet throbbed. The exhaustion and smoke inhalation of the night before had taken its toll. His mother came into his room and unwrapped his left arm, and once again applied aloe to it and to his feet. "I think you better just stay in bed fer awhile," she said. "You don't look no better this mornin' that I can tell."

She left the room, and Jeremy could hear her telling Lem that she was convinced that Jeremy was too sick to work that day. "His burns is purty deep, an' I'm worried about 'im."

His father consented to Jeremy's staying home, and he slept until noon. He finally got up in time to eat lunch, but he was still groggy, and he limped. Mrs. Stroop talked Lem into letting Jeremy stay home that afternoon also, and Jeremy spent a leisurely time lying on the settee in the living room. He slept most of the afternoon.

In his waking periods, he thought a lot about his experience of the night before. His attitude toward religion was different now. Before he had been curious about the church services; his attraction to Flancher and his preaching had grown, but now he was afraid. He was convinced that he was a sinner and that he must repent. Over and over, the image of the flaming field returned.

"Maw," he called to his mother.

"Yes, Jeremy," she answered as she came to the door.

"Maw, can I go tuh church tuhnight?"

"Now, Jeremy. Yuh know how yer paw feels about that. An' besides, I ain't at all sure yer feet er goin' tuh be up to it."

"But I just wanta go. If Miz McMillan comes tuh git me, can I go?"

"I'll have tuh check yer feet an' that arm. I'm really worried about yer arm. It's worse than yer feet. An' besides, we'll hafta check with yer paw about yuh even a-goin'. Ain't no tellin' what he might have tuh say. Frankly, I don't think yuh oughtta git yer hopes up. I don't much think he'll agree. He letcha stay home tuhday, an' I think he might be a little suspicious that yuh wuz sick all day, an' then here at night when yuh wanta go tuh church yuh just suddenly git well.

How do yuh feel now? Lemme see yer arm." She reached for his arm, carefully unwrapped it and examined it.

"I think I'm better."

"Well, yer arm still looks awful." She put her hand upon his forehead. "But you don't seem tuh have no fever." She gently rubbed her hand over his arm.

Jeremy winced when his mother touched his arm, but he tried to hide it. "Naw, Maw, I think I'm better."

"Well, we'll see. I'm a-gonna put some more aloe on it." She turned away in search of the salve.

That night, Mrs. McMillan showed up at the Stroop house, and she was her usual persuasive self. She was heavily made up and dressed in a bright yellow dress with a wide orange sash. She said, "Oh, but yuh must let th' boy go tuhnight. We're havin' our ice-cream supper tuhnight."

"Well, I donno. He ain't been a-feelin' well. In fact, he stayed home from th' fiel' all day," Mrs. Stroop objected. "He got burnt somethin' awful in a fire las' night."

"Oh, here at yer house?" Mrs. McMillan looked around at the room as if she expected to see evidence of a fire.

"Oh, no. It wuzn't here. It uz down in th' fiel', but he got too close an' burnt hisse'f somethin' awful. He didn' sleep a-tall las' night."

Mrs. McMillan looked sympathetically at Jeremy. "Oh, I'm so sorry. Poor baby." She patted Jeremy's shoulder. "You must be very brave tuh fight that fire thataway." Then, she brightened. "But I'm sure he feels much better now, an' besides, th' ice cream'll do 'im good. Don't yuh feel better now, Jeremy?"

"Yes, ma'am, I do." His mother gave him a distressed look.

"I'll just hafta check with 'is paw," Mrs. Stroop said and started to turn away. At that instant, Lem walked into the room.

"Oh, hello, Mr. Stroop," sang out Mrs. McMillan cheerily. "How are you tuhnight?"

"I'm fair tuh middlin'," Lem replied.

"I come tuh git Jeremy to take 'im tuh church. Thought some ice cream ud do 'im good." She winked at Jeremy.

"Well, I donno . . . . ."

"Oh, come on. Why don't you an' Miz Stroop come, too? We'd luv tuh have yuh. Why, I cain't remember you an' Miz Stroop ever a-comin' tuh our little ole church. Why don't yuh come tuhnight? We're a-havin' such a good meetin'. Ever'body's enjoyin' it. Brother Flancher is sooo good." She turned to look at Jeremy. "Ain't he, Jeremy?"

Jeremy did not look at his father or mother. He simply nodded his head.

Mrs. McMillan smiled. "Well, I know our little ole church ain't much tuh look at, an' we ain't got no new roof like th' Baptists, but we're all spirit-filled Christians, an' we're good folks." Her smile widened. "An' we're fren'ly too. We'll do our best tuh make yuh feel at home with us."

"Well, we cain't come tuhnight," Lem explained. "We never planned on it er nothin'. An' we ain't dressed fer church. We better just stick tuh home." Jeremy thought his father was speaking more gently than usual.

"But, my goodness, God accepts yuh just as yuh are. Ain't none uv us at th' church rich folks. We're just common folks that love th' Lord. You and Miz Stroop look jus' fine, an' we're a-havin' ice cream. Come on. Y'all come with us."

"I guess not tuhnight, ma'am. Maybe some other time."

"Well, okay, but we'll miss yuh. God'll miss yuh, too." She smiled prettily at Lem. "But just let Jeremy come. I'm sure that he wants tuh be with 'is frens and eat ice cream, don't yuh, Jeremy?"

"Yes, ma'am, I'd like that." Jeremy watched for his father's reaction.

"Well, then it's all settled. How 'bout it, Mr. Stroop?" Mrs. McMillan directed her full charm to Lem.

"I guess so." Lem's voice had its accustomed edge back in it. "But he shore better feel like workin' tomorrer, 'cause that's what he's a-gonna do."

Jeremy was delighted. He rushed back into his room to dress, ignoring his painful feet. His mother followed him. "Now, Jeremy, you put on yer shoes er you ain't a-goin' nowhere." She got down on her knees to retrieve Jeremy's shoes from under the bed, where they had been all summer.

"But, Maw, they'll hurt my feet."

"If yer feet hurt that bad, yuh ain't got no bizness a-goin' tuh that church."

"But, Maw."

"Just hush, Jeremy. If you go tuh church, yer a-wearin' shoes. I ain't a-gonna have alla them folks a-thinkin' you ain't got no shoes."

Jeremy sat on his bed and tried to put on his shoes. The pain was excruciating. "Maw, I cain't put 'em on. My feet hurts too bad."

Mrs. Stroop was frustrated. "Well, put socks on. Maybe that'll he'p."

Jeremy selected a pair of socks and gingerly slipped them on his feet. Then he tried his shoes again. They hurt, but not as bad as before—and Jeremy, afraid that if he complained again he might not be permitted to go to church, stood and declared that his feet now felt fine.

Mrs. Stroop stood and skeptically surveyed his feet. "Are yuh sure?"

"Fine. They're heaps better now."

She looked closely at Jeremy. "You sure? Try walkin'."

"Yes, ma'am." And he began to walk across the room to demonstrate how well he could walk. Every step was painful, but he was pleased to discover that the socks did seem to help.

"Well, okay," said his mother resignedly.

Jeremy walked very carefully back into the kitchen and joined Mrs. McMillan.

"Okay. You all ready?" she asked.

"Yes, ma'am."

"Well, let's go." She looked once again at Lem. "Shore wish you folks ud come tuhnight. Hot night like tuhnight, some ice cream ud really do yuh good."

Lem nodded without saying anything.

Jeremy walked carefully out to the car. His feet really hurt. He got into the back seat with Leland from the left side of the car and reached over his body with his right hand to close the door, protecting his left arm.

"What's wrong with yer arm, Stroop?" Leland asked. "Why have yuh got it all wrapped up?"

"I burnt it. We had a fire las' night in th' fiel'. I burnt my feet too, but my maw made me wear shoes."

"I burnt my arm once," said Leland, "but it didn' bother me all that much."

Sitting in the car, Jeremy discovered that he felt much better, and he and Leland spent the trip to church speculating on what kind of ice cream would be there and how much each would eat. But even in a conversation about ice cream, Jeremy wondered if he should respond to Flancher. Should he go to Flancher tonight and let him pray for him?

Mrs. McMillan directed a question to the two boys. "Have either uv yuh thought about bein' saved?"

"Nope," replied Leland curtly. "Not me."

Jeremy was more hesitant. "No, ma'am, I ain't."

"Yer both gittin' tuh be big boys now, and yuh should think uv th' Lord and yer souls. You remember th' baptizin' we had th' other night."

"Aw, I ain't inter'sted in that stuff," Leland said. "I'm a-gonna do like my paw an' Jeremy's paw when I grow up."

"You should be ashamed, Leland," Mrs. McMillan scolded. "I think that Brother Flancher has done some great preachin' this meetin', an' it seems tuh me that it ud touch yer hearts. Ain't you been touched, Jeremy?"

Jeremy looked at Leland. He pushed his hair back out of his eyes. "He's purty good," he said.

"Yes, he's wunnerful," said Mrs. McMillan, encouraged by Jeremy's response. "You boys outghta just think about it. Yuh don't hafta make up yer minds right now, but yuh need tuh think about it." They were arriving at the church building, and she dropped the subject.

The service that night was similar to all the rest that Jeremy had attended. He thought about what it would be like to get up out of his seat and actually walk down the aisle to Flancher, as he had seen so many others do. Many people responded to Flancher on this night, but when the service was over, Jeremy still had not.

18

OUTSIDE, AFTER THE SERVICE, Leland and Jeremy walked across the lawn to join other young people waiting for the ice cream. Jeremy's feet hurt worse now than they had earlier, and he walked cautiously.

A long table had been set up on the lawn underneath a string of naked light bulbs stretched between two poles. Insects swirled around the light bulbs. Around the table, the women scurried about, opening ice cream freezers of every size and description.

"I started not tuh even bring my ice cream," one of the ladies was complaining. "I just know it ain't no good."

"I'm sure it's fine, but I know just how yuh feel," replied her companion. "I feel th' same way about my cookies. It's a new recipe, an' I ain't sure how they turned out. I never made 'em before."

"Well, uv course," said another. "I don't use no recipe. I just put in a little dab uv this an' a little dab uv that. That's th' way my mother always did. People useta ast er fer her recipe, but she ud just say, 'Why I just put in a little dab uv this an' a little dab uv that.' I heard people say, 'Why, that ain't no way tuh make nothin'. Yuh gotta know how much flour an' sugar yuh use,' but my maw ud stick to 'er guns. An' I do th' same thin'. I never put no stock in recipes. My mother tole me that good cooks know their ingredients. My daughters don't unnerstan' that yet, but maybe someday they will." As she spoke, she triumphantly lifted a large chocolate cake from a cardboard box and set it on the table.

As the ladies talked, they set out plates of cookies, cakes, and pies of all sorts on yet another table. Between the two tables, on the ground, sat a tub filled with ice and soda pop. A short distance from the tables, there was a coffee pot over an open fire.

At last the food was ready. Mutchell called for everyone's attention and led a prayer of thanksgiving. As he ended his prayer, he stepped back with an exaggerated motion and shouted, "Come an' git it!" Jeremy, slowed by his painful feet, hung back as Leland and the other boys pushed and shoved their way toward the tables. He became separated from the boys and found himself standing among adults in the line. He was surprised to look up and see Flancher directly behind him.

Flancher nodded, smiled, and spoke. "Hello, there."

"Hi," Jeremy responded. He averted his eyes and pushed back his hair from his face.

"What's yer name, Son?"

"Jeremy. Jeremy Stroop."

"That's a fine name. Don't believe I know any Stroops. Do yer folks go tuh church here?"

"Naw. No, Sir."

"Didn' think I remembered th' name. Have I seen yuh before?"

"Oh, yeah. Yes, Sir. I been here before."

There was a brief silence.

"Have I met yer dad?"

"Yes, Sir."

"Here at church?"

"No, Sir. You met 'im out in th' fiel'." Jeremy had never been able to talk easily to adults.

"Out in what fiel'?"

"You an' Mr. Mutchell come out tuh th' fiel' an' ast my paw—an' me—tuh come tuh church."

"Oh. That's right. Now I remember. An' you've come. That's very good, Son."

Flancher and Jeremy were directly in front of the ice cream freezers now. Jeremy took the first bowl offered to him, although he saw that it was vanilla, and he would have preferred chocolate. He started to walk away.

"Here's yuh spoon," a lady said as she placed one in his hand.

Jeremy started walking away from the tables, thinking he might find Leland and sit and eat his ice cream with him, but he noticed that Flancher followed him. Jeremy walked aimlessly for a minute, and then Flancher said, "Yuh wanta siddown here?"

"Okay." Jeremy was glad to get off his feet, but he looked around, wishing that he could see some of the boys. He wondered why Flancher wanted to sit beside him.

Flancher lowered himself heavily to the ground, holding his bowl of ice cream carefully.

"Did yer folks come with yuh tuhnight?" Flancher's breathing was labored.

"Naw, they didn'." Jeremy continued looking down at his ice cream.

"Well, it's a shame they couldn't come."

"They uz both purty busy, I guess." Jeremy wished that Flancher had not sat down beside him.

"You said yer folks don't go tuh church here, didn't yuh?" Flancher was taking large bites of chocolate ice cream. Jeremy still had not taken a bite.

"Naw, they don't."

"Well, whur do they go?"

"They don't never go," Jeremy admitted, but he looked up quickly. "But my maw is saved. She tole me so. She's been baptized an' ever'thin'. An' she lissens tuh preachin' on th' radio ever' Sunday."

"That's fine. Good fer her. An' what about yer dad?"

Jeremy thought a minute and then said, "He works."

"He works? You mean he works on Sundays?"

"Yes, Sir. Sometimes."

There was silence as Flancher continued to consume his ice cream with gusto. Jeremy still had not taken a bite.

"So, yer paw works?"

"Yes, Sir. He don't believe that there's no Holy Ghost."

Flancher looked up from his ice cream and started to speak. Then he was interrupted by a lady that Jeremy did not know. "Oh, Brother Flancher, yer sermont was just divine tuhnight."

"Thankee, Sister," replied Flancher. He made an awkward move, as if to get up.

"Oh, no. Keep yer seat. I jus' wanted tuh tell yuh how I liked yer sermont, an' how much it hepped me."

"Thankee, Sister."

"I try," the lady continued, "tuh git my husband tuh come out an' hear yuh, but he just won't come. I git so frustrated."

"Now, yuh mustn't do that, Sister. God works in 'is own ways."

"Oh, do yuh think so?"

"I shore do."

"Oh, I hope so. My husband is Catholic, an' he won't come tuh church with me a-tall. But I keep a-tryin', an' I pray ever' night. We got two little uns, an' I worry so about them. Uv course they want tuh stay home with their paw, an' he won't encourage 'em tuh come tuh church with me, an' it's just so hard. All he wants tuh do at night is just lissen tuh his ole hillbilly music." She sniffled into her handkerchief. "I'm a-gonna tell my husband that I talked tuh you."

"You do that, Sister," said Flancher. "Praise th' Lord!" Then he turned to Jeremy. "Now, let's see. We were talkin' about you an' church. So, do yuh come tuh church here alla th' time?" He ate his ice cream rapidly, lifting large spoonfuls to his mouth. His breathing was still labored.

"I guess so."

"Whadda yuh mean, yuh guess so?" Flancher pushed the issue. He had finished his ice cream.

Jeremy changed the cold bowl of ice cream from one hand to the other. The cold bowl felt good on his burned left hand. "I been a-comin' a lot lately."

"You mean durin' th' meetin'?"

"Yeah, I guess so."

"That's good. Are yuh a member uv this church?"

"Naw, I ain't. Not yet."

Another person, an older lady, appeared before Flancher. "Could I talk tuh yuh, Brother Flancher?"

"Why, shorely." Once again Flancher started getting up from the ground.

"No, no. Keep yer seat. It'll just take a minute."

"All right, Sister. What is it?"

"I wuz a-wonderin'. Are we really gonna have a healin' service Sattidy night?"

"Yes, we are. We certainly are."

"Well, my little grandson, Johnny, he ain't been tuh church, but he's got a club foot, an' he ain't got no daddy. He uz killed in a automobile wreck, an' his mother ain't got no money neither. It's so pitiful. They jus' live out there on that lonesome ole place, an' they don't never see nobody er nothin'. It jus' breaks my heart. Would yuh look at 'im an' maybe just say a prayer fer 'im?"

"I shore will."

"Oh, if you'd do that, I'd be ever so grateful. I feel so bad fer that little boy. He tries tuh do what th' other little boys do, an' he just cain't keep up." She wiped a tear from her eye. "He just breaks my heart."

"I unnerstand, ma'am. Certainly. I'll be glad tuh look at' im. Th' Lord can do all thin's."

"I know that." Tears welled up in her eyes. "Well, thankee. I'll bring 'im tomorrer night." And she turned away, holding a handkerchief to her face.

"Lots uv interruptions, seems like. Now, what wuz we a-talkin' about? Seems I wuz astin' you if yer a member uv this church?"

"No, I ain't."

"Well, then, are you a member uv any church? A big boy like you oughtta be in church. Haven't yuh been saved?"

"Oh, I donno." Jeremy stirred his ice cream. He had not taken a bite of it yet.

"You don't know." Flancher seemed perplexed. "You don't know if yer saved? You should know that. It's very important tuh be saved, tuh have th' assurance uv salvation. Why do yuh think all them folks has been a-comin' up to th' front during th' meetin'?"

Jeremy did not answer. He studied his ice cream bowl.

"Have yuh discussed salvation with yer folks?"

"With my maw some."

"What did she say?"

"Not much. She says church is very important." He was not sure what to say. "An' she says yuh gotta be committed."

"Jeremy." Flancher had become solemn now, cupping his empty bowl between his hands. "Yuh shore need tuh be saved. Have yuh understood what I been a-sayin' this week?"

"Some, I guess." Jeremy looked at his ice cream. It was almost melted.

"Do yuh believe in hell?"

Jeremy looked up. He remembered the burning field. He carefully touched his left arm. "Yessir. I shore do."

"Well, th' only way tuh avoid that place is tuh let th' Lord save ye. Yuh gotta do that, Jeremy."

"Yes, Sir."

"Can I he'p yuh tuh make up yer mind? Yuh got any questions about anythin' I've said when I been a-preachin'? Er is there anythin' I kin do tuh help yuh? If they is, you let me know. Okay?"

"Yes, Sir." He tried to think of all the questions he had wanted to ask, but now he couldn't think of any. He said, "I guess I ain't got no questions. Leastaways not right now."

"Hey, Brother Flancher!" It was Mutchell, walking rapidly toward them. "I been a-lookin' ever'whur fer yuh. C'mere. I wanta show yuh somethin'."

"Whatcha got, Jacob?" Flancher rolled forward onto his knees, and then pushed himself up from the ground. He brushed himself off. He looked down on Jeremy. "You remember what I said, Son. If I kin he'p yuh, lemme know." Then he smiled and said, "Now finish yer ice cream." He turned and walked away with Mutchell.

Jeremy looked down at his ice cream, which had become a thick liquid. He sighed and rose to his feet and walked carefully on his aching feet out to the edge of the yard, where the shadows began to darken, and poured the ice cream on the ground. He stood for a minute. "I could have asked him about the holy laugh," he thought.

He continued to stand there, becoming increasingly aware of his aching feet and arm. Once again, images of the fire rose up in his mind. He could almost feel the flames again. He remembered his nightmare and shuddered involuntarily. I could have asked him about hell, he thought to himself, but I guess I understand it a whole lot better now.

He carried his bowl and spoon over to the table where the ice cream freezers were.

"Yuh want some more ice cream, Son?" a lady said. "We got lots more."

Jeremy looked at her, shook his head, and walked away. He headed for the McMillan's car.

Leland caught up with him as he walked toward the car. "Hey, Jeremy. I seen ole Flancher a-talkin' tuh yuh. Wha'd he want?"

"Nothin' much, I guess."

"Did he try tuh git yuh tuh come down tuh the front an' be prayed fer? I bet he did. He talked tuh Danny Williams that way once last year when he wuz here in a meetin'. Danny went down there, an' he said that he couldn' unnerstan' a word that ole Flancher said. Said he'd never do that ag'in. Ole Flancher ain't nothin' but a windbag. He oughtta mind his own bizness, always a-tryin' tuh git people tuh git religion. Wha'd yuh tell' im?"

"Nothin'," Jeremy said truthfully. "I didn't tell 'im nothin'." The pain in his feet was increasing. He wanted to get into the car and sit down.

"Good fer you, Stroop. I uz afraid that he'd git yuh alone, an' then he'd talk yuh intuh it. Boy, that uz good ice cream, wuzn't it?"

"Yeah."

"Say, how's yer arm, Stroop."

"It shore hurts."

Jeremy lay awake for a long time that night, his arm aching, his mind in turmoil. He tried to lose himself in his dream of the garden and the lovely girl, but his arm hurt so bad it distracted him. He was more convinced than ever now that he was a sinner. He remembered his guilt about the pictures in the catalog and how they aroused him. He felt sure that he was going to hell if he did not repent and—what was it his mother had said?—oh, yeah, commit himself. He still was not sure what commitment was. Flancher's concern about him had been further proof that he was a sinner, and yet he still did not know what to do. His father's contempt for "them Holy Rollers" and Leland's rejection of the church still bothered him. And there was the old crone. She must be Hazel. On the other hand, he thought that Flancher must be right when he talked about the Holy Spirit, in spite of what his father had said, for he had read about it in his Bible. He still had not read anything, however, about the holy laugh.

19

ONCE AGAIN, THROUGHOUT THE WEEK, Lem and Jeremy worked late into the evening, and Jeremy had no opportunity to go to church. All Saturday morning, Jeremy looked forward to the afternoon when he knew the family would go into town for groceries. Then at noon, during lunch, he was pleased to hear Lem say that he wanted to quit earlier than usual so he could check on the work that Mr. Soules was having done to the windmill before the family went into town.

"I wanta go over tuh th' windmill and check on what Sam an' Pookie has been a-doin'," Lem said. "I saw 'em come onto th' place this mornin', an' I figger they oughtta be done about now."

As Jeremy and his father approached the windmill, he saw Sam and Pookie sitting on their haunches under the shade of an oak tree. He had seen both of them on several occasions before, when they had come to service the windmill. "Howdy, Lem," they said in unison. They were both smoking. Pookie was drinking from a thermos.

"Howdy. You boys ain't a-gonna git no work done a-sittin' in th' shade."

Pookie, the smaller of the two men, drew on his cigarette. He was a young man with piercing blue eyes and bright, almost golden hair. He sat easily on his haunches, his shirt unbuttoned and outside his trousers. He had the bill of his baseball cap turned to the back of his head. "We're 'bout finished with 'er, Mr. Stroop. Just needed primin'."

"That's good. I figgered that uz all it needed, but Mr. Soules wanted you boys tuh come out an' take a look at 'er. He thinks you guys is th' onliest ones that knows anythin' about win'mills. An' I guess in this county that's prob'ly correct. Ain't many guys that works on 'em aroun' here."

Sam shifted his weight from his right leg to his left. He was older, heavier than Pookie. He wore overalls over a plaid shirt, and he had a straw hat pushed back on his head. "I useta do a lot uv work on win'mills. Hell, I musta climbed ever' win'mill in this county, but I don't do so much no more. My health has been porely th' past few years."

"Yeah," said Lem, "I heard."

"Oh, yeah. Mr. Soules called me 'bout a month ago, but I couldn' come then. 'Ole Arthur' has got me really bad."

"Arthritis can be tough," affirmed Pookie. "My uncle's got it turrible. Wife an' me uz down there two er three weeks ago, stayed with 'em a few days, an' he couldn' even git outta bed on a coupla mornin's. Knuckles on 'is right hand is all swole up."

"Yep," agreed Sam. "It's bad. You git arthritis like I got it, an' I guaran-damn-tee yuh that yuh won't be a-doin' no climbin' on no win'mills."

"Guess I'm lucky," said Lem. "I got arthritis, but it ain't that bad."

Sam shifted back to his right leg. "An' I'll just tell yuh somethin' else. My piles has been turrible now fer awhile."

"Ooh," groaned Pookie, shaking his head in sympathy. "Them's bad news."

"Shore as hell are. An' they ain't no way yuh can know how bad they are 'til yuh git a case uv 'em, always a-itchin' an' a-burnin'. It's hell."

"Well," continued Sam, "they ain't no cure that I know uv. I went tuh that chiropractor over in Milburn, an' I cain't tell no differ'nce."

"Onliest cure I ever heard uv," said Pookie, "is tuh wipe with careless weeds. My paw swore that ud work."

Sam heaved himself to his feet. "Ain't no shortage uv careless weeds, I guess. Well, less go, Pookie. Seems this win'mill is a-runnin' fine. Ain't nothin' more we can do fer it."

"Yep," agreed Pookie, standing to his feet and screwing the cap onto his thermos.

"Wish piles and arthritis uz this easy tuh fix." Sam walked with great difficulty. "Well, we'll see yuh, Lem. Yuh want us tuh give you th' bill er send it tuh Soules?"

"Just send it tuh him. He'll take care uv it."

"I know he will."

Sam and Pookie piled their tools into their pickup, climbed into the seat, and drove away. Lem and Jeremy continued on their way toward home.

It was late when he and his father arrived at the house. His mother was ready, waiting for them, and they were soon on their way to town.

Only Lem spoke, and that was to say that they were running late and would have to hurry to get home before dark.

Once in town, Jeremy stood outside of Ayers Store, watching the blacksmith shop. He saw Jackie once at the back of the shop, but he did not hail him, nor did he walk across the street to see him. He could see that Jackie was talking to Vincent, and Vincent made him nervous.

As he watched, Vincent left Jackie and walked across the street toward him. Jeremy started to go back into the store.

"Hello, kid," Vincent said. Vincent always called him "kid," and Jeremy wished he would not do that.

"Hi," Jeremy replied.

"How yuh been?"

"Okay."

"David White ain't been a-givin' yuh no hard time 'bout yer underwear, has he?"

Jeremy looked up and pushed his hair back from his eyes.

"I seen 'im pull up yer long johns an' show 'em tuh th' class that day. That woulda made me mad as hell."

Jeremy flinched. Why was Vincent bringing that up?

"I guaran-damn-tee yuh he wouldn't do me thataway. I wouldna put up with it no way. He comes aroun' me actin' like he's a-gonna do somethin' like that, an' I'll put a stop tuh it right quick." Vincent reached down into his pocket and pulled out a knife. He held it out in his hand, and then with a quick move snapped the blade from its sheath. Jeremy stepped back, his eyes on the slender, sharp blade of the knife. How had the blade appeared so quickly?

"I'da cut 'im," said Vincent. "Smart-aleck bastard. Why'd yuh put up with 'im, Stroop?"

Jeremy remained silent, watching the knife.

"You 'member ole Jerry Rawls?" Vincent closed the knife, then in another quick move reproduced the blade.

Jeremy nodded that he did. He had not taken his eyes off the knife.

"He come aroun' a-tellin' guys right there in front uv me that I uz a queer, an' I tole 'im he better shut up, an' he said, 'Why? Whatcha gonna do about it, queer?' So, I showed 'im what I uz a-gonna do about it. I cut 'im just about ever'whur." Vincent paused. "They put me away at th' state school fer two years, but I don't keer. I'd do it ag'in. Ain't nobody messes with me an' gits away with it."

Jeremy had heard something about Vincent going away to a "special school," but he had never known the details. He saw Jerry Rawls occasionally at school, and he had noticed the deep scars on the left side of the boy's face. He had heard that Jerry had a glass eye.

"You carry a knife?" Vincent asked.

"Naw, I ain't got one with me."

"Ain't never without mine."

"Did you cut up ole Jerry Rawls with that un?" Jeremy pointed at the knife.

"This un?" Vincent looked at his knife. "Naw. They took that un away frum me. But I got me another. It's a switchblade. Watch." And once again, Vincent closed the knife and then released the blade. "See? Yuh just touch this button, an' she opens up fer bizness." He repeated the process.

The conversation lulled, then Vincent said, "What er you a-doin' in town?"

"Nothin'."

"You got any plans fer tuhnight?"

"Naw." He decided not to mention his hope of attending church. He was not sure how Vincent would react, and besides, he had given up hope of getting to go now anyway.

"Boy, me and Jackie has."

"What er yuh gonna do?" Jeremy remembered Sally Leyendecker.

"We're goin' tuh Peach Springs. I bet you ain't never been tuh Peach Springs, have yuh?" laughed Vincent, folding the blade of his knife back into its sheath and dropping it into his pocket.

Jeremy hadn't, but he said, "Well, not lately."

"Aw, you ain't been. Yer folks wouldn' let their little boy go there, an' even if'n they did, you couldn' git intuh Peach Springs Dance Hall. They don't let guys young as you in there."

"I been a-thinkin' 'bout goin'," said Jeremy.

"Yeah, right. An' I been a-thinkin' 'bout goin' tuh th' moon." Vincent laughed again. "But maybe someday yuh'll grow up an' git tuh go. Hell, me and Jackie went las' Sattidy night. Boy, ole Jackie got drunk. He threw up three times on th' way home. I got so damn tired uv it. We'd have tuh pull over an' stop along th' road an' let 'im out. Once, he didn' make it, an' he puked all over hisse'f an' th' car. Stunk up th' car somethin' awful. I thought I'd never git th' odor outta th' car th' next mornin'."

Vincent shook his head. "That odor wuz somethin', 'specially since I wuzn't feelin' any too good. I'd had a few myself." Vincent laughed. Then he sobered and said, "Actually, they is still some uv that damn odor in my car."

Jeremy did not know anything to say.

"Yuh oughtta go tuh Peach Springs some day. Hell, some gal is likely tuh take a likin' tuh yuh. Likely one uv 'em ud think she uz a-gittin' a virgin. One uv them Peach Springs gals might git you in th' back seat uv one uv them cars, an' no tellin' what she might do tuh yuh. Hell, I know some that ud rape yuh." Vincent laughed again. "Man, I'd like tuh see that." He took a cigarette from his pocket and lit it. He offered Jeremy the pack. "Yuh want a cigarette?"

Jeremy shook his head.

"Boys' Town is better," Vincent continued, drawing on his cigarette, "but it's a long way tuh Mexico, an' they's lots tuh do in Peach Springs. Myself, I like tuh fight. Man, las' Sattidy night me an' this guy got in a fight over somethin'. I cain't even remember what we wuz a-fightin' about. I think maybe it uz some gal. Hell, I uz so drunk I cain't even remember who I wuz a-fightin. Anyways, we got out in th' yard an' we really went to it. I got 'im down over th' fender uv a car, an' I really beat up on 'im." Vincent was enjoying his story. "Then this bastard got up somehow, an' he got me down over that fender an' beat th' hell outta me. Damn, that uz a good fight."

"What about yer knife?" asked Jeremy.

"Aw, man. I ain't gonna cut up nobody like that. It uz just a good fight."

Vincent turned to walk away. "Well, I gotta go git ready fer Peach Springs. They'll be a party tuhnight." He turned back to Jeremy. "Maybe someday I'll see yuh there. Come on down. I'll show yuh th' ropes. Hell, I'll even do better'n that. I'll interduce yuh tuh one uv them gals I uz a-tellin' yuh about. They's women there that ud turn you ever'way but loose." Vincent turned his back to Jeremy and walked away, swaying as if to music, snapping his fingers. He was laughing to himself.

On the way home, Jeremy sat with groceries in the back seat, his feet on the quilt-wrapped block of ice. The ice felt especially good on his burned feet. He let his left hand rest on the ice as well. The sun had already set.

He was lost in thought when he became aware of a commotion, and he looked up to see that they were abreast of the church. The parking lot was full of people and cars. In fact, the commotion was the result of cars blocking the road as they waited their chance to turn into the churchyard and park. Two or three men with flashlights were trying to assist the flow of the traffic. One car had stalled, and men hustled about trying to get it out of the way. Jeremy had not seen so many cars and people at the church. Lem had no option but to stop and wait for the traffic jam to clear, so he turned off the ignition of the car and leaned back on the seat to wait.

As the Stroops sat waiting, Mrs. McMillan, standing in the churchyard, spotted their car, waved gaily, and came running across the parking lot to meet them. "Oh, hi there. I come by yer house tuh git Jeremy, but you wuz gone. And now here yuh are at church. Did y'all come fer th' special healin' service?" She placed her hand affectionately on Lem's shoulder.

"Well, actually, no," Lem said as he shifted his shoulder. "We just got back from groc'ry buyin', an' we got some ice in th' back seat that'll melt shore in this heat if'n we don't git home with it an' put it in th' ice box. And it's gittin' purty late, too."

"Oh, I see." Mrs. McMillan cast a glance into the back seat. "Well, then, let Jeremy stay!" She smiled beautifully at Jeremy. "Do yuh wanta stay, Jeremy?"

"Yes'm. I'd like to," Jeremy replied, watching his father, who looked at Olga and made a face.

"Good! We'll bring 'im home all safe an' sound soon as church is over," Mrs. McMillan beamed. "You folks sure yuh won't stay?"

"Naw, th' ice . . . ." Lem began.

"Oh, I unnerstand," Mrs. McMillan smiled. "But it is okay fer Jeremy tuh stay then?"

"I donno." Lem was struggling.

"Why, is somethin' wrong?" crooned Mrs. McMillan.

"Naw, naw, it ain't nothin' like that."

"Well, then, what is it, fer heaven's sake?" Mrs. McMillan pretended concern. "Don't yuh want tuh encourage yer boy tuh come tuh church? I make Leland come. He don't want to, but I make 'im."

"All right," Lem said to Mrs. McMillan, but he turned to Olga and, under his breath, he said, "Dammit!"

Jeremy climbed out of the car. The traffic jam had cleared, and Lem started the car. "Now, you behave in that church," Olga shouted to Jeremy as the car pulled away.

Mrs. McMillan put her arm around Jeremy's shoulders. "Yer mother is always concerned about yuh, ain't she?" She kept her arm around Jeremy all the way into the building.

20

INSIDE, THE CHURCH BUILDING WAS FILLED. Already people lined the sides of the building, looking for a place to sit down. Mrs. McMillan had her arm around Jeremy and was steering him and Leland forward. They had to walk up the aisle until they were almost to the podium before some people slid down a bench to make room for them. Mrs. McMillan sat on one side of the aisle, and Jeremy on another bench. People had to move down to make room for him, and he had to step around two kneelers. Jeremy felt squeezed onto the bench, but he was glad to find himself almost directly under one of the fans. Boy, he thought as he looked around the building, I've never seen so many people here. Behind him he heard people talking about the service that they anticipated.

"Lord, I wouldna missed tuhnight," said a man sitting behind him.

Jeremy did not look around.

"Me neither," a woman replied. "I been tuh healin' services before, an' it's just wunnerful tuh see th' hand uv God at work."

"I ain't never been," the man continued. "But I got a cousin in Oklahoma, an' she's been. She had a little boy that had a spot on 'is lung, an'she took 'im tuh one uv these services. An' he uz healed."

"That's wunnerful. Praise God! Th' spot went away completely, huh?"

"Well, no, it didn' go away completely, an' when she tole her husband, he said, 'Well, that ain't no healin'. He's still got th' damned spot,' but my cousin figgered that God had healed the boy. He just left some of th' spot there tuh remind us how we depend on God."

"Yes, yes, praise God. Yer cousin must be real spiritual."

"Yep, her whole fam'ly is. One uv her uncles is a preacher. She's seen lots uv miracles. Why, just las' week I talked tuh her, an' she had lost 'er keys. She tole me she prayed tuh God, an' she found 'em in just a couple uv days."

"Nothin's too big er too small fer th' Lord," the woman was saying as Mutchell rose and walked to the podium.

The kneelers suddenly ended their prayers and rose to their seats, and Mutchell made his usual announcements. He had on the same coat that he had worn at each service, and even from where Jeremy was sitting, he could see that Mutchell had not shaved recently. "I'm so glad tuh see each an' ever'one uv yuh," Mutchell said. "Yer gonna git a special blessin' tuhnight. Brother Flancher has called this meetin' a healin' service, an' I know we're gonna see th' hand uv God at work tuhnight. Hallelujah!"

Jeremy waited impatiently through the announcements, singing and prayers, but at last Flancher arose and heaved himself upon the dais. He was dressed in a white suit with a white shirt and a wide, bright blue tie. He turned to face the people, laying his handkerchief on the podium, and began to address the audience.

"Th' Holy Ghost is a-fallin' tuhnight! Hallelujah!" Then he said, "I been a-feelin' a great pressure on muh heart." He touched his chest. "I know they's people here that's sick an' in need. I feel it right here." He continued to hold his hand to his chest. "An' I'm concerned about these pore unfortunate souls. I been a-prayin' about it th' las' coupla weeks, ever since I got here, an' th' Lord's finally give me an answer. I wuz on my knees a-prayin' a coupla nights ago, and all at once th' Lord spoke tuh me. Praise God, he spoke tuh me, an' He said tuh me. . . ." Here Flancher paused for effect. "He said tuh me, 'Cleo, you heal these pore hurtin' folks. You heal their sick. It's th' devil that's a-makin' 'em sick, an' I wantcha tuh chase th' devil outta their lives.' Praise His blessed name. That's what he said!'" Flancher was already shouting. "An' I'm a-sayin', Devil, yer a-gonna take a beatin' tuhnight."

Hallelujahs rang throughout the building. The man behind Jeremy, the one with the cousin in Oklahoma, whispered, "Praise th' Lord. Wish my cousin uz here."

"God tole me tuh heal th' hurtin' here tuhnight," shouted Flancher again. "An' that's what I'm a-gonna do. I got up offa my knees after th' Lord tole me what tuh do, an' I said, 'Git thee behin' me, Satan. Git outta my way. Nothin' kin stop me now.' Hallelujah! Brethern, if th' Lord is fer yuh, who can be ag'inst yuh?" He looked around as if he expected a challenge.

"Amen!"

"Preach th' Word, Brother!"

"Come on, come on. Preach th' Word now."

"Give 'im th' power, Lord."

"So," Flancher continued, "I'm here tuh tell yuh, brethern an' sistern, yer gonna see mighty things tuhnight. Mighty things. Open yer hearts. Prepare yer souls. Open yerselves tuh th' possibilities uv God!"

Jeremy looked up to see Flancher staring at him. He fingered his mastoid bone. He was convinced that it was sensitive to his touch. Should he ask Flancher to heal his mastoid bone? Or should he ask Flancher to heal his burns? Should he ask Flancher how to be saved?

"I ain't got no sermont fer yuh tuhnight, just th' healin' power uv God. Oh, they's wunnerful things in th' scriptures that I could talk tuh yuh about; I been a-doin' that, an' they's lots more whur that come from, but tuhnight we're gonna drive Satan from our lives; we're gonna restore health tuh hurtin' bodies an' hope tuh hurtin' souls. Hallelujah!" Flancher walked out to the edge of the dais, put his hands on his hips, leaned forward from his waist, and fastening his eyes upon the congregation through his thick eyebrows, he said, "I want yuh to recall how th' Lord healed when he wuz on earth. You know that he healed th' blind. He put spit on their eyes, and they seen!" Flancher stomped and waved his arms. "Hallelujah! You know that he healed those who couldn't hear. You know that he cast out devils uv ever' description. Why, once he run a whole bunch uv devils off at one time. He run them devils intuh a bunch uv pigs, an' them pigs took off an' run plumb off uv a cliff. Yuh see, them pigs had more sense than most people do. They didn' want no devils in them."

Laughter swept through the congregation.

"That's right. They do."

Someone behind Jeremy said, "Even Brother Mutchell's pigs has got more sense than some people."

Jeremy looked at Mutchell, but Mutchell did not move or indicate he had heard the comment.

"Them pigs didn' want no demons in 'em, an' they just run offa that cliff tuh git rid uv 'em. Hallelujah! Praise God! An' I want yuh tuh remember how th' apostles healed after Jesus went back tuh heaven. Th' Apostle Peter raised Dorcas frum the dead. Oh, yes. He did. An' I tell yuh, that blessed power is still a-workin' tuhday, right here tuhnight, right here in Dorman! Praise th' Lord!"

Jeremy was thrilled. He had not read yet about anyone being raised from the dead.

"That's th' way tuh preach!" a voice from the rear of the church shouted. "You tell 'em, Preacher."

Flancher paused. The whole building seemed to throb with excitement. From somewhere in the building, Jeremy heard what he thought sounded like barking. Several people around Jeremy had begun to mutter incoherently. Flancher leaned on the podium and looked down at his feet for a moment. He mopped his face. Then he raised his head and continued. "I tell yuh, it's a great thrill fer me tuh see th' sick healed, tuh see th' lame walk, tuh see th' blind see. Such a blessin'. I cain't wait tuh see what th' Lord has prepared fer us tuhnight. An' it's all tuh th' glory uv God. Don't you go a-thankin' me fer anythin' that happens here tuhnight. You go home an' you git down on yer knees, an' you thank God. You tell yer little kids when yuh put 'em tuh bed tuhnight at home that God done th' healin'. When yuh kiss 'em good night, tell 'em that God done th' healin'." Someone began crying. "You tell yer wife er husband that God done th' healin'. Don't you go tuh sleep without prayin', an' in yer prayer, thank God fer His wunnerful healin' power. You tell yer frens that right here in Dorman, you saw th' power uv God at work. Right here, right here in Dorman!" Flancher rose on the balls of his feet and shouted at the congregation. "It's God that heals! Praise his name! Praise his blessed name! Amen! Amen!" The congregation rocked with energy, punctuated by shouts of rapture. The babbler had risen to his feet, but no one except Jeremy seemed to notice him. Jeremy could not see the crone.

Suddenly, almost as a unit, the people on the bench in front of Jeremy rose to their feet. They began to sway in unison, alternately clapping their hands and waving their arms above their heads. Many of them were singing. None of them was going forward to Flancher. No one seemed to expect them to do so. Jeremy looked around, and more benches erupted. He discovered that he was the only one seated on his bench, and he was not sure what to do. Then a man standing beside him reached down, seized Jeremy's arm, and pulled him to his feet. He looked down at Jeremy and smiled, then he began clapping his hands, nodding to indicate that Jeremy should do the same, but Jeremy only watched.

"Now, brethern. Now, brethern." Flancher was drenched with perspiration, his hair dishevelled. He pressed his palms together and beamed at the group. "Lissen tuh me. Lissen tuh th' invitation uv th' Lord tuh be healed. God don't intend yuh tuh hurt. Nossir. Amen! He's all powerful, an' he luvs yuh. He don't wantcha tuh hurt, an' he can cure yuh—of anythin'! Lissen! I said anythin'! Anythin'! Yessir. Ain't nothin' God cain't do. If he wants two an' two tuh be five, it'll be. You come an' be healed. Come praisin' th' Lord an' be healed."

Flancher stood silently. He motioned to the crowd to be seated. Sister Fowler paused in her playing, but she still stared at the piano. She seemed poised, ready to begin to play at a moment's notice.

Silence settled over the congregation. Everyone sat down, except the babbler. Finally, a man reached up and pulled him down on the bench. For a while no one moved. An air of expectancy had settled on the congregation. Then a little girl rose from a seat across the room and started forward. About halfway down the aisle, she coughed vigorously. She coughed again just as she reached Flancher.

"Now, I know they's others. So you just come ahead on. Join this brave little girl. See, she's sick, an' she's tired uv bein' sick, so she has come tuh th' Lord so's he can heal 'er. It's that simple. Just believe an' be healed. Amen! This little girl is a-gonna walk outta here healed. I don't know what's wrong with 'er, but I don't keer about that. I know God will heal 'er. She'll be th' first one healed here tuhnight. Hallelujah! Come on down here an' let yer requests be made known while I talk tuh this purty little lady."

Jeremy recognized the girl; she was in his class at school. Her name was Molly, and she was absent a lot. When she did come to school, she coughed frequently, attracting Mrs. Russell's attention. "We should all feel sorry for Molly because of her cough," Mrs. Russell had said, "but it is not polite to cough with your mouth and nose uncovered. Now, can anyone give me another reason why you should cover your mouth when you cough?" David White had raised his hand and said, "Molly ought tuh cover her mouth with 'er hand 'cause when she coughs, her breath stinks so bad."

An old, stoop-shouldered lady walked up to the front bench to talk to Flancher. As she walked, she rubbed her thin, withered arms. She stared at her feet as she made her way to Flancher. He hugged her. The lady put her head on Flancher's shoulder, and then she moved to a seat on the front bench beside Molly. Flancher returned his attention to Molly. After a couple of minutes of conversation, Flancher announced that Molly had a painful cough, and she wanted him to pray for her. "Says th' kids make fun uv her at school," said Flancher, shaking his head. "She wants tuh be healed, an' that's what God's a-gonna do, right now," Flancher announced. "We're gonna pray fer 'er an' we're a-gonna believe that God will heal 'er." He turned to Molly. She refused to look at him. She sat, staring at the floor, holding a handkerchief to her nose. "Molly, we're gonna pray fer yuh. Do yuh believe that God can heal yuh?" She still had not looked at him, but she nodded her head.

Flancher asked her to stand, and she rose to her feet. She still had not looked at Flancher. He placed his right hand on her head and began to pray: "Lord, yuh see this little girl's faith in yuh. We know she's one uv yores, one uv yer little angels, an' now, we just ast that yuh touch 'er an' heal 'er right now tuh yer name's honor an' glory. Take this cough away frum 'er." Molly stifled a cough. "Take it away completely, so she won't never cough no more. An' let ever'one who ever sees her after this know that she come up here sick tuhnight, but you healed her. Amen! Make 'er well, Lord, an' fergive 'er uv 'er sins as well." Jeremy watched closely. Flancher continued: "Thank yuh, Lord, fer hearin' our prayer an' fer healin' this little girl. Amen!" He turned to Molly and asked, "Well, little girl, how does it feel tuh be free uv that ole cough? Ain't it wunnerful?" Molly studied her shoes and nodded.

Flancher patted her on the head and gently pushed her toward the audience. Jeremy watched her all the way back to her seat. He watched her cover her mouth with her hand as she slid onto her seat.

Flancher next talked to an old, stoop-shouldered lady who had come forward. "Stand up, Sister. Now, what's yer request?"

The lady responded in a whisper.

"She says she's got arthritis real bad," Flancher said. Then turning to the lady, he said, "An' have yuh had it a long time?"

Another whispered response.

"She says she's had it near 'bout thirty years, an' it hurts awful." Then to the lady, he said, "An' yuh wanta be healed?"

For the first time the lady spoke up, turning to face the audience. "Oh, yes, Jesus. I want tuh be healed. I hurt so bad, I cain't git up some mornin's. I went tuh a healin' service last year up in Dallas, an' th' preacher there, he healed me, but it come back ag'in." She turned to face Flancher and began to cry.

"I unnerstan', Sister." Flancher patted her shoulder. "Do yuh believe th' Lord can heal yuh?"

The lady lifted her head to look at Flancher. "Yes, I do," she said, wiping tears from her eyes. Through broken sobs, she said, "I love th' Lord, an' I want 'im tuh just heal me. I just wanta feel good ag'in, an' I want tuh be able tuh come tuh church ag'in." She leaned into Flancher's arms and began to cry.

"I unnerstan'. I unnerstan'," said Flancher consolingly. Then to the audience he said: "Okay, let's pray fer this good Sister."

The congregation bowed and prayed.

Flancher asked, "Now, do yuh feel better?" Then quickly, without waiting for an answer, he patted her on the back and said, "Course yuh do. Praise God." He eased the lady back toward her bench. Flexing her left elbow, she walked toward her seat.

Jeremy heard a commotion behind him, and he turned and looked back. A man was struggling to get out of his seat, trying to make it to the end of the bench, and as soon as he reached the aisle, it became apparent that the clatter had been caused by his crutches rattling against the bench. Silence fell over the congregation. Jeremy turned to look at Flancher. Flancher beamed upon the man and met him partway down the aisle. He hugged him warmly and helped him to a seat. He patted the man on his shoulder. A murmur ran through the audience as the crippled man sat down heavily.

Flancher spoke to the man briefly; then he faced the audience and said, "This here's Brother Haygood." Flancher paused. "He tells me that he ain't been able tuh walk since he uz a boy. He had polio when he uz seven, an' he ain't walked since 'cept with these crutches. Cain't put no weight a-tall on 'is right foot. Ain't that right, Brother Haygood?"

Haygood nodded.

"Yeah," said Flancher. "This pore soul's right laig is plumb helpless. Worthless tuh 'im." Flancher stood, his hands on his hips, surveying Haygood. "An' his left laig ain't much better." Flancher mopped his face. "Ain't that right?"

Haygood nodded in assent.

"He tells me that he's been tuh doctors all over, an' they all tell 'im th' same thin'. They tell 'im that he may as well git used to these crutches 'cause he's a-gonna be usin' 'em fer th' rest uv 'is natcheral life. But he comes tuhnight a-tellin'me that he's tired uv these crutches, an' he's come tuh th' Lord tuh be healed, tuh git rid uv these crutches. Praise th' Lord!"

The congregation said "Amen," but it was subdued. They sensed a tension, and they were waiting.

"Now, I know God's a-gonna heal 'im," Flancher said confidently. "Yuh know, it's a funny thing. I felt they wuz somebody special here tuhnight that needed healin', an' I felt thataway even after these dear sisters come up an' wuz all healed. I still felt that they uz somebody else. Now, I know they wuz. It's Brother Haygood."

He turned to the man on crutches: "Brother Haygood, the Lord's a-gonna heal yuh tuhnight. I know he is. Yer gonna throw away them crutches! Praise th' Lord!"

Now, Flancher faced the audience. "Oh, th' wonders uv God. I tell yuh, brethern an' sistern, this just overwhelms me." He wiped tears from his eyes, and then blew his nose into his handkerchief.

"Praise th' Lord," murmured the crowd. "Hallelujah!"

Now Flancher stepped over in front of Brother Haygood and put his hand on his head. "Brother, do yuh remember that day at th' Gate called Beautiful when Peter and John healed a man who'd been lame fer so many years? You remember what Peter tole that man? He said, 'In th' name uv th' Lord, rise up and walk!' An' that's what that man did! Hallelujah! My frens an' neighbors, that same power is here tuhnight. Cain't yuh just feel it?" Flancher was shouting again. "Feel it! Oh, brethern. I feel it! It just sweeps over me like a river. Th' power uv God fills this buildin' tuhnight! Praise God! Praise God! That same power is a-gonna heal tuhnight. Brother Haygood, yer gonna throw them crutches away, an' yuh won't need em tuhnight er tomorrer er ever. Hallelujah! Do you hear that, Brother? Do yuh have faith, Brother?"

Haygood nodded.

Somewhere in the building, someone was barking. Two people on Jeremy's seat were babbling incoherently.

"God cain't do nothin' fer yuh less yuh got faith. James said tuh ast in faith, nothin' doubtin'. You must believe, an' I know yuh do. Praise God! I got faith. I don't doubt fer a minute. Hallelujah!" Flancher paused, took a deep breath, looked out at the crowd and said, "Let's all bow our heads an' pray."

A dead silence descended upon the room. Even the barking and the babbling ceased for a moment. Jeremy did not bow his head. He could hardly believe his eyes.

"Oh, Father," prayed Flancher, his hand on Haygood's head, his face lifted, glistening with perspiration, his eyes tightly shut. "Yuh healed so many when yuh wuz here on this pore ole sick earth. Now this Brother comes, an' he's got a real problem, Lord. He wants tuh walk, an' he believes you can heal 'im. Do it now, Lord! Do it to yore glory! Hallelujah!"

Flancher had begun to shout every word: "Heal 'im, Lord!" His raised right arm trembled. He pushed down hard on Haygood's head with his left hand, again and again. "Straighten 'is crooked laigs! Stren'then 'is bones! Let 'im walk outta here a healed man, an' we'll give yuh all th' glory through our Lord an' Savior Jesus Christ, fer it's in his name that we pray. Amen! Hallelujah! Hallelujah!"

"Amen," boomed the congregation.

And Haygood stood up!

A roar of amazement swept through the congregation. Flancher beamed and hugged Haygood. "Praise God!" he shouted over and over. "Glory be tuh God!"

Flancher shouted to Haygood above the din of the ecstatic congregation, "Take those crutches an' pitch em over there in th' corner. No more crutches! Walk outta here a new man, a healed man!"

Haygood took a halting step, and then he stopped. He took another step and stopped again. Then he reached down for one of his crutches. Flancher stepped forward to pick up the crutch and hand it to Haygood, who took it and flung it with a clatter into a corner of the church. Everyone cheered wildly, shouting, singing, praising God. The babbling and barking resumed. Haygood reached down and picked up his remaining crutch and threw it after the first. The crowd cheered lustily, whistling, lifting praises to God. Pandemonium reigned.

Jeremy watched Haygood carefully. Had Flancher actually healed that man? Haygood's face was strained with excitement. He reached out and gripped the end of the front bench to steady himself, and stood looking at the wildly cheering audience. Jeremy had to stand on the bench to see, as people were thronging Haygood, laughing, crying, cheering. Women kissed him; men shook his hand and slapped him on the back.

Haygood began slowly making his way down the aisle. Jeremy got down off the bench and moved out into the aisle so he could see him better. Haygood had difficulty getting through the crowd, but at last he was abreast of Jeremy. He put his hand on the boy's head, and looking down on him, smiled and whispered huskily, "Praise God, little brother." Then he passed on, still steadying himself by grasping each bench as he passed it.

Jeremy watched him until he disappeared out the door.

21

MUTCHELL, SEEING THAT THERE WAS NO CHANCE of restoring order, shouted an announcement about church services the next day and dismissed the crowd. Jeremy rushed outside, shoving his way through the people in the aisle. He wanted to see Haygood again. Once outside the church, however, he discovered that Haygood was nowhere to be seen. Jeremy walked completely around the building, but no Haygood. He had felt an attraction to this man who had been healed and had stopped to speak to him. He continued to walk among the cars, stopping to look into their interiors, thinking that Haygood might be sitting in one of them. Maybe his legs started hurting again, he thought, and he went to his car to sit down. He turned back to the building, searching from group to group, and although he heard much talk about Haygood and his miracle, he found no trace of him.

He did see Molly. She was holding her hand over her mouth, and between stifled coughs, explaining to some girls how much better she felt now that Brother Flancher had healed her.

"But yer still a-coughin'," one of the girls said.

"Well, I know," whined Molly.

Molly's mother arrived just in time to hear the girl's criticism, and she said, "Now, just leave 'er alone. That cough she's got now don't have nothin' tuh do with what uz wrong with 'er before." Molly and her mother walked away, her mother cautioning her to cover her mouth when she coughed.

At that moment, Leland spied Jeremy and called to him. "Maw's lookin' fer yuh, Stroop. Whur yuh been? We gotta git home." Jeremy had forgotten that he was riding with the McMillans. He cast one more hurried look around for Haygood, and then walked with Leland to the car.

In the back seat, on the way home, Jeremy asked Leland, "Say, Leland, do yuh know Brother Haygood?"

"Who's that?" asked Leland without interest.

"You know, th' man that uz healed."

"Oh, that guy. Naw. I never paid much attention. I never saw 'im before. Had you, Maw?"

"Had I what?" Mrs. McMillan said, steering the car out of the churchyard, looking into the rearview mirror.

"Had you ever seen Haygood, th' guy that ole Flancher claimed he healed?"

"No, I hadn't. He must've been one uv our visitors. We had so many tuhnight. Wasn't it wunnerful, boys, how th' Lord brought that poor crippled man tuh Brother Flancher, an' how Brother Flancher healed 'im right there in front uv th' whole church. I just tingled all over. I just think Brother Flancher is wunnerful. Such a man uv God."

Leland looked at Jeremy and raised his eyebrows. Jeremy did not say anything.

"And what's even more wunnerful," she continued, "is that th' Lord can heal our souls th' same way he can heal our bodies." She looked hopefully at the two boys in the rearview mirror.

Neither boy replied, and she did not pursue the topic. Jeremy sat quietly, gently rubbing his burned left arm. He fingered his mastoid bone once again. He wondered if Flancher could have healed him. He vaguely remembered the boy with the club foot, the one that the lady had asked about at the ice-cream supper. Could Flancher have healed him?

At home, Jeremy was greeted by Patches, who rushed out from under the family car, wagging his tail. Jeremy squatted down, caught the dog and affectionately rubbed his ears, then strode into the house.

"How wuz church, Son?" asked his mother.

"Fine. It uz fine," Jeremy replied. He thought about going on to his room but decided to sit down.

"Wuz th' preachin' good?"

"Oh, yeah."

"Wha'd th' preacher preach on?"

"Well, he didn' preach no sermon exactly, I guess."

"Why, whatta yuh mean? He didn' preach?"

"Not exactly. He sorta talked about how th' Lord kin heal yuh." His eyes darted from his mother to his father. He wondered what they would think about what he had just said. And especially what he had just seen. His father stirred, but said nothing.

"Anyone git th' Holy Ghost tuhnight?" asked his mother.

"I donno. Maybe they did," shrugged Jeremy. Now that he thought about it, he could not remember anyone at church claiming that they had received the Holy Ghost, nor had anyone acted as if they had the holy laugh or had seen Jesus. Of course, there had been the babbler.

"Th' service uz differ'nt," he volunteered.

"How wuz it differ'nt?" His mother continued her questioning.

Jeremy squirmed on his chair. "Well, Brother Flancher didn' talk very long, an' then some people went up tuh him tuh be healed. That uz all." Again he looked quickly from his mother to his father.

Now his father became interested. "Now wait a minute. I knew that uz bound tuh happen. You say that Prancer, er whatever 'is name is, actually tried tuh heal people?"

"He didn' jus' try, I guess. He healed some folks."

"You mean you saw people healed with yer own eyes?"

"Yeah, sure."

"Hell's bells," grumbled Lem.

"What uz they healed uv, Jeremy?" his mother interrupted.

"Oh, one girl wuz healed uv a cough, an' an ole lady uz healed uv arthritis." He did not mention Haygood.

"So," said his father. "You saw some kid go up there a-coughin', an' then you saw 'er an' she didn't have no cough no more?"

Jeremy remembered Molly out in the churchyard, coughing, as she explained that she was better. "Well, I donno. Maybe she wuz still a-coughin' some, but I heard 'er tell somebody that she felt a lot better."

"Damn nonsense," mumbled his father. "Yer either healed er not."

"But they uz a lady with arthritis, an' she uz healed too."

"Now how in th' worl' are yuh gonna know that?" asked his father in exasperation. "Arthritis comes an' goes. Hell, I got it, an' some days I feel purty good, an' some days I don't. Ain't no way yuh can tell in five minutes whether yer healed uv somethin' like that."

And then Jeremy blurted out, "They uz a man, Paw, an' he uz healed."

"An' just how do yuh know that? What uz he healed uv? A cold?"

"Naw, Paw. He uz on crutches, an' he went up tuh Brother Flancher, an' he prayed fer 'im, an' he th'owed away his crutches an' walked out uv th' building."

"Yuh seen that?" His father was sarcastic.

"I did, Paw. With my own eyes. I uz real close, closer'n I am tuh you, an' I seen it. He walked right by me."

"Damn nonsense!" snorted Lem.

"But, Paw, I seen 'im a-walkin'."

"Yuh see, Maw. That's just exactly why I didn' want this boy a-goin' down there tuh that church. We let 'im go, an' what happens? He gits filled with this nonsense about miracle healin'. I don't know why we ever let 'im go off down there."

"His name uz Haygood," said Jeremy.

"Whose name uz Haygood?" asked Lem.

"Th' man that uz healed. That could walk. Do you know 'im, Paw?"

"Why, hell, no. Uv course I don't, Boy. Don't yuh know nothin' a-tall?"

"Whatta yuh mean, Paw?"

"Jeremy, that preacher cain't heal nobody, an' he knows it better'n anybody else. Cain't you see that he had that guy brought in here, ain't no tellin from whur, an' had 'im act like he uz healed? That preacher shore didn' heal 'im."

Jeremy had not thought about that possibility. "But Brother Flancher don't claim that he can heal nobody, Paw. He says that God does it."

"He does, does he?" Lem spat indignantly. "Him ner God, neither one heals nobody these days. Th' age uv miracles is past. I know that. Yer always a-readin' th' Bible. See fer yer se'f. It says that th' age uv miracles is past. That preacher is so crooked he hasta screw his pants on, Boy. Cain't you see that? I bet him an' this guy, Haygood, is a-sittin' somewhur right now, prob'ly half drunk, an' a-laughin' their heads off at them fools at church."

"Well, he shorely thoo away his crutches." Jeremy would not give up on Haygood.

"Of course, he did. But that's just part uv th' act. Flancher prob'ly paid 'im tuh come in here an' act like he uz crippled, an' then Flancher ud heal 'im. It's one uv th' oldest tricks in th' worl', Jeremy. Tell me. Did yuh see 'im after church? Did yuh git tuh talk tuh 'im? Do yuh know anybody that knows 'im?"

Jeremy pushed back the hair from his eyes. "No, Sir," he said.

"Well, there yuh go. Uv course yuh didn't, an' yuh won't neither. Them bench-jumpin' preachers is a clever bunch. They oughtta be locked up, ever' damn one uv 'em. Deceivin' people like that. An' it's all fer money. Just fer money."

His mother tried to change the subject: "Jeremy, did anybody try tuh pray fer you?"

Jeremy remembered his mastoid bone, but he replied, "No, ma'am. Didn' nobody try tuh pray fer me that I know of."

125

"Well, it's a damn wonder," Lem said. "It's a waste uv time. None uv yer family ever did believe like them Holy Rollers, Son."

"How do we believe, Paw?"

"Huh? Well," Lem hesitated. He rubbed his jaw reflectively. "We don't believe like them. All that shoutin' an' carryin' on."

Lem turned aside. The conversation was over. The three of them sat in the room for a moment, and then Jeremy rose to go to bed. His father stopped him with a question. "Say, you ain't seen no stray dog aroun' here, have ye?"

22

JEREMY STOPPED AND AND TURNED TO FACE HIS FATHER. "No, Sir. Only dawg I ever see is Patches. Why?"

"I foun' a sheep tuhday, an' its throat had been slit."

You think a dawg did it?"

"I know a dawg did it. Ain't been no coyotes in these parts fer years, an' ain't no other animal aroun' here that coulda pulled down a sheep that size."

"Wuz th' sheep et up?"

"No, it had its throat slit. That's how I know it uz a dawg, 'cause that's th' way a dawg does. But once a dawg gits a taste uv blood, they ain't no stoppin' 'im."

"How do yuh tell a sheep-killin' dawg, Paw?"

"Well, they ain't no way tuh tell just by lookin' at 'em. But lemme tell yuh, my paw an' me useta take care uv a big herd uv sheep, an' we'd carry our guns with us when we went tuh see about 'em. If we ever even seen a dawg around 'em, we never ast no questions, and we never even stopped tuh think whose dawg it mighta been. We just shot it down right there an' let th' buzzards have it."

Jeremy moved off in the direction of his room. His father said, "Jeremy, I wantcha tuh go with me tomorrer tuh check on our sheep. I hoped tuh work in the fiel' tomorrer, but we gotta try tuh find that dawg if we can."

"What time yuh goin', Paw?" Jeremy hoped his father would not choose to go during the morning hours.

"Early in th' mornin'. I want tuh git started before it gits hot. Th' sheep er all over in th' east fiel', so I aim fer us tuh take a walk over there an' check on 'em. Then we'll prob'ly take a turn thoo them woods behin' th' fiel' an' see if we can turn up any dawgs in there. May not be just one dawg. They may be a pack. Sometimes dawgs run in packs, an' they might be a-layin' up in th' shade in them woods a-watchin' th' sheep, waitin' fer their chance."

Jeremy was disappointed. He disliked getting up early on a Sunday morning, and he also realized that his father's decision meant that he could not go to church tomorrow. He wished he could go. He wanted to see Haygood again. Beyond the possibility of seeing Haygood, Jeremy realized that he would like to see and hear Flancher again.

"Are you a-lissenin' tuh me, Boy? I said fer yuh to be ready early, yuh hear?"

"Yes, Sir," Jeremy agreed. He started toward his room, and then suddenly he remembered the time he had visited the Roosevelts and the huge dog that had growled at him there. "Paw, I did see a dawg. I know where they's one. I uz over at th' Roosevelts' an' this dawg came out frum under th' porch, an' he uz a-growlin' somethin' fierce. He scairt me."

"Th' Roosevelts', huh?"

"Yes, Sir. He uz a ugly dawg, all et up with mange."

"Well, now, that might bear lookin' into."

"It uz a big dawg, too, Paw. It could pull down a sheep easy."

"Well, we'll see."

Jeremy walked into his room and prepared for bed. He could hear his mother and father still talking. "I just don't like 'im a-mixin' with them Holy Rollers," his father was saying. "If he's gonna go tuh church, if he should go tuh church as you say, then let 'im go some place decent. They's other churches aroun' here. Ain't that a Baptist Church over here on West Road? That church that got a new roof recently? That ud be better than whur he's a-goin'."

"I just hate tuh hurt Miz McMillan's feelin's. I don't know what tuh say tuh th' woman when she comes over here tuh git 'im," explained Jeremy's mother.

"Miz McMillan is a busybody. Why don't she work on gittin' her own fam'ly tuh go tuh church? Her husband shore don't never go. He tole me so. An' what about her sons? That oldest boy, Ralph, don't never go tuh church. She oughtta work on him. Maybe th' Holy Spirit ud do him some good."

"Well, she does make her boy Leland go."

"He ain't nothin' but a kid."

"But you let Jeremy go with 'er th' other night," protested Mrs. Stroop.

"I know," Lem replied irritably. "I may not ever ag'in."

"Lem, I don't think that Jeremy's foolish. He likes tuh go tuh church, but I don't believe he goes along with all them Holy Rollers say an' do. He ain't said nothin' about gittin' th' Holy Ghost er nothin' like that. An' I'd a heap rather he went tuh some church than none a-tall. Th' boy is a-growin' up."

"He better not come in here a-claimin' tuh have th' Holy Spirit, 'cause that'll be th' end uv his goin' tuh that church fer shore. That kind uv thinkin' can drive yuh crazy. You 'member ole Hazel." Jeremy cringed at the mention of Hazel. He still worried every night that she might come into his room.

"She got all mixed up with that nonsense about speakin' in tongues. Remember? Couldn' nobody unnerstan' a word she said, just went around a-jabberin' all th' time, crazy as a damn bat. Started a-walkin' aroun' at night, goin' intuh people's houses, even when th' folks uz there an' a-tryin' tuh sleep."

"Well, now, Lem, don't be too hard on 'er. You 'member that she lost 'er boy in that huntin' accident just before she started goin' tuh church."

"I know. I know. But that don't make no differ'nce. An' somethin' else. Healin' is a bunch uv nonsense. Throwin' away crutches, my eye. What uz that guy's name?"

"I don't remember. I never heard uv 'im aroun' here before."

"Of course not. It uz some guy they brought in, I know. They're crooks, ever' one uv 'em. Damn hypercrites. Just want money. An' Jacob Mutchell. Let me tell yuh, he ain't no better. Him an' his damn pigs. Ever'body in town knows he cheats folks thirty ways tuh Sunday, an' then he's got th' nerve tuh come out tuh my fiel' whur I'm a-doin' honest work, an' a-astin' me tuh come tuh church. I shoulda run both him an' that preacher plumb off." Lem laughed.

"Now, Lem. I wish you wouldn' talk like that."

"Aw, I just want Mutchell an' Flancher tuh stay away frum my work."

The parents fell silent, and Jeremy lay in bed, thinking of all he had heard. What was he to make of Haygood, Mutchell, and especially Flancher?

He was almost asleep when he thought that he heard a strange noise, and he wondered if it was Hazel. He got up and stood at his window to see if he could see anybody, but it was dark, and he couldn't.

23

HIS FIRST THOUGHT WHEN HE AWOKE THE NEXT MORNING was that it was Sunday, and he would not have to work; then he remembered his father's decision to work the sheep and his countenance fell. Jeremy despised working with the sheep. Field work was monotonous, but at least he didn't have to deal with sheep. Lem always did the most. Jeremy mainly drove them from one place to another, but sometimes he was required to catch and hold sheep, and he hated even touching them.

Once he was out of the house, however, and walking with his father, his spirits revived. He enjoyed summer mornings; the heat was still bearable. He wore neither shirt nor shoes nor hat, and he enjoyed the heat of the sun on his naked shoulders and the feeling of the warm dirt beneath his feet, which by now had healed. Patches joined him this morning. He was not allowed to go with Jeremy to the field when Jeremy had work to do, but he was permitted to tag along this morning, and he trotted beside Jeremy, now and then venturing off to the right or left, his nose against the ground. Jeremy decided that all in all, it was not a bad morning.

The walk to the field where the sheep were grazing was not a long one, and soon Jeremy and Lem were walking among the sheep. Most of the sheep were lying down, but when Lem and Jeremy approached them they would rise awkwardly to their feet and move stiffly away. Jeremy was sure that they were the dumbest creatures on earth. He most despised marking and branding sheep.

Once a year Ted McMillan, Leland's father, would come over, and Lem, Ted and Jeremy would drive all the sheep into the corral. Lem rounded up the sheep for three reasons: to check them for injuries, to cut off the tails of all the lambs, and to castrate the young bucks. The sheep would stink, the dust would make Jeremy sneeze violently, and the sheep would step on his bare feet with their sharp hooves.

By evening, Jeremy's hands would have numerous grass bur needles embedded in them, and the tops of his feet would be raw from sheep stepping on them. He complained to his father about his feet: "Paw, these ole sheep keep a-steppin' on my feet."

"Well, wear shoes. We got tuh work these sheep, whether er not you got sense enough tuh wear shoes."

Jeremy also hated to deal with sheep, and that was in late winter when some of the ewes dropped their lambs. Lem always tried to round up the expectant ewes and pen them when they were due to give birth, especially if the weather was bad, but invariably some of the ewes would disappear. Then Jeremy and Lem would have to bundle up against the icy winds, after dark, and with lantern in hand, wander over the pasture. Jeremy had long since decided that when he grew up, he would not work with sheep.

As they moved about among the sheep now, they came upon an old ewe lying on the ground. She did not get up as they came near, although all the other sheep deserted her and fled. Lem walked up to her and stood, his arms folded, surveying the sheep. Then he kicked her, not hard, but speculatively. He watched for her response, but there was none. She lay there, her legs folded under her, her head held high at a dignified angle, her eye fixed on Lem. Only the rapid chewing motion of her mouth betrayed her nervousness. She did not get up.

"Git up," Lem commanded, and he kicked her again, harder this time. The ewe launched forward awkwardly a couple of times, but she did not get up. At last Lem leaned over, put his arms around the sheep's middle and lifted her to her feet. Jeremy could see the sheep still watching Lem. As soon as Lem released her, however, she flopped back down and resumed her rapid chewing.

"Git up, damn ye!" Lem hissed. He picked her up again; his face was red from exertion and frustration. Jeremy stepped forward and tried to help. "It's like they git down an' fergit how tuh git up," declared his father. "Maybe they lay there so long they lose th' circulation in their laigs."

He lifted her again and gave her a shove as he released her, but she fell forward to the ground in a tangle of legs where she flailed about, trying to get up but to no avail. Lem stepped forward and kicked the sheep hard in the ribs. Jeremy heard the dull thump of his father's brogan striking the sheep. Lem moved as if to kick the sheep again, but stopped. Jeremy watched to see what his father would do. Lem stood there, flexing his hands. "Ole bitch," he mumbled to himself.

Then he said, "C'mon, Son." He leaned over once again to try to lift the sheep. "He'p me tuh git 'er tuh walkin', so then maybe the ole bitch'll stay up."

Jeremy stood on one side of the sheep across from his father, and together they held her up and forced her to walk. At last, after several minutes of coaxing, she began to support some of her own weight, and finally she stumbled away on her own to join the other sheep.

24

ON THE FAR SIDE OF THE FIELD against a fence stretched a heavily-wooded area that Jeremy had never explored. He had always believed that if one went far enough into the woods, he would find Indians. He and Leland had often talked about someday making an excursion in search of them. Leland insisted that he had been told by eyewitnesses that Indians lived in the woods. "They got teepees built all over th' place. I know, 'cause my brother tole me. He seen 'em once when he wuz a-huntin'. Said they uz a big waterfall there, an' a river a-flowin' right by th' teepees."

Jeremy had mentioned the Indians to his father once. "Boy, they ain't been no Indians in this country fer years. Whur do you git such idees?"

Jeremy did not bring up the Indians now.

"I wanta take a turn thoo here," Lem said, indicating the pasture. "Might be we'll find us a stray dawg in there. A dawg might be a-layin' up in th' shade uv these trees." So saying, he climbed over the fence. Jeremy followed him, thankful now for the intermittent shade. He and Lem made a wide swing through the pasture, but they did not find any dogs.

"Mighta been one uv th' neighbor's dawgs that killed that sheep," Lem mused, as they stood once again at the fence to the field. "An' it mighta been a whole pack uv dawgs, maybe wild dawgs. I expect that lotsa people aroun' here has got dawgs, an' it coulda been one uv them."

"Paw, do yuh think it coulda been th' Roosevelt's dawg?"

"I guess it coulda been, but don't no dawgs seem tuh be aroun' here now, at least not whur we can find 'em. John Broman tole me he seen some dawgs a coupla days ago, but they uz way over toward

Dorman. But, hell, they may uv killed that sheep an' then high-tailed it tuh Dorman er intuh th' nex' county."

"I betcha it uz th' Roosevelts' dawg."

Lem ignored Jeremy. He watched the sheep in the field for a long while, and then he said, "Well, we might as well head tuh th' house. Yer maw'll have lunch ready before long." He stepped over the fence and began to lead the way home.

As Jeremy followed his father toward home, he thought about what Lem had said about John Broman. Jeremy knew he was the father of H.C. Broman, a boy in Jeremy's class. He remembered how H.C. had raised lambs for a hobby, and how several of the lambs had been killed by a dog or dogs a year or two ago.

He and H.C. were in the same Ag class at school. All the classes were taught by one of the most popular teachers in the school, Trevor Ward.

25

ALTHOUGH TREVOR WARD WAS HIS FULL NAME, people in the community always called him T. He had gone to high school at Milburn, then he had gone away to college, and when he got his degree, he had returned to Milburn to teach. After his return, he sang in the Methodist Church choir, and he played softball with the local team. He took pride in the fact that he not only taught the boys agriculture, but he also taught them about life. In his class, the discussions ranged from when to plant cotton to how to court a girl. Sometimes T took the boys on field trips, and once he demonstrated how to castrate a calf.

Jeremy remembered when the movie "The Truth About Sex" had come out. It had created a scandal in Milburn. Some of the people in town had boycotted it; others thought it was a good idea. No one was sure how the local theater owner, Fred Barton, had acquired the movie. He insisted that it was an educational film, but word spread quickly that it dealt with sex, and some parents would not let their children go to see the movie. When Jeremy had asked to go to see the film, his mother had told him that Milburn was too far for them to go to some movie.

Jeremy listened with rapt attention to the boys in his class as they talked and giggled about the film. Toward the end of the school year, T discovered the boys' interest in the movie and decided to join in their conversation, asking how many had seen it. The boys looked at each other and laughed. Some said that they had.

"That's a good film," claimed T. "All of you ought to see it." He looked over the room expectantly. "Now I mean that. You boys are getting old enough to see stuff like that and to be discussing it, too. What's some stuff you learned?"

The boys looked at each other and grinned self-consciously but didn't say anything.

"Well, come on."

Finally, Mark Whitten said, "It tells yuh whur babies come from."

"Sure it does," T said, "but what else?"

Jimmy raised his hand. "It tells yuh tuh be keerful 'bout syphilis an' stuff like that."

"You bet it does," said T. "You boys know how you get syphilis?" No reply.

"Well, do you know?"

"I heard yuh can git it off uv a toilet seat."

"No, that's wrong," T said. "But where can you get it?"

"Sex," somebody volunteered.

"That's right," said T. "And what that means is you better stay out of whorehouses. You never know what you might pick up."

All the boys laughed again.

"It's no laughing matter," said T. "I know that some of you guys have been driving down to the Mexican border to Boys' Town, and you better be careful. You might get clap, or crabs. A guy I knew in college claimed he got clap, and he said that when he went to take a leak it hurt so bad that he just wanted to smash his fist through the wall. Said that there was a pipe over the urinal, and he almost pulled it out of the wall, he hurt so bad."

"What happened tuh him?" the boys all wanted to know.

"I don't know. He dropped out of school."

Jimmy leaned over to speak to Bobby across the aisle. He whispered, "Ast 'im if he's ever had syphilis."

Bobby shook his head, but T had noticed the whispered conversation.

"What do you want, Jimmy?'

"Nothin'."

"Are you wondering if I ever had any of those things?"

Jimmy dropped his head and nodded assent.

"Well, I haven't. And you don't want it, young man. Syphilis is even worse than clap. It'll ruin you. I've read about people that have gone plumb crazy or blind."

Perhaps to redeem himself, Jimmy spoke again. "My brother got crabs."

All the boys riveted their attention on Jimmy.

"What did he do?' asked T.

"Yuh mean tuh git 'em, er tuh git rid uv 'em?" asked Jimmy. The class laughed.

"My paw tole 'im tuh use Blue Seal ointment."

"And did it work?" asked H.C.

Jimmy shrugged. "I guess so."

There was a brief silence. Then T looked directly at the class. Standing before them in full view, he cupped his right hand and made a sweeping up-and-down gesture from his groin to his waist. "What about this?" he asked.

A hush descended upon the room.

"What about it? What does the movie say?"

"It says not tuh do it," volunteered Bobby.

"Yeah, it does. And you know why? You know why? The movie doesn't say the real reason, but I can tell you. Every time you do this," and he made the gesture again, "you take a drop of blood from your brain. Not just from your body. From your brain. Think of that."

Jeremy had squirmed on his seat and looked around the room to see if anyone was looking at him.

From the back, H.C. called out, "Hey, Stroop, stop a-doin' that. Yer gonna lose alla th' blood in yer brain."

26

THE NOON MEAL WAS READY WHEN JEREMY AND LEM ARRIVED at the house, and the Stroop family sat down to "Sunday dinner," always one of Jeremy's favorite meals. The Stroops bought groceries every Saturday, so there would be special food on Sunday, and perhaps for another day or two after. Eventually the food bought on Saturday would be eaten, and the family would subsist for the rest of the week on corn bread, beans, and fried potatoes. But Sunday's lunch would be different.

One of Jeremy's main delights on summer Sundays was iced tea. Tea was a luxury for the family because of the shortage of ice. Since the Stroops had no electric power, they would buy a fifty-pound block of ice from Ayers Store on Saturday, wrap it in a quilt, bring it home, and store it in the icebox, which would preserve the ice until about Tuesday. By then, what the family had not used would have melted, and they would be without ice until Saturday. But on Sunday there would be plenty of ice for iced tea, and Jeremy loved it. He would put spoonful after spoonful of sugar into his tea until his mother made him stop; his father never seemed to notice how much he used. Jeremy loved to drain his glass of tea, then tilt back his head and hold the edge of the glass in his mouth, the ice resting against his upper lip while the partially dissolved sugar ran down the side of the glass and into his mouth.

On this Sunday, in addition to the fresh meat that Olga brought home from Ayers Store, there would be mashed potatoes—and while potatoes were a staple of the family diet, it was only on Sunday that they were mashed. Also for this meal, Mrs. Stroop would prepare special vegetables such as turnips and peas. Jeremy did not care for vegetables regardless of how they were prepared. He did like the desserts that his mother would fix for Sunday lunch, such as chocolate pie and sugar cookies.

Olga usually bought some kind of beef on Saturdays, but mostly the meat she bought was whatever Ayers Store had on sale. She explained that "meat is just so high, I don't see how a body can rightly afford it these days." Jeremy preferred the pork dishes his mother served, and he always looked forward to the coming of fall when pork would become readily available. Meatless meals were common, especially in summer, but in winter there would be lots of ham, sausage, and bacon.

Early every spring, Mr. Soules would buy two young pigs and bring them out to the farm. Jeremy knew he bought them from Mutchell. One of them Lem got to keep for himself, as payment for taking care of the two pigs; the other he delivered, butchered, to Mr. Soules. Some of the meat from the pig which Lem kept would be preserved in salt, some of it would be ground into sausage, and it would supply most of the family's meat for the winter and even into early summer.

Jeremy enjoyed "hawg-killin' day," as Lem referred to it. The weather would be cool, and there would be a lot of activity. Leland's dad would come over to help Lem with the butchering, and usually Leland would come with him.

Lem would take his rifle and a bucket of slop down to the pig pen. While the pigs ate, their heads buried in the trough, Lem would press his rifle to the head of each of the pigs and shoot them. Sometimes he had to shoot them more than once to kill them.

Once the pigs were dead, Lem would cut their throats and let them bleed for several minutes.

Meanwhile, Mrs. Stroop would have filled the fifty-gallon drum with water and have built a hot fire under it. While the water heated, Lem and Ted would rig a block and tackle over the branch of a tree growing beside the drum. To this block and tackle, Lem would attach a harness with two hooks riveted into it, and Lem would force these hooks through the pig's hind legs. Then, he and Ted would hoist the pig high into the air to lower it into the scalding hot water in the drum. After leaving the pig submerged for some time to loosen the hair on it, they would use the block and tackle to lift the pig's body out of the drum. Using the blade of a knife, they would scrape the carcass clean of bristles.

Next, Lem and Ted would butcher the pig, separating the meat that would be ground into sausage from the hams and other larger cuts that they would preserve with salt. Lem also would trim off most of the fat to use later in making lye soap. As a special treat, Lem would carve the backstrap from one of the pigs and cook it on the spot, frying it in a pan over the open fire that had been used to heat the water for scalding the pigs. Jeremy always thought it was the best meat he had ever tasted.

One of the last things that the two men did was to cut off the heads of the pigs. Mrs. Stroop would take each of the heads and cut selected portions from them, including the jowls and the tongues, to make what she called head cheese. She was a thorough woman. She not only made head cheese from portions of the head; she also took the backbone, the tail, and parts of the head of the pig to make souse meat. She would cook these meats until they assumed a jellied consistency. Later, she would serve it sliced thin, with pickles. Lem loved it; Jeremy despised it.

"Say, Jeremy, yuh know what they do with them eyes, don't yuh?" Mr. McMillan had asked at the last hog killing.

"Naw, whatta they do?" Jeremy concentrated more on his mother than on the question.

"Why, they make marbles uv 'em," said Mr. McMillan.

"Aw," Jeremy looked at Mr. McMillan. "They don't, do they?"

"Why shore they do."

"Paw, do they do that?"

"Do what, Son?" Lem was busy cutting up a section of ribs.

"Do they make marbles uv hogs' eyes?"

Lem looked at Ted and laughed. "I guess so."

Almost always at some point in the butchering process, Sam Sowell, a neighbor who lived close by, would arrive on his mule. Jeremy knew very little about the Sowell family. He knew where they lived, and he knew that the community considered them "white trash." Jeremy wondered how Sowell knew that Lem was butchering on this particular day, and once he had asked Lem.

"I don't rightly know. I guess he just figgers it's th' first cold day uv fall, and we're prob'ly butcherin'."

Sam would arrive quietly and not say a word, sitting patiently on his mule, casually smoking a roll-your-own cigarette, an old quilt wrapped around him against the cold. Finally, Lem or Ted would notice him and speak.

"Howdy, Mr. Lem, Mr. Ted."

"Hey, Sam."

"Looks like you a-butcherin' tuhday, Mr. Lem."

"Yep."

"I jus' thought yuh might be, it bein' so cold."

Lem smiled.

"Oh, yes, Sir. I had tuh break ice down tuh th' pond this mornin'."

"Cold as a witch's tit in Alaska, huh, Sam?" laughed Ted.

"I knowed it ud be cold this winter." Sam waited for someone to question him. When no one did, he continued. "I knowed it 'cause th' squir'ls all started gatherin' in nuts so early. Caterpillars is a lot fuzzier this year, too."

After a long silence, Lem said, "You an' yore fam'ly doin' all right?"

"Well, it looks like a hard winter," Sam would say. "We never got aroun' tuh raisin' no hawg this year." He smiled apologetically and tapped ashes from his cigarette. "Seems like with th' crops an' all, we just never had no free time tuh worry 'bout no hawg. I don't worry none 'bout myse'f, an' I guess th' ole woman can take care uv herse'f, but we worry 'bout th' chirren."

"That's all right, Sam. I'm shore that Olga has got more hawg meat than she can handle. Go over there an' talk tuh her. She'll he'p yuh out."

Sam's face broke into a wide grin.

"Yes, Sir. Thankee, Mr. Lem. I'll just do that."

Jeremy's mother was kind to Sam. "How is yore missus, Sam?"

"Well, now, she's tol'able. Just tol'able."

"An' yore kids?"

"Well, you know that Jimmy, that's my youngest, had a bout with th' whoopin' cough here a while back, but he's better. Thankee."

Mrs. Stroop offered him one of the hog's ham hocks.

"Now, Miz Stroop, I never came over here tuh ast yuh fer no meat. I just happened tuh be a-ridin' by."

"Just take th' meat, Sam. An' say hello tuh yer wife." Sam always took the proffered meat. Then he would leave as quietly as he had come, his old quilt pulled closely around him.

Olga would explain, "I know folks calls them Sowells 'white trash,' but I still feel sorry fer 'em, 'specially th' kids."

The butchering done, Lem would take the large cuts into the smokehouse to finish preserving them. After rubbing the cuts thoroughly with his own preparation of salt and spices, Lem would hang the cuts from the rafters. In the meantime, Mrs. Stroop would take the intestines, clean and boil them, and then set them aside to stuff with sausage.

But this was August, and hawg-killin' time would not come for some time—not until at least late in October or early November—and so the Stroops had no pork for their Sunday lunch. Instead, Mrs. Stroop had cooked a chicken.

27

AFTER DINNER, JEREMY SAT AT THE TABLE with his parents.

"We didn' find no dawgs, Maw," Jeremy volunteered. He watched Lem for his reaction.

"Maybe they left th' county," she replied. She was collecting the dinner plates from the table.

"Paw thinks it's one uv th' neighbor's dawgs, dontcha, Paw?"

"Could be," said Lem, rolling a cigarette. "They's lotsa dawgs aroun', but we'll git 'im sooner er later." He put a lighted match to his cigarette.

"Has anybody else lost any sheep?" asked Mrs. Stroop, moving between the table and the washstand.

"Not that I know uv," replied Lem, "but then I ain't ast nobody else. I just foun' th' first sheep yestiddy." He frowned at his cigarette and coughed.

"I'll he'p yuh git that dawg, Paw," Jeremy said. "I'll take my shotgun with me ever' evenin' when I git home, an' I'll go a-lookin' fer dawgs fer yuh."

"You ain't been home lately, Boy. Always down there at that church."

Jeremy had not expected that remark. Hearing his father speak of church reminded him that he would like to go to church that night.

"I'm surprised," Lem continued, "that yuh didn' try tuh go tuhday."

"Well, since I didn' go this mornin', can I go tuhnight?" Jeremy blurted out the request. Then he quickly added, "I'll do all uv my chores real good, an' I'll do any special chores yuh have fer me tuh do."

Lem studied Jeremy for a moment. "Well, now, you remember that patch whur we had our garden earlier this year? It's all grown up in

142

weeds now, an' I'd shorely like it tuh be cleaned out. If yuh'll clean out that patch an' do all yer other chores, yuh can go tuh church tuhnight."

Jeremy's heart sank. He remembered the patch. Lem had mentioned that he wanted Jeremy to weed the patch earlier, and Jeremy had gone out to look at it and had found it infested with weeds, with thick stalks of castor beans rising higher than his head. What a job, he thought. But he said, "I'll do th' patch, Paw."

Lem looked at Jeremy. "Have yuh looked at that patch lately?"

Jeremy nodded.

"All right, Boy. You do that patch this afternoon, an' yuh can go tuh church tuhnight, but now lissen. Lissen tuh me." Lem leaned toward Jeremy. "That's it. No more church after tuhnight. You hear me?" He crushed out his cigarette on the table's edge.

"Yes, Sir."

"I don't keer if Miz McMillan comes a-pussyfootin' aroun' here er not. You ain't a-goin' tuh that damn church no more. That's final. How long is that damn meetin' a-goin' on?"

"But Paw…" Jeremy started to complain, but he stopped when he saw how his father looked at him.

"Don't 'but paw' me. 'Stead uv sittin' there complainin' tuh me, yuh better git out there an' git on them weeds. You ain't a-goin' nowhur 'til yuh finish that job."

28

Outside, Jeremy did not go immediately into the garden. He headed instead for the shed. As he walked toward the shed, he remembered how the boys had teased him in Ag class, what the boys had accused him of.

He could still remember his first time. He had only been experimenting at first; he had not known what to expect, and then this strange thing had happened. Afterwards, throughout the day, he had thought about what had happened. He was vaguely aware that what he had done had something to do with producing babies, but he was not sure what. What had he ejected?

The next morning, as soon as he awoke, he had gone to the shed with great apprehension. He was not sure what he would find but he was afraid of what he might find there. Would something be there? Would it be alive? Had it been alive at first? Had it survived the night? Had some animal snatched it away? He had looked closely at the ground. Nothing. But even now, he wondered about the implications of what had happened.

He did not stay at the shed long. He was looking for a hoe. There were three standing in one corner of the barn, and he walked over to select one. Two of the hoes were garden hoes with slim handles; the third was a grubbing hoe with a short, stout handle. He selected the grubbing hoe and headed back to the garden. He wanted to finish in time to go to church.

He stood in the midday sun, looking at weeds higher than his head. There must be a million of them, he thought. He hesitated for a moment, and then walked into the patch and seized one of the weeds, intending to pull it by the roots. The weed resisted. Jeremy pulled harder, and finally the weed came out of the ground. Jeremy straightened and seized another weed, but pull as he would, this weed

144

would not come out of the ground. He looked around at all the weeds left, especially the castor bean stalks, and sighed. "I ain't never gonna git these weeds pulled tuhday."

He attacked the weeds with his hoe—first one at a time, and then he tried cutting wide swaths through them with the grubbing hoe—but nothing worked well. Each time he cut down a weed, it seemed that two grew in its place. "I ain't a-makin' no progress a-tall." He confronted a particularly large weed and swung at its base. He felt the blow throughout his arms and shoulders, and the hoe only bounced off the weed. "My God," he exclaimed.

Already an ugly blister had formed in the palm of his right hand. "I cain't do this," he thought aloud. He began to look for small weeds that he could cut more easily, but there were more large weeds than small ones. And he had not even reached the rows of castor beans yet. He wished that his father or mother would come to the door and tell him that he did not need to finish the job that afternoon, but only his mother came to the door, and she came only once to remind him to be careful of snakes in all those high weeds.

As the afternoon wore on, he regretted that he had decided to cut down the small weeds first, because more and more of the weeds that were left were thicker and taller. He had burst the blister on his hand, and it was now a raw, bleeding sore. He moved his hands down onto the very end of the hoe handle and flailed away, trying not to grip the handle with his right hand. Weeds filled the air; he was making progress when he felt a sharp, jarring impact in his hands, and the head of the hoe sailed across the garden.

"Eeeeeeyow!" He had hit a rock, and the blade of the hoe had flown off the handle. "Damn, I done broke th' hoe," he said aloud. "Paw'll git me shore." At the same time he realized that he had to tell Lem, so he went to the door of the house and called inside, "Paw, I broke a hoe."

His father appeared in the doorway. "Broke a handle, did yuh? Lemme see," he said, stepping outside and walking toward the garden. He did not seem upset, and Jeremy was relieved. Out in the garden, Lem surveyed the progress that Jeremy had made and seemed pleased. "Yer doin' purty good, Boy. Whur's th' hoe that yuh broke?"

"Down on th' other end," said Jeremy, massaging his injured right hand as he led Lem to the spot where he had dropped the handle. "Here's th' handle, an' th' head uv it flew off over there somewhurs. I'll fin' it."

He found the head and carried it to Lem.

"Well, yuh didn' break th handle, Son. Th' head just flew off. Gitcha another hoe, an' finish up. Yuh should be through before long."

Jeremy started toward the barn, but his father stopped him. "Here," he called after him. "Take this handle with ye an' put it over there by th' yard gate. I'll put th' head back on it a little later."

Jeremy set the handle down by the gate and went to the barn. There he selected another hoe and returned to the garden. Although this hoe was lighter, Jeremy had greater success with it in chopping down the weeds. Soon he was finished, but his right hand continued to bleed. He turned next to his chores and finished in plenty of time to get ready for church.

29

JEREMY HOPED HE COULD GET READY without attracting his mother's attention. He had not worn a shirt all day, and now he planned simply to select his best shirt, slip it on, and be ready for church. His mother had other plans.

She came into his room just as he was putting on his shirt. "Jeremy Stroop, just what do yuh think yer a-doin'?"

"I'm a-gittin' ready fer church," he protested.

"Not like that, yer not. My goodness, yuh been a-workin' out in that garden all afternoon, an' yuh been a-sweatin' like a horse, an' you ain't goin' tuh church like that. Now, you just take you a bath an' put on some fresh clothes. Here, give me that shirt, an' you clean up before you put it on. It'll be a-smellin' jus' like you."

"Maw, I ain't dirty."

"Uv course yer dirty. Now, don't give me no sass. You take a bath er else."

As he handed her the shirt she spied his right hand. "Jeremy, what have yuh done tuh yer hand?"

"Aw, it ain't nothin', Maw."

"Well, it shore is. Here, you jus' wait a minute, an' I'll git th' Mercurochrome."

"Maw, don't do that. That stuff burns like all git out."

"Well, it's good fer wounds like that. How did yuh do that?"

Jeremy wanted to hurry. "It ain't nothin', Maw."

She brought the Mercurochrome and insisted that Jeremy let her apply it to his hand. He squirmed in pain. "Ouch, Maw."

"It's good fer yuh. Now you wait, an' I'll git a bandage fer yuh."

Finished with the treatment, his mother said, "Now, go git yer tub."

"Can I go swimmin' down tuh th' creek an' just wash off?" asked Jeremy. He knew that his mother had on occasion consented to this alternative.

"No siree. You go down to th' woodpile an' git you a tub, an' you wash with soap. You don't want no dirty creek water on that there place on yer hand. An' you wash with this soap. It's good soap. An' you know it's th' onliest kind we got."

Jeremy reluctantly went down to the woodpile, selected a number 2 washtub, and carried it into the house. His mother had already laid out clean clothes for him. He filled the tub with water from the water barrel outside the house. Then he stripped himself and with some difficulty settled himself into the tub. He seemed always to bark his shins whenever he took a bath. Sitting in it, his knees came up to his chin; his shins rubbed one edge of the tub and his backbone the other. Further, it was impossible to wash his entire body while he was sitting in the tub. He stood now, but he rushed, for he was afraid that his mother would come in and see him. Then he quickly splashed water on his head, in case his mother asked him if he had washed his hair, and he climbed out and dressed quickly.

"Jeremy," his mother came into the room. "Are yuh already through?"

"Yes'm."

"It shore didn' take long. Are yuh shore yuh washed good? I want yuh to smell clean when yuh go tuh church."

"I'm clean, Maw," Jeremy assured her. "I got tuh go."

His mother pulled him to her and smelled his hair. "Yer hair don't smell any too clean. You shore yuh washed it?"

"I washed all over, Maw. I gotta go." And he strode toward the door.

"Just wait a minute. How does yer hand look?"

"It's fine, Maw. I gotta go."

"Well, wait a minute. Now look. Yuh got th' bandage all wet when you uz a-bathin'. I shoulda known you ud do that. Here, I got tuh change it."

"But, Maw."

"Hush. It'll just take a minute."

A fresh bandage on his hand, Jeremy stepped outside. His father lifted his head as Jeremy passed. "What did yuh do with th' hoe handle?"

"I put it over there against th' fence like yuh tole me to."

"Okay. Just leave it there. I don't wanta fool with it right now."

Jeremy started out again, but then his mother called to him, "Jeremy, you be keerful. They's a storm a-comin' up outta th' northwest. I can see th' lightnin' already. It could be a bad un."

Jeremy did not reply.

"An' don't you git caught out in no hailstorm. You be keerful."

Jeremy kept moving, but as he walked away, he could hear his mother say, "Lem, don't yuh think that there cloud looks sorta green? I bet they's hail in it."

He didn't hear his father's reply, but as he continued his walk, he could hear his mother chiding his father, "Oh, Lem, how many times have I tole yuh we need a cellar? An' now here's this turrible storm a-comin', an' we ain't got no cellar yet."

Jeremy felt a mix of moods as he walked across the pasture toward church. The figure of Flancher kept rising in his consciousness. He could see Flancher, coatless, his tie loose about his neck, mopping his face with a large white handkerchief. As he preached, he jabbed his finger into the air, and it seemed to Jeremy that Flancher was looking directly at him through his thick eyebrows, demanding that "all sinners come an' be saved." The image of the old crone intruded, leaning over him, her filthy dress hanging loosely away from her shoulders as she asked him if he were saved. He could smell her foul breath. He shook his head.

He looked to his left and saw the windmill, and he dropped his head and grinned as he remembered the night when he had mistaken the windmill for the returning Christ. He hurried a little.

To the northwest, Jeremy could see the jagged streaks of lightning arcing from the clouds down to the earth. But it would be a long time after the lightning flash before he would hear the thunder, and he knew that meant the storm was far away. He knew he could make it to the church building before the storm arrived. He also knew that it was common for storms so far away to die out before they reached the farm.

30

THE CHURCH WAS ALMOST FULL when Jeremy arrived. Boy, another big crowd, he thought. He walked into the building, recognizing the room now, the benches, and the podium. The ceiling fans turned slowly overhead. He felt a new confidence; he felt that he belonged. He waved to some of the young people that he recognized. Due to the large crowd, he was forced to sit near the podium. All around him people were laughing, talking, fanning themselves with songbooks—all except the kneelers, who remained motionless, their heads buried in their arms.

"Reckin that storm is a-gonna hit?" someone behind him asked.

"Hard tuh say," another voice replied. "It's still a long way off yet. Mebbe it'll hold off 'til we git home."

"I don't think so. I got a feelin' that it's movin' purty fast."

"Well, we need th' rain."

"We do fer a fact. An' I knowed it uz gonna rain. My rheumatism has been actin' up awful."

"Yeah, hope we git a real gully-washer," someone behind him said. "My stock tank's a-gittin' mighty low. I had tuh haul water frum th' river durin' th' drouth, an' I don't wanta do that ag'in."

"Well, that's th' way it is aroun' here. It don't rain very often, but when it does, it comes a chip-floater."

"Yeah, ole Joe Bob uz a-tellin' me that he uz a-talkin' tuh some city folks that he had a-visitin' him, an' they ast 'im how much rain he got in a year, an' he said 'Oh, 'bout ten inches.' They thought that wuzn't much rain, an' they tole 'im so, but he said he tole 'em, 'Well, yuh oughtta be here th' day we git it.'"

Jeremy turned, surveying the benches, trying to see Haygood, but he couldn't find him. He also looked for Leland and Mrs. McMillan, but they were nowhere to be seen, and he was glad. He did not want Leland to see that he came to church by himself.

He leaned back on his bench. He even smiled at a woman that he did not know. He knew what to expect as the services started. Mutchell made the announcements, and they were the same as always—a welcome to visitors, an admonition to those present to come every time they could. He still spoke gazing out of the windows on the sides of the building. When the singing began, Jeremy even tried to sing along, but he still did not understand any of the songs, so he quit.

A boy sitting beside him punched him in the ribs. "What th' hell is an Ebenezer?"

Jeremy looked at him. He had seen the boy at school but didn't know his name. "What?" he asked.

The boy grinned at his songbook; it was opened to the song the congregation was singing. He pointed to the line, *Here I raise my Ebenezer*. "What is that?"

Jeremy shrugged his shoulders.

"Well, I got my Ebenezer right here," said the boy, seizing his crotch. "An' I shore as hell know how tuh raise it."

Jeremy looked away from the boy. Flancher was approaching the podium, and silence descended upon the crowd. He began to speak, slowly, with little volume. He seemed weary. He moved slowly, and his shirt had come unbuttoned at his belt, revealing a slender triangle of white flesh. He carried a freshly starched white handkerchief in his left hand. Jeremy noticed for the first time that Flancher wore a gold cross that hung almost to his waist. He lifted the cross for all to see and said, "Yuh see this cross? A dear sister in th' church give it tuh me. Ast me if I ud wear it ever' now an' then in memory uv her husband. I told 'er that I would, an' I do. Tuhnight I just felt like a-wearin' it, an' so I did."

Flancher then addressed Mutchell. "Brother Mutchell, ain't this a good crowd?"

"It shore is," Mutchell answered from the front seat.

"Yes, yes, it shorely is. Thank th' Lord. Praise God! I think we may have a record crowd tuhnight. Ain't we had a time durin' our meetin'? I ain't never seen th' Holy Ghost so active in alla my preachin'."

Amens echoed all over the building.

"Brother Mutchell, why don't yuh count all these good people here tuhnight? Count 'em ever' one, babies an' all. They're all God's childern, an' he loves ever'one uv 'em. I'd just like tuh know how many is here."

Now Flancher turned his attention to the audience. "I'm so glad all uv yuh come tuhnight. I know th' Lord is a-gonna bless yuh fer bein' here. You wait an' see." Flancher beamed at the crowd as he looked at them through his bushy eyebrows. "Lemme tell yuh," he said. "If th' Lord don't git aroun' tuh blessin' yuh here, they's all eternity fer that." A few scattered amens followed.

Flancher paused. Then he said, "Ah, brethren, it's so good tuh be here with yuh tuhnight. I'm so glad that we extended this meetin'. I just don't believe th' Lord's work is finished here in this little community uv Dorman. They is still lost souls here. I feel it in muh heart."

Jeremy could have sworn that Flancher looked directly at him.

"Now I know that we cain't continue this meetin' ferever, 'cause they's other work tuh do fer th' Lord. I got another meetin' after this un, an' I gotta git ready fer it. Th' Lord's work is never done." He smiled. Then he said, "I know that I ain't got much time lef' tuh preach tuh yuh, an' it's hard tuh decide what tuh preach on. An' I know th' devil keeps a-tryin' tuh hinder me."

"Oh, yes. Beware th' devil," someone intoned behind Jeremy.

"Git thee behin' me, Satan," shouted someone else.

Flancher was pleased. "You tell 'em," he said.

Flancher paused, and then he said, "I know some uv yuh lissenin' tuh my voice tuhnight is lost. I know yer lost, an' I wantcha tuh be saved tuhnight. I wantcha tuh give yer heart tuh God an' receive eternal life." Flancher's voice was rising. "They ain't no doubt that God is a lovin' God. They ain't no doubt he is all powerful, an' he can save yuh. Ain't no doubt about it! Praise God!"

Flancher leaned forward, his right hand on his knee to emphasize his point. The audience cried, "Amen!"

"But tuhnight I wanta impress on yuh how important it is, once a person is saved, that they be faithful all their lives. You know that, dontcha?"

Jeremy could see heads in front of him nod.

Someone said, "That's right, Preacher." Another said, "You tell it like it is, Preacher."

"Yuh gotta live fer him who died fer you! Now, think about it. Jesus died fer yuh. Do yuh believe that?" The crowd shouted its approval. "Uv course yuh do. An' don't yuh see what a small thing it is tuh live fer him? After all, he died fer you!"

Jeremy looked up, and his eyes met Flancher's.

Now lightning flashed, its eerie light filling the church, and thunder rumbled. A fresh, cool breeze blew through the open windows. People sitting against the windows tried to move away from them, toward the center of the benches. Flancher stopped and looked at the open windows on the north side of the church. Then he said, "Brother

Mutchell, some uv you brethern better close them winders over on that side. Some uv th' ladies is likely tuh git wet." Then he addressed the ladies on the north side of the building. "But a little rain ain't gonna hurt you ladies. They ain't gonna be no Noah's flood, I guess." The congregation laughed. "But I'll tell yuh one thing, that sprinklin' yer gittin' ain't gonna count as no baptism neither."

Flancher continued his sermon. "Now let me tell yuh somethin' else. If yuh do come tuh God an' git saved, an' then yuh just start a-sinnin' ag'in, then yer a backslider. Ain't nothin' worse, brethern. Remember Esau. That pore man sold his birthright, and then found no place fer repentance, though he sought it carefully with tears. So, you think hard. God knows yer hearts. You can come down here a-blubberin' tuh beat th' band, an' a-speakin' in tongues, but it's what's in yer hearts that counts. God knows if yer lost. If yer sincere, an' if yuh love God, an' if yuh commit tuh him, then he'll change yer life. He'll give yuh strength tuh live, an' yuh can pray tuh him, an' he'll hear yer prayers. Give yerself tuh God, an' then yuh can ast anythin' in th' world as long as yuh ast in faith, an' God is a-gonna give it tuh yuh. Anythin' in th' world."

Jeremy listened closely to Flancher's reference to prayer. He remembered his desire for a bicycle, how he had wished for one, how he had talked to his mother about his wishes and how she had told him simply to wish harder. Flancher was suggesting another approach. But how was one to pray?

A brilliant flash of lightning filled the room; simultaneously, a crash of thunder shook the whole building. For a moment the lights dimmed, and the overhead fans slowed. The congregation shifted about in apprehension. "There's th' power uv God," shouted Flancher, jabbing his finger toward the ceiling. "An' that same power can save yer soul, er it can send yuh straight tuh hell. Which'll it be, sinner?"

Now the storm arrived with full force. The sound of rain falling on the tin roof above almost drowned out Flancher's words. Thunder rumbled constantly. Flashes of lightning illuminated the room. "Oh, sinner. Cain't yuh see yer lost condition?" Flancher was shouting, trying to make himself heard above the storm. "Wontcha come tuh him and faithfully promise 'im that yuh won't sin no more. Send th' devil tuh hell whur he belongs! Hallelujah!"

Lightning flashed again and again, accompanied by loud peals of thunder. Torrents of rain whipped against the closed windows, blowing through the broken panes of glass. People scrambled to get away from the rain. The roar of the falling rain on the tin roof and the thunder drowned out all sounds, even the grinding of the fans—all sounds except the voice of Flancher.

Someone behind Jeremy shouted, "Oh, praise his blessed name!" Another shouted, "Oh, Jesus, calm this storm just like yuh did on Galilee." Jeremy was not sure what Galilee was.

"Th' Lord knows yuh," Flancher declared, jabbing his finger at the audience. "He knows if yer a sinner." He leaned forward across the podium. "Even yer secret sins." Jeremy thought about the privy and the Sears catalog. A tremendous peal of thunder shook the whole building; lightning seemed to envelop Flancher with a mystical glow. Jeremy stared at him in fascination. And then the lights went out.

There was a moment of silence, and then Jeremy heard someone say, "Oh, Lord, I'm a-comin'." A commotion arose. Jeremy strained to see Flancher in the dim light. "I wanta be saved," the voice continued. "I wanta come tuh Jesus. Oh God, oh God, save me, save me, save me!"

"Come on down here, Sister. Praise th' Lord!" In the dim light, Jeremy could barely make out that Flancher was smiling, his arms wide, beckoning with both hands, shouting above the storm. "Now, who else will come? Who will promise their lives tuh God? Come an' be made whole." Cries could be heard throughout the building between the claps of thunder. Flancher had never semed so large, so powerful.

Somehow for Jeremy, the energy of the storm and of the congregation seemed focused in Flancher. He felt his throat constrict. He looked back to see the aisle filling with people, streaming down to the podium and to Flancher. They came, some laughing, some crying, some with their eyes fixed on Flancher, but they came, and Flancher hugged them one after another. The storm continued its fury.

A man on the bench in front of Jeremy rose and began a spastic dance. He turned toward the crowd. His eyes were set back in his head, and his body jerked convulsively. He began to sing.

The babbler was on his feet. Everywhere Jeremy looked, people were swaying in the aisles, their arms above their heads. A rumble of voices punctuated by peals of thunder created a terrific uproar, and a grotesque fluorescence bathed the whole scene, especially Flancher. *I can't stand it*, he thought. *I got tuh git out of here*. He stepped out into the aisle and turned back toward the main door. He wanted to go home, but the onrushing crowd of people coming to Flancher stopped him. He tried to push through them, but there were too many. The crush of the crowd engulfed him, and he found himself forced to face the podium. He looked up at Flancher, standing behind the podium, his hair dishevelled, the cross askew on his chest, and Jeremy could have sworn he beckoned to him.

At that instant a tremendous crash of lightning burst into the room. Women screamed. Somewhere a baby began to cry. The people behind Jeremy surged forward, pressing against his back, shoving him toward the podium and into the arms of Flancher.

31

THE STORM HAD ABATED. There were still pale flashes of lightning, now through the south windows of the building, but the thunder had moved far away, and the rain on the tin roof had lessened. Flancher began to move from person to person. Jeremy remembered that he had watched this ritual before, and he had always wondered what Flancher talked about. As Flancher shifted his heavy body from person to person, his cross dangling awkwardly from around his neck, Jeremy wondered what Flancher would say to him.

By the time Flancher reached him, Jeremy had lost much of the nervousness that he had felt at first—but when he started talking to Flancher, a tremor crept into his voice. Flancher laid his arm heavily over Jeremy's shoulder, and Jeremy was aware of an unpleasant odor.

"What's yer request, Son?"

"What?" Jeremy looked down and twisted his hands in his lap.

"What's yer request?"

Jeremy shrugged his shoulders. He did not know what his request was.

"Do yuh wanta be baptized?"

Jeremy pushed his hair back from his eyes. He did not look at Flancher. He did not reply.

"Son, do yuh wanta be baptized?"

"I donno." Jeremy was shaking. He had difficulty controlling his voice.

"Is yer parents here?"

"Naw. They ain't."

"Well, you jus' sit here, an' I'll talk tuh yuh some more in jus' a minute."

There were many people for Flancher to talk to, and he took a long time. At last, he stood and faced the audience. "These pore sinners has come forward and confessed their need fer God. Praise th' Lord. An' they've ast us tuh pray fer 'em. Now, I wantcha tuh bow with me as we pray."

As soon as the prayer was finished, many of those seated around Jeremy headed for their seats. Somewhere in the audience, a little girl sang out, "Here comes Mama."

Jeremy remained seated. He did not know what to do. Flancher walked over to Mutchell and began whispering to him. Once he looked over his shoulder at Jeremy.

Mutchell rose from his seat and peered out into the night. He whispered something to Flancher, and then went over to the windows on the north side of the building. He stood and stared out of the window for a while, then returned to Flancher. Jeremy sat in his place. What happens next, he wondered. He began to wish he had not responded to Flancher, but it seemed too late to get up and walk back to his seat.

Mutchell continued his whispered discussion with Flancher.

At last Flancher came to Jeremy and sat down beside him. "Son, do yuh wanta be baptized?"

"I donno. I guess so," said Jeremy. He had himself under control now.

"Well, yuh see, they's a little problem. Usually we have all th' baptizin's over tuh Brother Mutchell's tank, but it's shore been a-rainin', an' Brother Mutchell don't think we kin git tuh his tank. He's got a coupla low places in his road, an' he's shore that they're filled with water now. So, we ain't got no place tuh baptize yuh tuhnight."

Flancher stood up and consulted Mutchell again. Then he returned to Jeremy.

"Yuh see, Son, we cain't baptize yuh tuhnight."

Jeremy did not look up at him.

"I ain't never had nothin' like this," said Flancher.

Jeremy still did not look up.

"I did pray fer yuh with these other folks, an' we'll git th' baptizin' done soon. Stick aroun' after th' service. Okay?"

Jeremy nodded. He glanced up at Flancher, smiling down upon him.

"Are yuh prepared tuh promise him that you'll give 'im all yore life and accept Jesus as yore personal Savior?"

Jeremy looked up at Flancher, then down at his hands, twisting in his lap. He pushed his hair back from his face. Then he nodded.

"God bless yuh, Son. We'll take care uv yuh."

Flancher stood up and addressed the congregation. "Now they's a bit uv a problem here. This young man has come forward tuh be baptized, but we cain't git tuh th' tank tuh do th' baptizin'. Never seen it when they wuz too much water fer baptizin'."

"But th' young man is a-gonna come back another time, an' we'll do th' baptizin' then. Now, this ain't th' best way, but th' Lord unnerstan's. Th' boy is saved."

Flancher continued: "Now I want those uv yuh who responded tuh know they's special blessin's fer yuh. I been a-tellin' yuh about th' good life in Jesus fer a long time now, and tuhnight, if any uv yuh wants tuh know th' deeper life, th' prayer life, yuh can stay here at th' buildin' after services is over, an' I'll tell yuh my own experience an' what a differnce prayer can make. I tell yuh, brethern, prayer changes things." Flancher paused. Then he said, "Joshua prayed, and th' sun stood still fer a whole day. Did yuh know that?"

Jeremy's interest increased. He had never heard of Joshua. He wondered where that story was in the Bible. He tried to understand. How could that be? And yet Flancher had said that the man prayed, and the sun stood still. He was deeply impressed. He thought of all the times he had wished for a bicycle. Perhaps prayer was better than wishing. He decided that prayer must be a wonderful thing. I'll try it, he thought to himself. Maybe I won't make the sun stand still, but I'm going to pray.

32

JEREMY ROSE TO GO.

"Son," said Flancher. "Wouldn' yuh like tuh know more about God an' prayer an' them things?"

"I don't know," replied Jeremy. He studied the floor.

"Well, I betcha would. You come by yerse'f tuhnight, didn' yuh?"

"Yes, Sir. I did."

"Ain't no need tuh check with yer folks, then. An' I'm shore a big boy like you knows his way home. It's stopped rainin'. Yuh'll be all right."

Jeremy nodded and sat back down. The church behind him had emptied except for Flancher and two ladies he did not know.

"I 'preciate you folks a-stayin' fer a few minutes," Flancher said. "I hope all uv yuh believe in prayer." The ladies nodded vigorously.

Jeremy watched to see what would happen. Then Flancher addressed him. "Son, didn' we have ice cream tuhgether?"

"Yes, Sir."

"That uz good ice cream, wuzn't it?"

Jeremy nodded.

"So, do yuh believe in prayer?"

Jeremy shrugged. He just didn't know what to say.

"Well, I certainly do," said one of the ladies. "An' you ought to, young man. I pray alla th' time, an' God hears me. I jus' know that he does. Las' week I had a quarter that I owed Ethel Robinson, an' I uz a-goin' over tuh pay 'er, an' when I felt in my pocket, it uz gone. I couldn't fin' it tuh save my life. But I kep' a-goin', an' I uz a-prayin' all th' way, an' when I got there, I uz a-talkin' tuh Ethel, an' I reached in my pocket, an' there it wuz. I know God put it there."

"Course he did, Sister," soothed Flancher.

Then he turned to Jeremy. "So, Son. Do you believe in prayer?"

Jeremy looked up to see the two ladies studying him. "Yeah, I guess so."

"Praise th' Lord. Son, did yuh know that th' Lord prayed, an' th' waves uv the sea wuz calmed? Did yuh know that Jesus prayed an' raised a dead man?"

Jeremy tried to think carefully about these incidents that Flancher was describing. He realized that he knew very little about prayer. He had never seen his father or mother pray, and he had never prayed himself, except to repeat the lines, "Now I lay me down to sleep." But Flancher had opened a whole new world to him. Prayer could raise the dead. Stop the sun. He looked at Flancher with deepening respect, even awe.

"Now, I must caution yuh," Flancher said. "Prayer ain't just sayin' some words tuh God."

"It certainly ain't," said the lady who had prayed about the quarter. "Yuh got tuh work at prayer alla th' time. I pray ever' mornin' an' ever' night. An' I pray at church too. Ever' time Brother Mutchell asts us tuh pray, I pray with 'im."

"Yes, uv course yuh do, Sister. I know yuh do. But two things is required. Do yuh know what they are?" Flancher directed his attention to the two ladies. "How 'bout it, sisters? Do yuh know?"

"Well, yuh gotta say 'Amen' when yuh finish," one of the ladies spoke up.

"Well, that's right," Flancher agreed.

"An' yuh got tuh hollow th' name uv God," the lady continued. "I remember we had a preacher here, an' he taught us that."

"Well," said the other lady, "if yer talkin' 'bout ole Brother Wooley, I ain't so sure about him. I had 'im over fer lunch one Sunday, an' he never thanked me once, an' I got up early that mornin' tuh fix my special tomaters an' squash fer 'im."

Flancher smiled tolerantly. "Jesus, said, 'Whatever yuh ast, ast believin', an' yuh'll receive.' Whatever yuh pray fer! But yuh must believe.Yuh must believe that yuh'll git what yer astin' fer when yuh pray."

Jeremy listened carefully. He felt a deepening resolve to try the power of prayer.

The lady who had lost the quarter and cooked the squash raised a question. "Brother Flancher, don't you think that a preacher ought tuh be thankful fer somebody a-fixin' 'is lunch?"

"Course I do," Flancher replied.

"Well, so do I. But that Brother Wooley, he just come out tuh my place an' set hisse'f down at my table an' et an' et. An' when he finished, he never said a word 'bout my lunch. An' I fixed tomaters an' squash special."

Jeremy ignored what the woman said. He was excited to hear that a person could get whatever he prayed for. But he wondered how one could know if he believed enough.

Flancher continued. "Whatever yuh ast, ast in faith, nothin' doubtin'. That's what th' Bible says. He that wavereth is like a wave uv th' sea," Flancher went on.

"Oh, I believe," said the lady who prayed for the quarter. "I believe ever'thin' in th' Bible."

"Good fer you, Sister," Flancher approved.

"But I got a neighbor that don't. I wish you'd talk tuh her, Brother Flancher. She don't even go tuh church er nothin'."

Flancher shook his head in consternation.

"An' she's got a houseful uv kids too. I uz a-tellin' Ethel Robinson that it's a shame not tuh take them kids tuh church."

"Yes, Sister," agreed Flancher. Then he continued: "But they is somethin' else. Once yuh give yerself completely tuh God, th' most wunnerful things can happen in yer prayer life. All uv yuh saw what happened tuh Brother Haygood th' other night. That uz th' power uv prayer."

Jeremy looked up. He was tempted to ask about Haygood. He wanted to know if he still walked without crutches, and he wanted to know why he had not been to church since he was healed. He started to ask, but when he looked up, Flancher was not looking at him.

"I've seen it happen many times," said Flancher. "God wants yuh tuh have th' power. It's yores fer th' astin'. You can accomplish all thin's through prayer. You can pray an' raise th' sick, an' you can pray, an' do miracles yerse'f." Flancher paused. He stood to his feet.

"Well, I shouldna kep' yuh so long. I know yuh got tuh git home. Are they any questions?"

"Yeah, I got one," said the quarter-loser. "My momma never went tuh church er nothin' all 'er life, an' then on her death bed, she repented an' ast fer a preacher tuh say a prayer fer 'er. An' I've just always wondered if'n she uz saved er not."

"We must trust th' grace uv God, Sister," replied Flancher.

The lady nodded soberly. "Oh, I trust God, but I just wondered if she uz saved er not. My husban' said he didn' think that she wuz. But him an' Momma never did quite see eye tuh eye."

The group rose to leave.

"Now before we go," said Flancher. "I want us tuh pray that God will give yuh th' deeper prayer life."

Jeremy bowed his head as Flancher prayed. He was not listening. He was still thinking of the prospect of praying for a bicycle.

When the prayer ended, Jeremy rose from his seat.

"Son," Flancher said to Jeremy. "Can yuh stay a minute?"

Flancher smiled at Jeremy. "Yer name's Jeremy, ain't it?"

"Yes, Sir."

Flancher paused reflectively. "I uz just a young man about yer age when I obeyed th' Lord, Jeremy."

Jeremy looked up. Flancher was staring into space. "That uz a long time ago," he smiled. "Lotsa changes since then, but I been true tuh th' Lord, an' he has shore been true tuh me. He made me a preacher, an' he has healed lotsa folks through me. An' I still preach th' same truth that I preached when I started out. Yes, Sir. I ain't changed a thin'. I ain't changed a word. Still preach th' same gospel. Maybe yuh'll be a preacher, Jeremy." Flancher slapped him on the back.

"Oh, I donno," stammered Jeremy.

"Well, that's up tuh God. We'll see. But be that as it may, I wantcha tuh remember yer promise tuh God. Yer his now, Boy."

Flancher continued, "Now, Jeremy, afore yuh leave, I wanta give yuh this." Jeremy looked in curiosity at Flancher, who was digging in his pocket. At last he extracted a small, burnished metal cross. It was heavy in Jeremy's hand when he took it.

"I've always had a cross like that un, Jeremy, long as I can remember. Ever since I became a preacher, prob'ly before that. An' I want you to have one, too. When yer troubled, take this cross and hold it in yore hands an' pray, an' yuh'll feel better. Seems like tuh me it makes me more shore that my prayer is gonna be answered."

Jeremy took the cross and turned it over and over in his hands. He looked up at Flancher. "Thankee," he said.

Flancher started to walk away.

"Brother Flancher," Jeremy suddenly addressed Flancher.

"What, Son?"

"I ... Oh, nothin', I guess."

"Don't you worry, Son. Yuh gave yerse'f tuh God tuhnight. You pray in faith, an' see what God can do fer yuh. Pray tuhnight, an' feel th' power. Amen!"

"Yes, Sir. Thankee."

33

OUTSIDE, JEREMY REALIZED THAT EVERYONE ELSE had left, and he was glad. He did not want to have to confront Leland and to explain to him why he had come to church by himself, and especially why he had responded to Flancher. He took out his cross and turned it over in his hands, then placed it in his shirt pocket and began his trip home. It was almost too dark to see.

The thunderstorm had moved far away by now. There were only dim flashes of lightning on the southern horizon, and the thunder and rain had stopped. The effects of the rain could still be felt, however, in the cool damp air, and the world seemed refreshed. To Jeremy, it was as if the world had been washed clean. He held his head high and walked with a firm step, enjoying the heavy tug of his cross in his shirt pocket. He felt very good.

He tried to remember everything that Flancher had said about prayer. He recalled Flancher's saying that Jesus had raised a dead man, and Joshua had prayed and stopped the sun. Prayer is wonderful, he thought. He resolved to look up the stories about prayer that Flancher had preached on.

And Flancher had said that anybody could pray. He had told him that he could pray, and Jeremy believed it. And he would pray. It was a wonderful prospect.

He became aware again of the cross in his pocket, and its weight seemed reassuring. He patted his breast pocket appreciatively. The cross was already becoming one of his prized possessions, but he decided that he would not tell anyone about it, not yet. Not even his mother.

As he walked, he sank more and more into a quiet, almost mystical mood, and the girl of his dreams appeared. She was dressed as always in a white dress, but tonight the dress seemed to be cut lower than before. She joined him in their garden, and she was more beautiful than ever. As she leaned back against a tree, Jeremy saw that a burnished metal cross was nestled in the cleavage of her bosom, and it drew him with a strange power. He bent over her to see it better. Her breasts gently rose and fell. A fragrance, an intoxicating aroma enveloped him, and he felt stronger urges than he had ever felt before.

He broke into a run, leaping over small ponds that the rain had left glinting in the pale light of the moon under a sky laden with white stars.

When he got home, he went straight to his room and prepared for bed, but the last thing he did was to lay his cross upon his Bible. Somehow it seemed the appropriate thing to do.

34

HIS MOTHER WOKE HIM THE NEXT MORNING. "Git up, Jeremy. Tuhday's a workday."

"But it rained las' night. It's too muddy."

"Not accordin' tuh yer paw it ain't, an' I guess he has th' final say."

"Aw, Maw. Ast 'im if he's checked. I know it's too muddy. I saw lotsa water standin' las' night."

"'Spect yuh better ast 'im yerse'f. Now git up 'fore he comes in tuh git ye up," she said as she left the room.

Jeremy rose and dressed and started to leave the room, but he remembered his cross and went back to retrieve it. He picked it up and started to put it in his drawer, then thought better of it and put it in the bib of his overalls. He buttoned the bib pocket, patted it once, and went in to eat. His father was still at the table.

"Shore rained las' night," ventured Jeremy.

No response.

Jeremy was delighted to notice water dripping off the eaves. "Man, just look at that water," he said.

"It'll dry up soon. Eat yer breakfast an' come on," said his father, pushing back his chair from the table and walking out of the room.

Jeremy hated the prospect of work, but in a way, he was relieved. Neither his father nor mother had brought up church. He did not want to have to admit to them that he had responded to Flancher. He sighed, got up from the table, and joined his father outside.

The field was wet, but his father seemed not to notice, and he and Jeremy began their morning work. But Jeremy found himself in a good mood. He began his work energetically. He thought and thought about what he should pray for, but it was a hard decision to make. He had thought about praying for a bicycle, but now he wasn't sure. At one point at midmorning, he thought he had resolved his problem. He decided he would pray to be muscular.

He would pray just before going to bed, and the next morning when he got up, he would notice how thick his arms and legs were, how flat his stomach was. He would pull a gleaming white tee shirt over his muscular shoulders. On the bus, all the kids would notice. He could imagine Opal Jones noticing him.

"Why, Jeremy. Yuh look so differ'nt tuhday. Yuh look so strong."

Jeremy would hardly notice her.

Opal would call to her girlfriends, "Hey, girls. Look at Jeremy. Don't he look fine?"

"He shore does," the girls would chime in. They would get up out of their seats and come down the aisle of the bus. "Come on, Jeremy," they would say. "Come sit with us."

"Why don't yuh sit with me?" Opal would ask, sliding over on the seat of the bus to make room for him. As she slid over, her breasts shifted, and her dress rose above her knees, revealing her shapely legs. She did not pull her dress down.

Now Mona Tyler, the most popular girl in school, appeared in his reverie, standing beside him, stroking his muscular arms. Perhaps she would even insist, "Jeremy, I ud a lot rather go with you than with that awful David White."

Why shouldn't I pray for muscles, Jeremy asked himself? I saw Haygood healed, and if God can heal a crippled man, then I guess he can give me muscles. I could pray for them right now, he thought. Heck, I might have muscles by lunch.

But he didn't pray. A disturbing idea intruded. He had watched Flancher pray and heal people at church, but all these people had been sick. Maybe God only answers prayers for people who are sick. He thought about prayer all day without deciding what to pray for. He was still thinking about prayer when he sat down at the supper table.

"Yer shore quiet," said his mother.

"Yeah, I noticed," said Lem. "He didn' say nothin' all day. Didn' even complain about workin'. Never ast if we uz about thoo fer th' day. Most likely he's just been on another uv them daydreamin' trips uv his."

"What is it, Son?" asked his mother.

"Might be that he's disappointed 'cause I won't let 'im go tuh that church no more," said Lem. Then he addressed Jeremy: "Is that it, Boy?"

"Naw. Ain't nothin' wrong."

"Well, it better not be that church."

"Ain't nothin' wrong," insisted Jeremy. "Can I be excused?"

"Yeah, tuh do yer chores," Lem said.

He stepped outside and whistled for Patches, but there was no response. He whistled again. Still no response. He walked down toward the barn, looking about intently for his dog. He had not seen him all day, and he missed him. Finally, he spied Patches far across the big open field to the north of the house. Jeremy whistled as loud as he could, but the dog was so far away that he did not hear. Then Jeremy shouted at the top of his lungs, but Patches still seemed unaware. He stood and watched the dog. It seemed to Jeremy that Patches was concentrating on something on the ground, and at last Jeremy decided that he would go see what the dog was doing. He looked up at the house to see if his father was watching, and then he headed across the field. As he neared the dog, it became apparent that Patches was chewing on something.

"Hey, Patches, c'mere. Did yuh fin'ly catch a rabbit?"

The dog looked up, wagged his tail in recognition, and then returned his attention to the object on the ground. Now Jeremy was almost beside the dog, close enough to see that Patches was not eating a rabbit. He was chewing on the woolly leg of a sheep!

"What th' hell er you a-doin'?" he yelled. He rushed toward the dog, and Patches sprang back and then stretched flat, his stomach pressed to the ground, his ears laid back, wagging his tail rapidly. Jeremy reached down and picked up the foreleg. He swung it viciously at the dog, and Patches yelped and jumped back. He threw the foreleg at Patches, who slunk away to one side and then sat down on his haunches, closely watching Jeremy. The dog dipped his head and licked his chops with exaggerated motions.

Slowly, the boy gained control of himself. "What have yuh done?"

The softened tone of the boy's voice prompted Patches to wag his tail more vigorously, but he still kept his distance. Jeremy walked over and picked up the leg again.

He sat down and continued to look at the leg. It was dry and dusty; the wool had begun to disintegrate, and slowly Jeremy realized that the sheep from which this leg had come must have been dead for a long time. Patches had only found the carcass of a dead sheep somewhere and had picked up the leg. Jeremy looked carefully at the leg. There certainly was no blood on it.

"Hey, Patches, c'mere."

Patches moved nearer, grovelling on the ground. Jeremy reached out and took Patches' head in his hands and pulled the dog to him. The dog tried to roll over on his back. His ears were laid back, the whites of his eyes showed, and he licked Jeremy's hand wildly. Jeremy looked at the dog's mouth carefully. No sign of blood. He hugged the dog. Patches squirmed and licked his face. "Oh, Patches. You ain't never killed nothin." Jeremy rocked back and forth, hugging the dog closely. "Yer a good dawg."

At last, Jeremy pushed the dog away. "Now lissen, Patches, you must leave them ole sheep alone. Don't you never bother them sheep. Don't yuh even chase 'em. Now, you come on home with me."

Jeremy reached down, picked up the foreleg, and hurled it as far as he could into the field, and then he hurried to the barn and finished his chores. His mother and father were already in bed when he came into the house.

As he was undressing for bed, his cross fell out of his pocket and to the floor. He picked it up and rubbed it gently. Then he placed it on his dresser. The cross reminded him of his resolution to pray for something, though he realized that he still had not made up his mind about prayer. He wished he could talk to someone.

35

HIS MOTHER WOKE HIM THE NEXT MORNING as usual and then went back into the kitchen. He lay still for a few minutes, enjoying his bed as long as he could, and then he sat bolt upright. He had left his cross out on the dresser the night before. What if his mother had seen it? He didn't expect her to be angry, but she might be curious—and she might tell his father about it, and he was not sure how his father would react to it. He got up and went over to his dresser. The cross lay where he had left it the night before, but he could not be sure that this mother had not seen it.

His father had already left the breakfast table, and if his mother had seen the cross, she gave no indication of it. Jeremy began to feel better. He was already turning his attention to what he perceived to be his central problem—what to pray for. He would not pray for a bicycle, and neither would he pray for muscles. Somehow, he wanted the first prayer to be just right.

He got up from the breakfast table and walked to the outhouse. He had forgotten to close the catalog after he had been looking at the lingerie section, and somebody had torn out the best pages. Now that he had made a commitment to Flancher, would he have to give up his experiences in the privy? He rose from the seat, quickly checked it for spiders, and walked out into the morning sun.

It was about mid-afternoon when his inspiration came. He and his father were working close to the dirt road that formed the western boundary of the farm when a shiny car came tearing down the road, leaving a cloud of dust. He recognized the car and the driver. It was David White's father in his new car. Lem stopped work and watched the car go by. "Damn," he said. "Shore would be neat tuh have one uv them suckers."

"You like that car, Paw?" asked Jeremy.

"Hell, yes. That there machine is some expensive, but it shore is worth it, ever' cent. Man, if I had one uv them thin's, I ud love tuh drive up at Ayers Store in it. Damnation! I guess I'd raise some attention in a car like that. But ain't no use a-dreamin'; I'll never have one uv them. It ain't like yuh can just pray fer one uv them cars."

Pray for a car like that. That was what his father had said. Why not? Immediately, Jeremy was caught up in the idea. Why not? Think how his father would feel, how the family would ride in style. Why not? Jeremy watched the car as far as he could see it, and when he went back to work, he had begun to formulate an idea. It was simple. He would pray for a new car. "It oughtta git God's attention, I guess," he said aloud.

"Wha'd you say, Son?"

"Nothin'. I uz just a-talkin' tuh myself."

His father looked at him for a moment. Then he laughed.

The idea would not go away. In his mind, he could imagine his father's surprise. He began to dream of how he would present the car to his father. It would be best, Jeremy decided, if the new car arrived late in the afternoon, after he and his father had arrived home from work. Perhaps the car would come while Lem was in the house. Jeremy realized that just how the car would be delivered was not yet worked out, but he thought that could be left to God. Once it came, however, he would be the first to see it as it sat gleaming at the front gate of the yard. After admiring it for a bit, he would go into the house and call his father outside.

"Hey, Paw, come out here. They's somethin' I wanta show yuh."

His father would probably complain about "bein' dragged outside," but he would come, and there the car would be.

"Whatta yuh think uv that?" Jeremy would ask.

He could hear Lem's response. "What in th' worl'?"

"It's a new car, Paw."

"Whur'd it come from?"

"I prayed fer it."

"What?"

"I prayed fer it, just like Brother Flancher said, an' it worked. Here she is." Jeremy could imagine how excited his father would be.

Lem would walk around the car. Perhaps he would kick a tire speculatively. "My God. It shore is a new car."

"Yep. I prayed fer it, an' I got it, too."

His mother would come outside and join them. "Oh," she would say. "It's jus' too wunnerful fer words. A new car. Oh. Lem, I wanted one uv them fer so long. Whur'd it come from?"

Lem would look at Jeremy. He would say, "Why, I guess yuh better ast Jeremy here that question."

She would cast an adoring glance upon Jeremy. "You got it, Son? How'd you do that?"

Jeremy would swell with pride. "I prayed fer it."

"You prayed fer it?"

"Yep."

And then Lem would say, "Well, Jeremy, I guess I uz wrong about church."

His mother would smile broadly. "I'm so proud of you, Jeremy."

Then Jeremy had a thought. Hey, if Paw had a new car, I could ride to school in it. Perhaps Paw would even let me drive it to school. What a thrilling prospect! To drive a new car. He might even ask Mona Tyler for a date.

They would go for a ride. Jeremy would drive, sensing how well the car performed. Occasionally, he would say something clever, and Mona would laugh and tell him what a smart boy he was and how glad she was that he had asked her out. In his dream, they would stop beside a garden, a full moon overhead, and Mona would get out of the car in her long white dress. They would stand close together in the garden, Mona leaning back on a tree, and Jeremy, leaning over her, would discover that she wore a burnished metal cross on her breast. "Say, that's a fine cross," he would say.

"Do yuh like it?" she would ask with a smile.

"Yeah."

"Well, why don't yuh look at it closer?" Even in his dream his throat constricted, his body tingled.

"Yuh can touch it if yuh like," Mona would say huskily.

Jeremy would reach out for the cross, and touching Mona's skin would electrify his whole body.

"Jeremy, what th' hell er yuh a-doin'? Yer off on th' wrong row, an' yer way behin'." His father's voice shocked him. Jeremy had to reach down and adjust his trousers.

36

JEREMY WAS EMBARRASSED TO SEE HOW FAR BEHIND HE WAS, but the idea of praying for a car lingered. Praying for a car was much better than praying for a bicycle. It seemed much more appropriate to pray for some significant gift. At last, he couldn't control himself. "Paw, how'd yuh like tuh have a new car like Mr. White?"

"Huh?"

"I said, how'd yuh like tuh have a new car?"

"Well, fine, uv course," his father said.

"No, I mean it. Wouldn' yuh like tuh have a new car?"

His father stopped and directed his full attention to Jeremy. "Now ain't that a silly question? A new car! A new damn car! Yes, an' how 'bout throwin' in a new house, too?"

"No, Paw. I'm serious."

"I don't doubt yer serious, Son, but yer a fool first. Now what is this nonsense about a new car?"

"I can git one."

"Well, now that's nice. That's wunnerful. And pray tell how?"

Jeremy thought about his father's question for a moment. Now that he had brought up the car, he wasn't sure that it had been a wise thing to do. "Aw, nothin', I guess."

"Nothin' is right, an' nothin' is how much sense yuh've got fer thinkin' uv a new car. I guess that nex' time yuh'll be astin' me if I heard that yuh've been made king uv Sweden. Don't be so damn stupid, Boy."

Jeremy was stung. "All I got tuh do is pray fer it."

Immediately he wished he had not spoken, for his father stopped in his tracks, turned slowly, and looked fully upon Jeremy.

"Wha'd you say?"

"Nothin'." Jeremy feverishly began clipping maize heads.

"Boy, I ast yuh a question. Wha'd yuh say?"

"Nothin'." Jeremy ducked his head over his work.

Lem seized his arm. "You answer me, Boy, er I'll tear yuh up right here in this fiel'." He seized Jeremy and jerked the boy toward him. He retained his grip on Jeremy's arm, and he began to strip his belt out of its loops. "Now, wha'd you say?"

"I said I could pray fer it." Jeremy's heart beat wildly.

"That's what I thought yuh said," sighed Lem. He released the boy but kept looking at him. "I'll be damned. I will be damned. Whur th' hell did yuh ever git such a fool idee as that?"

Jeremy pushed his hair back out of his face. He rubbed his aching arm. "Brother Flancher said so. I can pray fer it an' git us a new car, an' I will, too. An' I'll drive it, too."

Lem shook his head. "Boy, are ye plumb damn crazy? You cain't pray fer no new car. An' what if yuh did, an' what if yuh got it—whur would we keep some fancy new car? Ain't no room in th' barn fer it. It ud just rust down like our ole car's done. An' as fer you drivin' it, why, you couldn' drive no new car if yuh had one. Yuh don't know how. An' yuh ain't got no license. An' even if yuh had a license, I shore as hell wouldn' let yuh drive a car if we had one. Likely yuh'd just drift off intuh one uv yer damn daydreams an' run off in a ditch an' ruin th' car, an' kill somebody tuh boot." Lem flexed his hands.

"Now, Boy, you lissen tuh me real good." Lem leaned down into Jeremy's face. He reached for Jeremy's arm again, but Jeremy drew back. "I only intend tuh tell yuh this once, an' yuh better hear it, 'cause I don't wanta hear no more nonsense about some new car. Think! Does Flancher have a new car? I reckin not. And Mutchell? Why, he drives an ole car worse'n mine. Now, if yuh can pray fer a new car, why don't they have new cars? I can tell yuh. Nobody can pray fer a new car an' git it. That's just some Holy Roller nonsense. Jeremy, I work hard fer ever'thin' I got. Now I ain't got much, but what I got, I worked fer, an' I'll tell yuh somethin'—th' only thin' yuh'll ever have is what you work fer. You mark my words. You lissen, Boy. Now, one more time. Git tuh work, an' fergit about prayin'. A new car. My God."

Jeremy thought about what his father had said. Perhaps he had been foolish to think of praying for a new car. He had seen Flancher's car, an old rusted station wagon with one of the back doors wired shut and a right front fender missing. And his father had been right about Mutchell's car. Jeremy had ridden in it the night he and his father had gone with Mutchell on the turkey hunt, and he could remember how the springs in the back seat had stuck through the upholstery, and especially how the foul odor of pigs permeated the car. He despised himself for even thinking of a new car. He fell to work resolving that he would never mention prayer again.

37

AT THE SUPPER TABLE THAT NIGHT, Lem brought up the incident about the car. "Maw, you best git yerse'f some new clothes."

"Why, what er yuh a-sayin', Lem?" she asked. She smoothed the front of her dress.

"Why, we're gonna start a-ridin' in style, an' we might as well dress th' part."

"I don't unnerstan'…"

"It's all true. Jeremy tole me all about it out in th' fiel' tuhday. He's gonna git us a new car, ain'tcha, Jeremy?"

"What? A new car?" Olga was confused.

"Yeah, he's gonna pray an' git us one. Ain't that right, Boy?"

Jeremy refused to look up from his plate, but he could feel his mother's eyes focused on him. His face burned hotly.

"Yep, that's our boy. He don't need tuh work like normal folks. He just prays an' gits a new car." Lem paused for a bite of food. "Yuh see, Olga, we're jus' plumb damn lucky tuh have a son like this here boy. Hey, Jeremy, what kind?" Lem put down his spoon. "How 'bout a new Buick? I like them new Fords, too."

Olga had stopped eating. "Lem, what's this all about?" She looked first at Lem, and then at Jeremy.

"Why, ast him. This is all new stuff he jus' learned down tuh that church. He's done learned how tuh pray fer cars. One uv them fancy ones like ole man White bought. You seen that car, haven't yuh? Why, that thin' is slick as a button. An' Jeremy's gonna git us one jus' like it. Course we don't have tuh buy ourn; Jeremy is a-gonna pray fer one fer us. I cain't hardly wait fer it myse'f. You have any pref'rence, Maw? Is they a color yuh like best?"

His mother looked at Jeremy. "Oh, Jeremy. It's them Holy Rollers, ain't it? What have they told yuh, Son?"

Jeremy was not eating. He buried his head in his hands and stared at his plate.

"Yeah," said Lem. "It's them Holy Rollers an' this harebrained damn Boy. I tole yuh we shouldna let this boy go off down there, but no, you insisted. Didn' wanta hurt ole lady McMillan's feelin's. Now yuh see what's happened. Hell, if all a man had tuh do tuh git a new car wuz tuh pray, why then ever'body in th' whole damn worl' ud have one."

Jeremy could stand no more. He stood up. "Can I be excused?"

"Not just yet." Jeremy dropped back into his seat. "I already tole yuh this once, but seems yuh don't remember things too good. Yuh ain't a-goin' tuh that church no more. Yuh hear that?"

Jeremy did not look up. He did not respond.

"Did you hear me?"

"Yes, Sir."

"Now go do yer chores, an' by God, you better do 'em yerse'f. Don't be a-prayin fer 'em tuh git done, 'cause if they ain't done right, I ain't goin' lookin' fer no Holy Spirit tuh whip. I know exactly whur tuh look. I'll take a ploughline tuh yuh."

Jeremy looked up, frightened. He remembered Lem taking off his belt in the field. "No, Sir. I'll do 'em. An' I'll do 'em all my own se'f."

Outside, Jeremy was met by Patches, jumping up on him and nipping his hand. "C'mon, dawg," he said, patting the dog. He continued to the barn, went inside and sat down in disgust on a bale of hay. What a fool I've been, he thought. Of course no one ever prayed for a new car. Why hadn't I thought of that? He thought again of Mutchell and Flancher. Either they had never prayed for new cars, or they had prayed for them and not received them. And now, he said to himself, Maw and Paw both think I'm a fool.

He reached into his pocket, took out his cross, and sat looking at it. He did not view it now as he had the night Flancher gave it to him. When Flancher first gave it to him, it had symbolized power, some kind of link with God. As he looked at it now, the cross seemed almost to mock him. Tears burned his eyes, and he pitched the cross away from him. He sat looking at it for a long time; then he walked over and picked it up. Still, he stared at it, turning it over in his hands. At last, in frustration, he hurled it to the ground. He kicked at it awkwardly.

After he had finished his chores, he entered his room. He noticed his Bible lying on the dresser but did not pick it up. He went straight to bed.

38

THE NEXT EVENING, JEREMY SAT ON HIS BED, his eyes roving about the room, mildly conscious of boredom. His eyes came back to the Bible. He picked it up, opened it at the front page, and as he began to leaf through it, he came upon a page that he had seen before but had forgotten about—a page listing verses in the Bible that had to do with specific topics. He idly scanned the page, and then he discovered a bold-faced heading: "Prayer."

Even with the verses identified, Jeremy had difficulty finding them because he was not that familiar with the Bible, but he kept trying. The first verse he looked for was Matthew 7:7. He flipped through his Bible for several minutes, finally found the book of Matthew, and read: "Ask and it will be given to you; seek, and you will find. Knock, and it will be opened to you." He grew excited. This is what Flancher preached about, he said to himself. He eagerly hunted down another verse, Mark 21:22. There he read: "And whatever you ask in prayer you will receive if you ask in faith." Now Jeremy had come almost full circle. He began to see prayer in a different light. Flancher was right. The Bible said the same thing that he had said. Jeremy re-read the passage in Mark: "And whatever you ask in prayer you will receive if you ask in faith." Ask in faith, he repeated. Flancher had said that also. And yet the idea was still hard for Jeremy. Maybe what had happened the day before, when he had decided to pray for a new car, had happened because he had not had enough faith. Maybe I lack faith. But how much faith is enough?

He reached into his bib pocket for his cross but could not find it. He searched his other pockets to no avail. He stood up and searched all his pockets again. He looked on his dresser and under his pillow, but he couldn't find it. Then he remembered throwing it on the ground in the barn. *I need to go get it*, he thought, but he abandoned the idea. He didn't want to wake up his parents.

39

AS SOON AS HIS MOTHER WOKE HIM THE NEXT MORNING, before he ate breakfast, he hurried to the barn to search for his cross. He found it on the ground where he had thrown it. He picked it up, dusted it off, and put it away in his pocket. As he walked back to the house, he once more experienced a sense of well-being in the weight of the cross in the bib pocket of his overalls.

As Jeremy worked beside his father that week, he was constantly devising a plan of what to pray for. One thing was certain. He would not include his father in his plans, and he wouldn't pray for a new car. But Flancher had said to pray in faith, and the Bible said the same thing. Paw must be wrong, thought Jeremy. Still, he had to admit that praying for a car did not seem to be a good idea. But he would pray for something.

Jeremy had hoped to go to church during the week, but that had not worked out. Now he hoped to go on Sunday morning, but his father announced plans to move the sheep from one pasture to another on that day, and as he explained to Jeremy, Sunday morning was the only free time for such a task. "We gotta move 'em," he explained. "They'll eat th' grass down tuh nuthin' if we leave 'em too long in one field. Besides, I wanta see if that dawg has been after 'em ag'in. We might even slip up on that dawg an' catch 'im after th' sheep."

His father's plans disappointed Jeremy on two counts: first, he still held to dim hopes of getting to go to church that day, and second, he dreaded working with the sheep. As he walked beside Lem that morning, hatless, shirtless and barefoot, he thought about how much dust the sheep would raise. We'll probably find another sheep lying down that can't get up, and we'll have to wrestle around with her. And she will stink, and her wool will be full of grass burs.

"Paw," Jeremy asked, "have yuh seen any stray dawgs yet?"

"Yestiddy I seen some uv th' sheep a-runnin', but I couldn' figger out why they wuz. May uv been a dawg after 'em."

"I hope we find that dawg tuhday. I bet we could chase 'im plumb offa this place if we do find 'im, an' he wouldn' ever come back."

"Well, we might chase 'im off, but that don't mean nothin'."

"You ever seen a sheep-killin' dawg, Paw?"

"Oh, sev'ral years ago they uz one on this place. I found 'im one day. He had a sheep down, a-tearin' at its throat. That's how these dawgs do. Like I told yuh, they ain't inter'sted in eatin' th' sheep. They just tear out its throat."

"Wha'd yuh do, Paw?"

"I killed that bastard." Lem flexed his hands.

When Jeremy and Lem found the sheep, they were all lying down in the hot August sun. They circled them in order to get on the other side and to drive them back toward their new pasture and then moved toward them. The sheep scrambled to their feet, raising an acrid cloud of dust. Jeremy sneezed violently. Once a sense of direction was established, however, the sheep moved along easily. Occasionally some of the younger, friskier sheep tried to break away, but they always returned to the flock.

Jeremy realized, however, that the real problem was yet to come. The sheep were to be driven into a field that was fenced and could only be entered by a single narrow gate. He had driven sheep into this field before, and he could remember how the sheep would walk right up to the gate, and then turn and run away, scattering in confusion. Lem had explained to Jeremy: "Th' trick is tuh git one uv these bastards tuh go in, an' then nothin'll stop ever'one uv 'em frum a-goin' thoo that gate."

They continued to drive the sheep. "Paw," said Jeremy. I bet we have trouble a-gittin' these sheep tuh go thoo that gate."

"Yer prob'ly right, Son," replied Lem. "I tried tuh git Mr. Soules tuh buy a bellwether, but he don't see no use in it."

"What's a bellwether, Paw?"

"It's a goat er a sheep that's been trained tuh go through gates. When yuh git ready tuh move sheep through a gate, yuh just put that there bellwether in front, an' when he goes thoo th' gate, alla th' damn sheep will foller 'im er die tryin'. But we ain't got no bellwether, so we might as well git ready tuh force these damn sheep thoo th' gate however we can."

At last the sheep reached the gate, and just as Jeremy had expected, when the sheep neared it, they turned aside in a wild scramble. Jeremy had to run around them and drive them back toward the gate, but once again confronting the gate, the sheep turned aside. He ran after them again in exasperation. "Git back in there, you bitches," he shouted.

"Wait a minute, Son," called his father. "Let 'em go. Cain't yuh see yer just a-runnin' 'em off? Let th' bastards go. We'll git 'em in a minute."

Finally, he said, "Okay, come on. They're halfway back tuh th' other fiel' by now. Let's go git 'em."

"Kin we git a drink first, Paw?"

"That's a good idee. May as well let them damn sheep settle down fer a little bit, an' my throat's all dry after alla that dust."

Lem and Jeremy turned toward the nearby stock tank, the family's water supply. There they drank their fill of water, lying flat on their stomachs, dipping their lips into the shallow, tepid water. Jeremy plunged his head under the water, and then splashed water all over his upper body. "Shore would like tuh go swimmin'," he said wistfully.

Lem ignored the remark, and the two of them started in the direction of the sheep again. By now the sheep had moved across the pasture, back toward their original position.

"Now, Jeremy, you go aroun' behin' 'em, and work 'em this way real easy."

"Okay, Paw."

"An' you keep an eye out fer any dawgs."

Jeremy began a wide circle to come up behind the sheep and was about to close in on them when he saw the bloated sheep lying on its side on the ground, its legs sticking out at an awkward angle. For an instant he thought it might be a sheep like the old ewe he and his father had found and had helped up. Then he saw the blood, and he knew that the sheep was dead.

"Paw! Paw! C'mere! Here's a dead sheep!"

His father, still on the other side of the flock, came directly toward him, scattering the sheep as he waded through them. "Whur, Son?"

"Here, Paw! Here by this bush."

Lem joined Jeremy, and they stood looking at the body of the sheep. Large, blue-green blowflies swarmed around its mouth and nose. They crawled over the blood clotted in its neck wool and around a torn gash in its neck. A pool of blood, black and crusted now, had spread on the ground. Lem knelt for a closer look. He picked up a handful of dirt and threw it down in disgust.

Lem stood and looked around, as if he hoped to see the sheep-killing dog. "Another un," he said bitterly. "God, I wish I could fin' that dawg fer just a minute." He took off his hat and slapped his leg with it. "Well, come on, Boy. We got tuh git them sheep."

Once again Jeremy and Lem drove the sheep across the pasture toward the field and the narrow gate. The sheep approached the gate. For an instant they milled about, and some of the leaders seemed about to make another break. Then one of the sheep darted through the gate, and all the others rushed forward, pushing and shoving, climbing over each other, raising a cloud of dust. Jeremy watched the sheep crowd through the gate. He sneezed, and then sneezed again.

But he sighed with relief to see the sheep go into the field. He knew that they would be kept there grazing for some time, and while they were there, he would not have to deal with them.

40

THROUGHOUT LUNCH JEREMY HAD BEEN FORMULATING A PLAN, and now he was sure what to do. He remembered that when Lem had first brought Patches home with him, he had been leading the dog on a leash. Jeremy had removed the leash and put it in the barn. He entered the barn now, walked over to a large bin, and rummaged around among tools and pieces of harness until he found the leash. He wrapped it around his arm and went outside to call his dog. "Here, Patches. C'mere!"

The dog trotted to him, and Jeremy knelt and secured the leash around the dog's neck. Then he led him back toward the house until he reached the fence. There, he tied the loose end of the leash to one of the fence posts. Jeremy dropped to his knees and took the dog in his arms. "I know yuh don't like this bein' tied up, but I'll see that yuh git lots uv food an' water. Don't yuh worry none about that." Jeremy hugged Patches close, and the dog squirmed and licked the boy's face. "It's okay. I luv yuh, dawg, but it's gotta be this way fer now."

He rose and started toward the house. Patches struggled against the leash, alternately barking and whining, but Jeremy wouldn't look at him. He entered the house and went in search of his mother. He found her sitting in the living room.

"Maw, I think I fin'ly solved a problem fer me."

"Oh, how's that?"

"Well, we found another sheep that some dawg had killed, but jus' now I tied Patches up so he cain't chase no sheep. So if another sheep is killed any time soon, Paw will be able tuh see that Patches didn' do it."

"Now, Jeremy, do yuh really think that yer paw would kill Patches if he found out he had killed a sheep?"

Jeremy remembered the time he had watched Lem beat the horse to its knees. In his mind's eye, he still could see the bloody eyeball hanging on the horse's cheek. He said, "Yeah, I do."

41

AS THE EVENING APPROACHED, Jeremy made up his mind that he was going to ask permission to go to church. He went into the room where his mother and Lem were sitting and sat on the floor between them. Country music played on the battery-operated radio.

"Can I go tuh church tuhnight?" he asked.

"I figgered that uz a-comin'," said his father. "I just wondered how long it ud be before yuh ast us that question."

Jeremy's mother did not look up from her sewing.

Jeremy sat quietly. He did not look at his father. Then he said, "Well, can I?"

"Now, Boy, I thought our talk earlier had got some uv that nonsense outta yuh. Whatcha want tuh go tuhnight fer? Yuh wanta git Flancher tuh he'p yuh pray fer that car?"

Jeremy remained silent.

"You stay here. I wantcha tuh he'p me start th' ole car. I don't know what's wrong with it. I hope it's just the batt'ry. If they is somethin' wrong with th' engine, I don't know what we'll do fer a car, less you hurry up an' pray fer a new car fer us. How you comin' on that project, Boy? You 'bout got us a new car? I shore wish yuh'd hurry up. A car shouldn' be no problem fer folks like Flancher. Er maybe yuh could git Mutchell tuh he'p yuh." Lem laughed. "Now, there'd be a good un fer yuh. Yeah. Git ole Mutchell." Lem sobered. "Hell, Mutchell ain't had a prayer answered in no tellin' how long. Fact is, I doubt if he ever got one answered. Likely all he'd ever pray fer is some way tuh make some money offa some honest folks, or some chance tuh do some illegal huntin' er fishin', an' I don't reckin th' Lord hears prayers like that. No, you quit worryin' about church. I need you an' yer mother tuh help me start th'car."

The family trooped out onto the rock sidewalk and through the yard gate, past the tied Patches, who strained against his leash. Jeremy stopped momentarily to stroke Patches' back.

Starting the car proved not to be difficult after all. Jeremy and his mother pushed the car while Lem jerked the car into gear. Smoke boiled ominously out from under the hood, but the car continued to run. Keeping the engine running, Lem got out of the car and announced: "Well, that's good. It started an' it's a-runnin'. So it's prob'ly just th' batt'ry. While I got it a-runnin', I'm a-gonna take it over tuh Bill Milburn's place. He's got a batt'ry charger, an' I gotta git th' batt'ry charged, so th' car'll start in th' mornin'. Maybe th' charge will last fer a while. Batt'ries er expensive, an' I ain't got no money fer one." And with this announcement, he headed for the house.

When Lem came out of the house, he seemed in good spirits. "Shore glad tuh git that car started. If it had been th' engine, no tellin' what it mighta cost. I can git th' batt'ry charged fer free, an' maybe Jeremy'll come up with a new car er at least a new batt'ry 'fore long."

Seeing his father's mood, Jeremy sensed an opportunity and brought up church again. "Paw, can I go tuh church now? Th' car's started."

Lem was climbing into the car. He stopped. "Boy, is church all yuh ever think uv? Why don't yuh wanta go swimmin' er fishin' er wanta go chasin' after some little split-tailed gal like other boys do? I swear, I never thought that I'd see th' day when a boy uv mine wuz such a religious nut."

"Why don't yuh let th' boy go this time, Lem? He hepped with th' car."

Jeremy looked at his mother. Encouraged, he continued, "Please, Paw. I ain't been in a long time now."

Lem climbed into the car and slammed the door viciously. "Oh, what th' hell. All right." Lem slammed his hands down on the steering wheel. "Git on down there, an' join in with them damn Holy Rollers. But don't expect me tuh take yuh. It's late, an' likely they've already started, but I guess they'll still be plenty uv whoopin' an' hollerin' goin' on when you git there. Maybe yuh'll git th' Holy Spirit er th' holy laugh er whatever nonsense you been a-talkin' about." He put the car in gear and pulled away. Then he stopped the car, stuck his head out of the window and said, "An' see if Flancher can he'p yuh pray fer that new car." He started to drive off, then stopped again. "An' see if yuh can git one uv them new Buicks, like ole man White has got. An' you be damn shore tuh tell 'im that we don't want no used car." He laughed loudly. Then he turned again toward Jeremy. "Tell 'im that I prefer a bright red un." Then he turned his attention to the road.

Turning to his mother, Jeremy said, "Maw, Paw said that I can go."

"I heard him, Jeremy, but you go clean up first."

"Aw, Maw. Paw's done said I can go. Lemme go now."

"Oohh, Jeremy, you frustrate me so. Go ahead on, but first at least you put on a clean shirt. I ain't gonna have yuh goin' down there lookin' like some white trash."

"Okay, Maw, I will," shouted Jeremy as he rushed into the house and into his room to select a clean shirt. He was in excellent spirits.

42

JEREMY QUICKLY SELECTED A CLEAN SHIRT, and he was on his way, but as he headed to church he had many thoughts. He wondered if Haygood would be there. What would he say to Flancher if he got an opportunity to talk to him? Then he reached into his pocket and felt his cross. "I bet if I show 'im this cross, he'll remember me," he said aloud. He took the cross out of his pocket and looked at it. He viewed it now with mixed feelings. He had had it for some time, and he did not see any advantage in it as yet. His attempts at prayer had been frustrating. He had thought about praying for a car, but that seemed foolish now. Perhaps the preacher could explain all the mystery of prayer. Jeremy respectfully slipped his cross back into his pocket.

He was nearing the church as he put away his cross. Now he looked up expectantly. Something was wrong! There were no cars in the parking lot, and the building was deserted. He stopped and looked about. No sign of anyone coming or going. Had he come too late? Were services already over? Surely not. The sun still hovered just above the horizon. What could have happened? He stood still on the churchyard, wondering what to do.

"Well, maybe they's somebody in th' buildin'," he mused aloud. He started toward the church building and walked up onto the small porch before the main door. There was still sufficient light to see into the building, to see that there was not a soul there. He reached for the doorknob. It turned easily in his hand, and the door swung open. He had never been in an empty church building before. Now there was only the drone of a wasp high up in the ceiling. He stepped inside and was surprised by the sound of his own bare feet. He stopped, and all sound stopped.

He stood still a long time, surveying the empty building. The last rays of sunlight cast long shadows of the trees outside across the floor.

He looked up at the podium. He could picture Flancher moving about on the speaker's platform, jabbing his finger in the air, a large, gleaming white handkerchief clasped in his hand. It was as if he could hear Flancher saying, "Oh, sinner, hear me! Escape th' fires uv hell."

As he stood there, he could remember previous nights here in this building—the large, enthusiastic audiences, the people singing and shouting, raising amens to heaven. The silence just did not seem right. He remembered the night when a young lady had come forward, laughing and crying at the same time, stepping over the backs of the seats with a triumphant shout as she made her way to Flancher. He could still see her, clearing the last bench and leaping forward into Flancher's arms, knocking him back against the podium. How she had clung to him, wrapping one arm around his waist while with the other she tried to tug the hem of her skirt below her knees. How at last she had slumped at his feet and remained there, hugging his knees as he had stroked her head.

He started timidly down the deserted aisle. Somehow he felt like an intruder in the quiet, empty building. A board squeaked under his foot, and he jumped involuntarily. As he neared the front of the building, an increasing weight descended upon him, pressing upon him. His chest constricted. A pale light bathed the rostrum and pulpit area. Jeremy pushed back his damp hair. At the front bench, he sat down and rubbed his perspiring hands together. He sat very still.

Maybe, he thought, it makes a difference where a person prays. Yes, it was an inspiration. Now that he thought about it, the only prayers he had ever heard had been prayers in the church. Perhaps trying to pray out in the field or down behind the shed was not appropriate. The idea grew in significance for him. It had been here in the church building that Flancher had prayed for Haygood. Maybe you have to pray in church.

Jeremy decided that here, perhaps, was the place to pray. He took his cross from his pocket and held it in both hands, very close to his face. He found himself slipping to his knees, his eyes fixed upon the pulpit.

"Who th' hell is in here?" a loud voice boomed, and all at once the lights of the building came on. Jeremy sprang guiltily to his feet and whirled to face the intruder. It was Jacob Mutchell.

"Well, hey, Boy. What th' hell uz you a-doin' on the floor? An' fer that matter, what er yuh a-doin' here in th' church when they ain't nobody here? This is private proppity, don't yuh know that? You can go tuh jail fer trespassin' in a church, same as anywhur else. What th' hell do yuh want?"

"Nothin'." Jeremy cast about for something to say. "I come tuh see Mr. Haygood," he blurted.

"Th' hell yuh did. Who's Haygood?"

Jeremy was surprised. "Why, he's th' man that Brother Flancher healed."

"Flancher healed a lot uv people."

"Mr. Haygood uz th' one with th' crutches, an' after Brother Flancher healed 'im, he thoo 'em away."

"Oh, yeah. That ole guy. Well, no tellin' whur he is at now. He ain't been back tuh church since he got healed. An' he shore ain't here tuhnight." Mutchell stared at Jeremy. "Ain't I seen you before?"

"I'm Jeremy."

"Oh, yeah, that's whur I seen yuh. I thought I recognized yuh. Yer Lem Stroop's boy. Well, they ain't no church. Th' meetin's over. An' you damn shore ain't got no bizness in this here church."

"I didn' know."

"Yuh didn' know. Why, it uz announced this mornin'. I made th' 'nouncement my own se'f. I always make th' 'nouncements."

"I wuzn't here this mornin'."

"Well, there yuh go. That's what yuh git fer not comin' tuh church like yuh should. Yuh oughtta come tuh church when they's a service, not come pussyfootin' aroun' when they ain't no church. Whur wuz yuh this mornin'?"

"I had tuh he'p my Paw move th' sheep."

"Hell, that ain't no excuse. Yuh ain't supposed tuh work on Sunday, an' neither is yer paw. An' he knows better, too. He knows that he ain't supposed tuh make you work thataway. It's one uv th' commandments. Remember th' Sabbath. Hell, don't you know that?"

"You an' yer paw is a-screwin' up bad, Boy." Mutchell stared hard at Jeremy. "Prob'ly both goin' straight tuh hell." He had moved even closer to Jeremy by now, and Jeremy could see his scrubby beard. The long hair on the left side of his head that was normally combed over his head to cover his baldness had slipped down across his left ear. His stomach bulged against his overalls. "But th' meetin's over. Flancher had to leave right after th' services this mornin'."

"He's gone?"

"Why, I jus' tole yuh he is. He's been gone since lunch tuhday. Why?" Mutchell watched Jeremy closely.

Jeremy ignored Mutchell's question. "Whur'd he go?"

"Clean tuh Oklahoma. Gonna hold a meetin' there, I think. Why? You plannin' tuh foller 'im? Whatta yuh wanta see 'im fer?"

"I just wanted tuh talk tuh 'im." Jeremy studied his naked toes as he flexed them on the floor.

"Brother Flancher's a busy man. He's got meetin's all over," said Mutchell. Then he looked closely at Jeremy. "You shore that's why yuh come tuh this church? Just tuh see Flancher. Why didn' yuh come some other time? Why wait till th' meetin's over? I still think yuh come in here a-plannin' tuh steal somethin'."

"I just wanted tuh see 'im." Jeremy pushed back his hair.

Mutchell turned and looked out the windows on the right side of the building. "I uz up at th' house, an' I thought I saw somebody come in here, an' I rushed right over here tuh see what uz a-goin' on, an' I guess it uz a good thing that I did. Caught yuh red-handed. I just live a piece from here, so I could see yuh purty good. I couldn' tell fer sure who yuh wuz, but I figgered yuh wuzn't up tuh no good, so I come tuh check. Started tuh bring my gun." He turned back to face Jeremy. "But Flancher's gone, Boy. He won't be back fer no tellin' how long. Maybe never." He stared at Jeremy. "Why did yuh want tuh see 'im?"

"I just wanted tuh talk tuh 'im." Jeremy did not look at Mutchell.

"Well, maybe yuh did, an' maybe yuh didn't. I oughtta take yuh tuh th' sherf, but yer Lem's boy, so I'm a-gonna let yuh go this time. But you better not let me catch yuh a-foolin' aroun' here ag'in, yuh hear me? Now you git home. It's a-gittin' late, an' th' meetin's over."

Jeremy hurried past Mutchell and headed for the door. Outside, he fled into the peaceful night. He ran all the way home.

In bed at home, he tossed restlessly. There were so many things he did not understand. That Mutchell had accused him of trying to steal something from the church made him angry. His attempt to pray in the church frustrated him.

Jeremy flopped over in bed and pounded his pillow. "Ever' time I try tuh pray, somethin' goes wrong. Ever' time! It ain't no use. Ain't nothin' to it. That ole cross ain't no good, neither. It ain't no use."

But even as Jeremy was thinking these things, in the back of his mind a thought persisted: Haygood had been healed. He had watched that man throw away his crutches, and he had seen him walk down the aisle. He had stood at the end of the bench and watched Haygood pass by.

Flancher had healed Haygood. "I know he did," Jeremy muttered to himself. No question. Flancher had healed him. Prayer had worked. "Don't I have enough faith? Ain't I committed enough?" He turned over again, and finally dropped into a troubled sleep.

43

THE NEXT MORNING AT BREAKFAST, JEREMY SAT EATING SLOWLY.

"Maw, do you an' Paw pray?"

"Why, shore."

"An' are yer prayers always answered?"

"Well, I guess so."

"What do yuh pray fer?"

"Lots uv things, I guess."

"Well, name one."

"What are you a-gittin' at?"

There was silence. His mother smoothed her apron.

"Do you ever pray anywhere except th' church?"

"Why, uv course. What are yuh astin'?"

"I jus' thought maybe yuh had tuh pray at th' church."

"Well, I don't know whur yuh ever got such an idee, Jeremy. Yuh can pray anywhur." "Whur do you an' Paw mostly pray?"

"Anywhur, I guess."

Jeremy looked at his mother. "An' it don't matter whur? Yer prayer is always answered?"

"Yeah. I guess so." She turned her coffee cup in her hands. She did not look at Jeremy. "Jeremy, I swear yuh can ask so many fool questions."

Jeremy persisted. "Is some things easier tuh pray fer than others? Tell me some things yuh pray fer."

His mother looked closely at Jeremy. The conversation had taken a new turn for her. "What is it, Jeremy?" she asked softly.

Jeremy sighed deeply. "I been a-tryin' tuh think uv somethin' tuh pray fer, an' I cain't do it."

"Jeremy. There's lotsa things tuh pray fer. Health an' blessin's."

Jeremy looked at her. "Brother Flancher tole me that I could pray fer stuff, an' I ud git it, but it's so discouragin'. I thought about prayin' fer a car an' fer muscles, but that didn' work out, an' fin'ly I just gave up. I ain't prayed fer nothin' yet." He watched his mother. He was relieved to see that she was not laughing.

His mother responded slowly. "I expect those things yuh just mentioned ud be hard tuh pray fer."

"But th' Bible says tuh ast in faith, an' yuh'll git anythin' yuh ast fer, don't it? I read it myse'f."

"I donno. Them things just seems hard. Maybe God he'ps them that he'p themselves. Yuh might need tuh work fer a car before yuh pray fer it."

"Is God more likely tuh give yuh some thin's than others?"

"Why, yes. Yes. I'm shore that's so. Some thin's is easier than others."

"So, what's some easy thin's?"

"Oh, blessin's, I guess."

Jeremy pressed his question. "What kind uv blessin's?"

"Prayin' fer others, fer other people, is easier. Prayin' fer those you love is easier."

Jeremy had an inspiration. "So, I could pray fer Patches?"

His mother hesitated. "Well, I think so."

She turned her cup in her hands.

The more he thought about it, the better Jeremy liked the idea.

"Jeremy! Jeremy! Git out here, Boy. You plan tuh eat all day?" It was his father.

His mother rose. "Now, go on, Jeremy. Yer father is a-callin' yuh."

Jeremy stood from his chair, hurried around the table and out the door. He felt good about his conversation with his mother. He had a new sense of direction about prayer.

His father met him at the gate. Patches, overjoyed at seeing Jeremy, lunged against his leash and barked excitedly.

"Shut up, dawg," ordered Lem as he walked past the dog. Patches wagged his tail.

Jeremy bent to pat the dog's head as he walked past. "You be a good dawg now," he said gently. Patches strained against the leash and whined.

The morning passed quietly. Church never came up, nor did praying for a car. Jeremy's thoughts were mostly occupied with the night before. He was still embarrassed that Mutchell had found him.

And, he still wondered what had drawn him into the the the church? He shook his head. "Crazy," he said out loud.

"What?" his father asked without looking at him.

"Oh, nothin'. I uz just talkin' tuh myse'f."

"Hmmm. Never learn, do yuh? They uz a time I thought yuh only talked tuh yerse'f when yuh wuz behin' that shed. Now yer likely tuh talk tuh yerse'f any time. Guess yer worse than I thought."

Once or twice that morning, Jeremy tried composing a prayer but quickly gave up. The field just did not seem like the appropriate place.

Jeremy and Lem took their usual lunch break. Jeremy ate hurriedly.

"Son, will yuh slow down?" his mother said.

Still, Jeremy hurried. His plan was to finish eating as quickly as he could, and then to go behind the shed, and there he would pray for his dog. Now he had a new sense of direction.

At last he was finished. "Maw, kin I be excused?" He shifted back on his chair, scraping its legs along the kitchen floor.

"I swear, I ain't never seen yuh in such a hurry."

"Damn kid cain't wait tuh git behin' that shed an' start talkin' tuh hisse'f," his father grumbled. "He uz even talkin' tuh hisse'f ag'in this mornin' out in th' fiel'." Lem watched Jeremy as he moved toward the door. Then he said, "Now, Boy, I better not have tuh come down tuh that shed an' git you."

Jeremy ignored his father and headed for the shed. He hurried down the walk toward the tethered Patches. There, he stopped and took Patches' head in his hands. "Don't yuh worry none, Patches. Ever'thin' is gonna be all right.'

Patches whined and tried to jump up on Jeremy, but the leash restrained him.

"It's okay, dawg. Just a little while. Then yuh'll be loose." Jeremy fell to his knees and hugged his dog. Patches strained to the end of his leash, standing only on his hind legs and whining toward Jeremy. "It's okay, dawg. Just a little while."

Jeremy headed for the shed. He stood still for a minute, trying to decide what to do next. He thought about all the prayers he had heard at church. Almost all of the people who prayed at church knelt when they prayed. Jeremy looked around, and then slowly knelt. The gravel hurt his knees, and he shifted his weight. Still uncomfortable, he scraped a spot clean of gravel and at last found a comfortable stance. Now, what next? What do I say? Most of Flancher's prayers had beeen whispered. At the healing service he had prayed loudly, but Jeremy was not sure that the kinds of prayers Flancher raised at that service were appropriate now. Patches was not sick.

He remembered when he was young, his mother had encouraged him to clasp his hands when he prayed. That had been a long time ago, but Jeremy decided to try it now. "Oh," he said out loud. "I gotta have my cross." He reached into his bib pocket for his cross. It seemed bigger and heavier than he remembered.

How did Flancher begin? He remembered a phrase: "Our heavenly Father, hallowed be thy name." He remembered the woman at church and Flancher talking about the word "hallowed," but he wasn't sure what that meant.

The ground was becoming unbearable to his knees. He hurried his prayer. "God, please lissen tuh me. I ain't astin' fer nothin' fer myse'f. An' I don't keer if I don't git no car er nothin' like that." His throat was so tight, he could hardly speak. "Please, God, Patches is a good dawg. You know that. He ain't never kilt nothin', not even a rabbit, an' he don't wanta kill no sheep."

"You don't hafta do much, God. Just keep Patches away from them ole sheep, an' I aweady got 'im on a leash. If he got a-loose an' chased one, all it ud hafta do is turn aroun' and butt at 'im, an' he ud run away." He shifted his cross in his hands. What to do next? Had he said enough? He started to get up, but then he remembered how Mutchell and Flancher always said "Amen" once they had finished their prayers, so he knelt once again and said, "Amen."

"Jeremy, git up here tuh this house." It was his father.

Jeremy quickly replaced his cross in the bib of his overalls and joined his father.

The two returned to the field. The sun glared down. "Gonna be a hot un," observed Lem.

Jeremy barely heard him. He was still thinking about his prayer. He wondered if it had been all right. As he reflected on it, it seemed it should have been all right. Perhaps he should have put in a few more "Amens" and "Praise the Lords." *I may have screwed up*, he thought to himself. What if he had? Had God even heard him? Would God give him a second chance?

They had been working for about an hour when Jeremy looked up and saw a car parked beside the road at the end of the rows that he and Lem were working. A man had gotten out of the car and was waiting for them. It was Jacob Mutchell.

44

"HOWDY, LEM" SAID MUTCHELL as Jeremy and his father reached the end of the row. He ignored Jeremy.

"Howdy, Jacob," replied Lem.

"Mighty hot day." Mutchell removed his hat and wiped his forehead with his forearm. He pushed up the long hair on the left side of his head so that it fell across the crown of his head. Then he put his hat back on.

"Yep," replied Lem.

"'Bout gotcher work done?"

"Nope."

"I ain't neither."

There was silence. Both men studied the ground. They did not look at each other.

"Well, looky, Lem," began Mutchell. "I know yer busy, but I think they's somethin' yuh oughtta know." Now, for the first time, he looked at Jeremy.

"What's that?" Lem began to roll a cigarette.

"Well, I got kids, too. An' I wanta know whur they are. If'n somebody found one uv my kids somewhur whur he warn't supposed tuh be, I'd wanta be tole, wouldn't you?"

Lem looked fully at Mutchell now for the first time. "What's on yer min'?"

"Well, las' night I seen somebody down tuh th' church about dark, an' I uz a-watchin' 'im, an' I seen 'im go intuh th' church, yuh see, so I walked down there tuh th' buildin'. I don't live very far frum it, y'know. I allus have liked tuh live near th' church house, Lem. Makes me seem closer tuh th' Lord somehow." Mutchell smiled benignly. "Anyways, I walked down there, an' I walked in, an' there uz yer boy. It uz Jeremy, Lem."

Jeremy fixed his gaze on his father.

"Well, hell," said Lem casually, "you been a-tryin' tuh git 'im down there, ain'tcha?"

Mutchell looked surprised. "Uv course. Shore. But that uz durin' th' meetin'. An' see, th' meetin's over. Ended yestiddy mornin', so they wuzn't no church las' night. I'm sorry yuh missed th' meetin', Lem. Shore missed some good preachin'. I kep' a-hopin' ever' night that yuh'd come. But, see, las' night, th' buildin' uz empty. Th' meetin' uz over, an' Jeremy shouldn't uv been in there."

"Maybe he didn' know that yuh wuzn't a-havin' church las' night," observed Lem, still in his casual tone.

"But he could see they wuzn't nobody there." Mutchell seemed puzzled at the turn in the conversation.

"Ain't th' church fer ever'body?"

"Uv course. But shouldn' be no young people like Jeremy a-wanderin' aroun' in there when they ain't no adults."

"Jacob, my boy ast me tuh let 'im go tuh church las' night, an' I let 'im. I didn' cotton none to his a-goin' tuh that church, what with all that hollerin' an' carryin' on, but I let 'im go. He went there with good intentions, an' if you folks didn' have church las' night, I don't see it uz any fault uv his."

"But, Lem, he coulda carried somethin' off." Mutchell spat the words.

"Did he?" Lem addressed the question to Mutchell. Then he turned toward Jeremy. "Did yuh?"

Jeremy quickly shook his head. Mutchell looked at Lem for a second, then he said, "No, not that I know uv, but that ain't th' point. He could've, Lem. Damn it, Lem, he could've."

"I got work tuh do, Jacob. My boy does somethin' wrong, I'll be th' first tuh git with 'im, but I ain't a-gonna git all over 'im fer showin' up at church one day late fer some damn Holy Roller meetin'." Lem turned back to his work.

Mutchell called after him: "Don't say I didn' try tuh warn yuh. Nex' time yer boy gits in trouble, don't come a-runnin' tuh th' church fer he'p. Someday when he breaks in an' steals somethin' frum Ayers Store er some place like that, you jus' remember I tried tuh warn yuh."

Lem made no reply. He had returned to his work.

"These damn kids is a-runnin' wild," shouted Mutchell. "Ain't nothin' but th' church between them an' hell. Yuh better remember that, Lem."

Lem never looked back.

Jeremy felt like he was walking on clouds. He had been so afraid. And now, not only had he escaped punishment, but his father had defended him to Mutchell. Jeremy walked along, watching his father's broad, sweat-stained back. He smiled to himself. Mutchell better stay away from us. His father had come to his defense. His father had taken his side. Jeremy swaggered as he walked.

Lem, observing Jeremy's stride, said, "Watch whur yer a-goin'."

"Yes, Sir," said Jeremy spiritedly, and he smiled as he said it.

Work now went much better. The sun seemed not so hot. There were fewer cockleburs and grass burs. Jeremy's recent frustrations seemed to melt away. He had found something to pray for; he had prayed for Patches. And perhaps the prayer was already working. He felt like a new person.

They continued working through the afternoon as usual, but Jeremy remained in high spirits. They had just come to the end of the row when his father turned to him and said, "We're gonna quit early tuhday, Boy. I gotta go intuh town tuh git a batt'ry fer th' car. We never could charge it up right th' other night."

"It's a-gittin' purty late anyways, I guess," Jeremy observed.

"Yeah, right." Lem squinted at the sun, still well above the horizon.

"You go on tuh th' house, an' I'll be along in a minute. I wanta walk over here a piece an' check a place in th' fence across that dry wash. I thought it looked like it uz down when I came by here this mornin'."

Jeremy was off like a shot. No more work today. "Hallelujah!" he shouted. No more work, and he had not gotten into trouble because of Mutchell. Perhaps his good fortune was already an indication that God had heard and was answering his prayer. He dashed across the large, flat rock formations, the domains of the mountain boomers. A couple of the large lizards, surprised by Jeremy, scurried for cover, but Jeremy paid no attention to them. He had no fear of them at that moment. He jumped low bushes, dashed in circles around larger ones, and he was in the midst of the sheep before he realized it.

He stopped. What were the sheep doing here? He and his father had put them in another field far across the pasture only the day before, and yet here was what looked to be the whole flock—some of them grazing nonchalantly, most of them lying down under whatever shade they could find.

But what were they doing here? Jeremy was perplexed. He had stood and watched the last sheep file into the field, and he had closed the gate behind them.

The gate! That was it! He had not closed the gate! He remembered his father telling him to close it, but he did not remember closing it.

He had not closed the gate! And now here were the sheep, all out of the field and into the pasture. Oh, Boy, he thought. I'll catch hell now. Paw will be furious when he sees these sheep out. I better try to drive them back over there to the field myself.

The prospect was overwhelming. Jeremy knew that just getting the flock together by himself and driving them to the field would be a monumental task. And yet, something had to be done, for his father would be along soon.

"Boy, just as I uz gittin' along good with Paw, an' a-learnin' how to pray, somethin' like this has tuh happen. Why'd these ole sheep hafta git out anyhow?" He picked up a rock and hurled it at the nearest sheep. The sheep trotted awkwardly away. "Damn ole sheep. I hate yuh! I hate yuh!"

"Well," he continued to talk with himself. "I gotta do somethin'. Maybe I can at least drive 'em all over tuh th' fiel' so Paw won't see 'em when he comes by here, an' then after he goes tuh git his batt'ry, I'll come back an' git 'em intuh th' fiel'. Maybe Maw'll he'p me." It was an emergency measure, but it seemed the only thing to try at the moment.

He began circling the sheep, intending to bring them all together and then to drive them across the pasture. The sheep were scattered, and Jeremy had to make a wide circle to be sure that he had not overlooked any stragglers. He watched the trees and bushes closely, afraid that one of the sheep might be lying close up under a bush in the shade and he would not see it. It was critical that he not overlook a single sheep. His father might see it, might try to drive it over to the field, and discover the open gate.

It was because Jeremy was searching so intently that he saw the sheep lying in a clump of algerita bushes. He yelled at the sheep to get up, but it didn't move. He picked up a rock and threw it at the sheep and hit it squarely in the side, but the sheep did not move. He went nearer to the sheep, picked up another rock and threw it. He hit the sheep again solidly.

"Lazy damn sheep," muttered Jeremy in exasperation. He remembered the time earlier when he and his father had found a sheep that refused to get up. It worried him that here was a similar situation, for he had no idea how he would ever get the sheep on its feet. He remembered that he and his father had struggled to make the sheep stand.

As Jeremy approached, he could see that the sheep was lying on its side with its back to him. He walked up and kicked the sheep. "Git up," he ordered, but the sheep did not move. He reached down to seize the sheep by its wool to try to pull it up, and then he saw the blood. He knelt down for a closer look. The sheep was bleeding from a large, gaping hole in its neck. Bright red blood trickled down over the dirty grey wool and dropped in clots into the dust. "My God!" Jeremy exclaimed.

But as Jeremy considered this turn of events, he felt a wave of security. At least Patches was tied up at home. He would not be blamed. The prayer. The prayer. Maybe it was working.

Jeremy's first thought was to go and find his father immediately, and he started back toward the field to intercept Lem, but then he thought about all the sheep. What was he to do about them? He knew his father would be angry about the sheep being out. But wouldn't he be pleased to learn that Patches was not a sheep-killing dog? Jeremy thought about it, and he decided that he could not be sure how his father would react. "If I coulda found that ole dawg a-killin' that sheep, an' if I coulda killed 'im, then I guess Paw woulda been happy."

And then he had an idea. The sheep could not have been dead very long. The blood was still fresh. It was still dripping from the wound. That meant the dog must be somewhere nearby. "I'll fin' that dawg, an' I'll kill 'im," he said. "Then Paw'll be proud uv me, an' I reckon then he'll fergive me fer leavin' that gate open, too. Maybe I can fin' that dawg before Paw gits here an' gits mad about th' sheep."

As Jeremy hurried toward the house, he constructed his own idea of what it might be like to find the dog and to kill it. He could see himself going to his house and getting out his gun. Then he would begin to hunt through the pasture until he found the dog. "I bet that dawg is that big ole black un," Jeremy thought aloud, "an' I bet its mouth is all covered with blood. I'll have tuh be keerful, 'cause that ole dawg might charge me an' try tuh bite me."

Jeremy's vivid image of the charging dog aroused his emotions. "I'm a good shot, an' I'll shoot that dawg an' kill 'im dead." Jeremy, in his imagination, could see the dog, its mouth covered with blood, a pink froth dripping from its jowls. Its hair hung in ugly patches from its sides. Jeremy could imagine the dog looking up and seeing him. As his dream unfolded, the dog lowered its head and began to growl in low guttural tones. It began to bark ferociously, snapping its teeth, and then it charged. Jeremy calmly stood his ground, raised his shotgun, and fired. The charging dog dropped dead, right at his feet.

Later, in his imagination, Lem would join him and would congratulate him. "Son, that uz a brave thin' tuh do. I'm proud uv yuh an' how yuh stood yer groun'. Then Lem would say, "Jeremy, just fergit about that gate being left open. It uz no big deal. We can always git them sheep back intuh th' fiel'. Main thing is we got that sheep-killin' dawg." It was a wonderful possibility.

Jeremy ran all the way home. He flung the door open and rushed into his room, where his shotgun stood in a corner.

"Jeremy, is that you?" called his mother.

"Yeah," yelled Jeremy, rummaging around in his drawer, trying to find his shotgun shells. He had not used them for awhile, and he didn't remember where they were.

"What're yuh doin' home so early? Does yer paw know yer here?"

"I come tuh git my shotgun," replied Jeremy, still searching for the shells. He threw everything out of his drawer and onto the floor in his search.

His mother appeared in the doorway to his room, drying her hands on her apron.

"Whatta yuh mean, yuh come tuh git yer shotgun? Why ain't yuh still in th' fiel' with yer paw?"

He answered without turning around to face his mother. "Paw sent me home early."

"But why do yuh want yer shotgun?"

He had found the shells by now and was stuffing them into his pants pocket. "I foun' another sheep that's been kilt. Just a minute ago. It uz that sheep-killin' dawg, an' I inten' tuh find it an' kill it."

"But whur is yer paw?"

"He's a-checkin' th' fence," said Jeremy over his shoulder as he headed toward the door. He was formulating a plan. He would untie Patches, and the two of them would find the sheep-killing dog. He flung open the door and looked expectantly toward the fence. His blood froze as his eyes swept the yard fence. He saw only a short piece of the leash hanging from the fence post. Patches was nowhere to be seen. He dropped his gun in the dirt and rushed to the fence. "Maw, did you untie Patches?" His question was a scream.

"What, Jeremy? What er yuh sayin'?"

"Patches is gone!"

"Oh, yeah, I noticed that this mornin', an' I wuz gonna tell yuh. How do yuh think he got a-loose?"

Jeremy looked at the short, ragged piece of leash. It had been chewed through. "Oh, no," he thought. "Oh, God, no!" Jeremy was frantic. He must find the sheep-killing dog, and he must find Patches and re-tie him, and both of those things needed to be done at once. And there was still the problem of the sheep out in the pasture instead of being in the field where they should be, and where they would be if Jeremy had not left the gate open. He struck the fence post with his hand. "Damn! What a day this has turned out tuh be."

He slammed his open hand against the fence again. His mind swirled in turmoil. Still, he realized that just because Patches had chewed the leash through did not mean that he had killed the sheep. All he had to do was find that other dog. Quick!

He walked over to pick up his gun, and as he bent over, he was almost bowled over by the leaping Patches.

"Patches!" Jeremy exclaimed, and the dog was bounding upon him, wagging his tail in ecstasy. He seized the dog's head and caressed it roughly in his hands. The dog leaped away and then back again. "Boy, yer a-slobberin'. Whur yuh been?" laughed Jeremy, and then he looked at his hands. They were stained with blood. He looked down at his pants and saw the bright red streaks of blood on them. He caught Patches and held him close. "Oh, Patches, what have yuh done? My God, Patches, what have yuh done? No, no. Stop a-jumpin' aroun', an' let me look at yuh." He restrained the dog while he looked at its muzzle and paws. They were covered with blood!

"Patches! Oh, Patches." He said it over and over as he hugged the dog to himself. And now a fierce urgency began to take shape. He must get the blood off the dog before his father saw him. Then he saw the shotgun lying in the yard where he had dropped it. "Oh, God," he declared. He released the dog with a curt command. "Now you stay here, yuh hear me? Don't you go off." Then he ran over, picked up the gun, and carried it back into the house. First, he stood it in the corner where it ordinarily stayed; then he thought better of it and knelt down beside his bed, and pushed the gun as far back under his bed as he could.

He rose to his feet and looked down at his clothes. They were streaked with blood. "Oh, God, Patches. What have yuh done?" He rushed back outside to check on Patches. The dog had stayed in the yard. Jeremy went into the kitchen and took the washpan and a towel from the rack over the washstand. He filled the pan with water from the water barrel, and then turned to look for Patches. "C'mere, Patches. Come quick. We ain't got no time."

Patches rushed to his master, ready to play with him.

"Now, be still, dawg," said Jeremy huskily. "We gotta git this blood offa yuh." Jeremy sat on the ground, awkwardly trying to hold the squirming Patches still and to wash him at the same time.

Immediately Patches stepped into the pan of water and turned it over, spilling the pink water out onto the ground.

"Damn it, Patches!" screamed Jeremy. "Be still. Oh, God, cain't yuh see what yuh done?" He pushed the dog away from him roughly, wiped his eyes with the back of his hand, and rushed back to the barrel to refill the pan. The blood was drying now and did not come off easily. Jeremy sloshed water over Patches' muzzle and legs, and the dog tried to jerk away and turned the pan over again. Jeremy rocked back on his haunches and began to cry. He rose to go to the barrel again.

"What's a-goin' on?" asked his mother from inside the house.

"Nuthin'! Nuthin'!" yelled Jeremy in frustration. "Ain't nothing wrong, Maw, not a damn thin'." *She must not see the dog*, he thought to himself. "You stay in th' house, Maw. Don't yo be a-comin out here!"

Once again he filled the pan and went back to call his dog. Jeremy could see that he had made almost no headway in getting the blood off Patches. While he was scrubbing Patches, the dog wagged his tail and tried to lick Jeremy's face. He tried to scrub the dog, but the stains were becoming more stubborn. And then, Jeremy became aware of a shadow, a presence. He looked up to see his father standing over him, watching.

In an instant Jeremy was on his feet, turning the pan over in his haste and spilling the water onto the ground. Patches leaped back in alarm.

Jeremy lunged against his father, pounding him with his fists, screaming, "He didn' do it, dammit! He didn' kill no damn ole sheep. I tell yuh he didn' kill no sheep. He killed a rabbit. I seen 'im do it. He caught th' rabbit, an' he killed it and et it. I seen 'im. I seen 'im!" He jumped up and down, continuing to scream and to pound Lem's chest. He tried to kick Lem, all the time swinging furious roundhouse blows at him.

Lem shoved him roughly aside, so hard he collapsed to the ground. "He didn' do it," Jeremy pounded the ground as he sobbed, "He didn' do it. I seen another dawg do it, an' I come home tuh git my gun tuh kill it..." His voice trailed off.

His father ignored him and called to the dog. "C'mere, poochie," he called soothingly, snapping his fingers as he did so.

Jeremy sat up in fright. "No, Patches," he screamed. "Don't!"

Lem turned toward him. "You shut yer damn mouth, Boy."

Patches looked from Jeremy to Lem, anxiously licking his pink muzzle.

"C'mere, poochie," said Lem.

Patches stretched against the ground; he licked his muzzle and wagged his tail. His ears were laid back against his head. Jeremy could barely contain himself. He wanted to scream.

"C'mere, poochie." Lem flexed his hands.

Patches crept forward on his belly, his head outstretched, his tail wagging.

Oh, Patches, Jeremy said to himself. Please run away. Don't let Paw catch you.

Now the man and dog were much closer. Lem still held out his hand invitingly, speaking gently. The dog grovelled on the ground. His eyes were white-rimmed with fright. He thrust out his tongue. Then with a sudden movement Lem seized Patches by the foreleg and jerked him up from the ground.

"Got you, damn you!" Lem shouted triumphantly. The dog yelped in terror and pain as Lem began carrying him across the yard, still holding him only by one leg, which was twisted at a terrible angle. Jeremy was up on his knees. "Paw, don't! Don't! Yer a-hurtin' 'im."

Lem ignored him. Patches howled in pain and then, twisting and snarling, tried to bite Lem's arm. When Patches tried to bite him, Lem swung viciously, striking the dog again and again, the dog's head jerking with each blow, and Patches' snarls quickly dissolved into whines of agony and terror.

Then Jeremy saw his father's intention. Lem carried Patches to the fence and, holding him securely, looped the piece of leash which was still tied to the fence around the dog's neck and knotted it. The leash was so short now that the dog's front paws would not touch the ground. Patches desperately tried to find footing against the mesh wire fence.

"Now, damn yuh," said Lem. "I'll shore as hell teach yuh not tuh kill sheep." So saying he picked up the broken hoe handle lying by the gate.

"Oh, Paw, please don't," begged Jeremy, and he moved toward Lem, who turned, raising the hoe handle. "Stay outta my way, dammit, er I'll break this damn hoe handle on yore head, and by God, I mean it. You shore as hell don't want what this mutt is about tuh git."

Jeremy couldn't stand it. He fled toward the shed. His heart beat crazily; tears streamed from his eyes and down his face. He was crying loudly, wildly. He ran as hard as he could, as if to escape what he knew would happen. He reached the shed and tried to make a turn behind it, but he was running so fast that he lost his footing and fell headlong, sliding across the gravelly ground. He felt a thousand sensations of sharp pain as he slid across the gravel. Instantly, there was a sharp stabbing pain in his chest. Simultaneously, he heard the first loud whump and a high–pitched, yelping whine of pain. He was almost out of his mind with fear and terror. Another sharp whump, another shriek of pain. Jeremy's thought patterns were shattered, obsessed by an image of his dog being beaten to death.

He heard his father's voice: "Yeah, try tuh git away, you bastard. Kill sheep, will yuh? I'll teach yuh better'n that. Take that, damn you! I'll see tuh it that yuh never kill another damn sheep, you sorry bastard dawg."

Jeremy dug his hands into the dirt. His mouth was filled with an acrid taste; he kicked the ground with his feet and pounded it with his fists. He clapped his hands against his ears, trying to shut out the noise, but he couldn't. The pain in his chest increased. Pray! He thought. Oh, God, he thought. Pray! Oh, God. All the time the beating continued. He heard the dull thud of wood striking flesh, the weakening cries of the terrified, dying dog. Jeremy lifted a scream: "Oh, damn you! Damn you! Oh, damn you tuh hell!"

And everything became quiet.

Jeremy lay face down on the ground for a long time, half-conscious. His body was wracked with huge, convulsive sobs. The pain in his chest became unbearable. Something was dreadfully wrong. He rolled over and reached to his chest, felt his cross in his bib pocket, removed it, and the pain lessened. He lay still, looking at the cross without emotion. He sat up and leaned against the barn, still holding the cross. The knees of his pants were torn; his hands and arms were speckled with blood. He couldn't open his right eye. He turned the cross over and over in his hands. He leaned back against the shed and stretched his legs out in front of him. In kicking the ground, he had torn the nail from the big toe on his right foot. It bled profusely. Jeremy stared at it dully, barely aware of it. He lay the cross on his leg and fingered it. Then he slowly rose to his feet.

The sun was very low in the western sky now, and the day was beginning to cool. He walked through the yard gate, not looking to the right or left. He knew what he would not see. He lifted a blood-flecked hand and pushed back his forelock. He shook his head as if to clear his thoughts, walked straight into his bedroom, and pulled up a chair in front of his dresser. He sat down and placed his cross before him. Then he pushed it away from him, and it fell with a clatter between the dresser and the wall.

About the Author

DR. RAY WRIGHT was a native of Texas and spent his younger years in Salt Gap and Brady. His teaching career of 32 years was spent at the University of Houston Downtown teaching Literature and Philosophy. In 1985, he was privileged to spend a year in Guilin, China teaching American Literature. He is an honorary professor of literature at Guangxi Teachers University.

In the 20 years thereafter , he took student groups from the university to China for study and adventure before his retirement. He devoted much of his academic career to the study of world religions. His publications include *American Religion: Its Dynamics and Diversity*, and *A Handbook of Philosophy*, both published by McGraw-Hill.

He wrote this novel — part fiction, part life — over a number of years reminiscing about his early life.

Dr. Wright lost his battle with Alzheimer's in 2015.

www.ingramcontent.com/pod-product-compliance
Lightning Source LLC
Chambersburg PA
CBHW011510170626
46810CB00009B/3301